In memory of my father

James Aubrey Robbins, Senior
December 6, 1919–December 6, 1984

A proud member of the Civilian Conservation Corps

Acknowledgments

This work was written in part through the support of a mini-research grant provided by the University of South Dakota Office of Research, Dr. Howard Coker, Director. A special thanks goes to Pat Peterson, Managing Editor, USD Press, for her editorial assistance.

The characters in this novel are entirely fictitious and bear no reference whatsoever to real people, living or dead.

KR
1994

The Baptism of Howie Cobb

Happy Feet

"Dear Mr. Howell Madison Cobb..."

Howie read the sentence, pleased that somebody in the world considered him a "mister," and enjoyed the ring the word gave the rest of his name. He read on, deciphering the easy words and skipping over the more difficult ones, as the Georgia landscape slipped past the bus that was taking him farther and farther away from home.

> "Welcome to the Civilian Conservation Corps. Your one-year commitment to the Corps will commence on May 15, 1936, by 4:00 p.m., at which time you are to report to the commandant of Camp Iron Mountain in the Black Hills of South Dakota, who has been informed to expect your arrival."

He had never before seen so many ten-penny words written on a piece of paper. His Poppa, Alexander Stevens Cobb, changed "commence" to "start" for him, but nobody in the house he was leaving behind could help him with phrases like "in accordance with" or "commandant of." He skipped over them, but tried to memorize them for possible use in the future, just in case he needed to impress somebody.

The movements of the bus made the paper jump up and down in his hands as he read on.

"Enclosed with this letter is a voucher, issued from the Corps Office, Atlanta, Georgia, to provide you with interstate bus transportation from your home in Douglasville to Sturgis, South Dakota..."

"Sturgis." There was a manliness about the name. He chewed on the word and its spelling and uttered it aloud under his breath. The woman sitting beside him on the bus gave him a sidewise look. He grinned and said, "It's a city, Sturgis," but she didn't grin back. He shrugged. "Actually, I don't know what the—heck it is." He had almost said "hell," but he wasn't certain of a seventeen-year-old was allowed to use cuss words when around total strangers. He returned to the well-read, crumpled letter.

"...where you are to report to the regional office of the Corps at Fort Meade, South Dakota, for transport to Camp Iron Mountain. Questions related to this assignment should be addressed to me at the Atlanta office.

Sincerely and again welcome to the Cs,

Walter Nomad,
Assistant to the Associate Director
Office of Enrollees
Civilian Conservation Corps."

Howie folded the letter and stuffed it in his hip pocket. He had spent a full half-day trying to find out how to use the voucher. Eventually, the fellow at Buddy's One Stop, the Douglasville bus depot, figured out the complicated instructions and had given him a one-way ticket to Sturgis, South Dakota. Now, several weeks later, it was happening. He was using the ticket, leaving Douglasville for the first time. The thought of finally being on the road made his gut twist into fist-sized lumps. Discovery and adventure were ahead of him. Family and friends behind. Would he come back? Would he want to? If he did, would he finally be the man he so determinedly wanted to be? Would Indella Shealy be waiting for him? She said she would be. He said he wanted her to be. He took the photograph she had given him from his pocket and held it so nobody else could possibly see her face and then brought the image to his lips and kissed it.

He closed his eyes, laid his head back on the stiff bus seat, and felt the rhythmic beat of the tires on the road.

He had dreamed of this for so long. When he had been more a kid, he and his younger brother Pierson would stand on the far side of the heap of tire carcasses at Buddy's One Stop on the edge of town and watch the buses come and go, dumping passengers at Buddy's gas pumps and taking others away toward Birmingham or Atlanta, Savannah or Chattanooga...or who knows, maybe even New York City or Chicago. Pierson was the one, even when he was an awkward twelve-year-old with snot still hanging from his upper lip, who had dragged Howie down to Buddy's. The two would stand around and drool over the thought of being aboard anything that moved, on their way to destinations unknown.

By the time he turned thirteen, Pierson was bragging about journeys to Lithia Springs or Villa Rica or Tallapoosa, or Birmingham, or even Chattanooga, though everybody knew he was lying about Birmingham and Chattanooga and probably Tallapoosa—after all, who in his right mind would want to go to Tallapoosa? Now it was Howie on the bus, heading for a place that wasn't on any map that he could find: Camp Iron Mountain. He had finally located the Black Hills on a world globe kept in the high school library. On the map the Black Hills seemed so close, less than six inches from the speck named Atlanta. "Piece of cake," he had told friends and relatives and anybody else who would listen. Getting to the Black Hills was going to be as easy as slipping eggs from beneath a setting hen.

He was especially pleased when Pierson got all puffed up with envy. Now, he, not Pierson, was on his way to find out how the rest of the world's folks managed their lives.

He checked his ticket, folded and tucked inside his ball cap. Government issue. The ticket told him all he needed to know. Atlanta, then a connection to Nashville, another connection to Memphis and on and on, connection after connection, through towns he had never heard of. He was heading toward that huge blank space some folks he knew referred to as the "heart of America"—the Black Hills of South Dakota. The words held magic for him.

Georgia was slipping past him at a pace that boggled his mind. Beulah, McWorter. Lithia Springs. Houses and houses and fields and more houses. Austell. Before today Howie had never heard of Austell; yet, wouldn't you know it there it was.

Howie felt like he was on a conveyer belt. His stomach churned. He needed to upchuck and get things settled; otherwise, all the movement inside the bus might do it for him.

"Where you heading, buddy?" a man with a full gray beard asked from across the aisle.

Howie grinned and said "South Dakota."

"No shit," the fellow said. "Where the hell's that?"

"Ain't got the foggiest."

"No shit." And the gray beard nodded and returned to the view through his window.

Less than an hour before, Howie had stepped onto the bus down at Buddy's One Stop, grinning bigger than a hungry hog at a full trough, and had waved to his Momma May Lou and his brothers and sisters with full swings of his arm. Pierson had been there, with hatred at being left behind etched all over his face. His Poppa Alexander Stevens and older brother Hev had to work, and Indella hadn't shown up, either. She had spent their last night together crying. After all, she reasoned, nobody had twisted his arm to get him to enroll in the C.C.C. He had done it out of spite; he didn't love her. Once signed up, why had he asked for an assignment so far away? He was heading off to South Dakota because he didn't love her.

"Just don't go!" Indella had argued.

He tried to explain that he had a contract with the Cs. If he didn't go, he would be absent without leave, AWOL, and he couldn't do that. Never.

Going AWOL would be an impossibility for him. After all, he was a Cobb, and Cobbs, once committed to something, saw it through to the end. No matter what.

She cried even more. He felt awful, but what could he do?

The sign beside the road said, "Atlanta City Limits." Howie was on top of the world. He had made it and after so short a ride. The city was so much nearer his home town than he had realized. Maybe he had slept some of the way? He knew he hadn't. His stomach wouldn't have let him sleep.

The buildings grew bigger and bigger, until he had to crane his neck to see the tops. Cars and buses were everywhere. And people! He had not known so many people lived in the world.

They were like ants in a turmoil. Going everywhere. Doing nobody knew what. This was a damn sight better than sitting home. Suddenly, his stomach did a surge that almost emptied his innards there in the aisle of the bus. Oh, Lord, just see me through this, he prayed, suspecting deep inside his head that there was no Lord anywhere around who would pay the least bit of attention to him.

The bus pulled into the terminal in downtown Atlanta. The driver opened the doors, and everybody but him got off. The driver glanced back at him before stepping to the ground. If he wanted to sit on board for half an hour, it was up to him.

Howie debated inside his head. He needed to relieve himself, but he didn't know if he dared. The bus might take off without him while he was looking for the facilities. After sitting in the empty bus for ten minutes or so, he found his nerve, eased down the narrow aisle to the open door, stepped off, stretched his legs, and said out loud for anybody in the world to hear, "I've done it. Set foot in Atlanta! How about that, huh?"

The urinal he found deep inside the bus terminal was a most welcome sight. And the bus driver didn't leave without him. A truly amazing thing, he decided, this life on the road.

He slept much of the way to Chattanooga in spite of his excitement. His stomach had resolved itself to the sway of the moving bus. He dreamed he was riding a bus, being jerked this way and that. He dreamed of sitting on his rear end until it throbbed, of getting a crick in his neck from staring out the window, of growing wheels on his legs in place of his feet. Then he woke; it wasn't a dream, except the part about the wheels.

He peered out the window. The scene hadn't changed. The bus must have been sitting still. From the landscape outside, he was sure he was as far from Chattanooga as ever.

The the hills became a little taller and the trees more dense, more hardwoods and fewer pines. The bus shifted into a lower gear as it began the steep climb up the mountain. The vehicle was less than half full, yet Howie felt as if somebody, himself most likely, would have to get out in order for it to make it to the top. The machine lurched but continued to roll ever forward. Oh Lord, he sweated, what if this damn machine can't make it all the way to South Dakota? What if he could only get so far and then not be able to get home? What if he got stuck out here so far away from home?

What if the bus cleared the hill and began to coast down and down and down? The whole world seemed to open up in front of him. Howie looked out over a sprawling valley that contained the beginnings of another city much like Atlanta, and the bus began its descent into Tennessee.

Tennessee. He was free. Howie expressed himself with a slightly audible "Wow!" He wished Indella was there with him, so he could hug her close and share his elation with her. He was finally out of Georgia. The words were like sugar cubes to be sucked on. He was finally, after so much dreaming and longing, in another world.

This new world, whatever shape it might take, was his to do with as he wanted. Nothing was going to stop him. Nothing. Maybe someday he and Indella and their brood of kids, nine of them, all boys if he had anything to do with it, a home-made baseball team, would go to Tennessee and he would share with them the elation he felt this first exciting time.

Three days later, his great adventure had been reduced to sleeping on a cement floor behind a wooden bench inside the bus depot in Des Moines, Iowa. He used his duffel bag as a pillow and his light-weight jacket, the warmest garment he owned, as a quilt. Even with that for covering, he shivered.

May nights in Iowa were like December ones back home. Des Moines. He said the name over and over to himself. He pronounced both "s"s and put the emphasis on the "i" until somebody laughed at him.

"It's Des Moines" they told him, pronouncing the word with true midwestern glee.

"That so?" Howie answered. "Well, how come they don't spell it that way?"

"Where the hell are you from, kid?" somebody asked.

"Georgia," he said with pride.

The Iowan yelled too loud and with too much scorn, "Hey, Hans, we've got us a real down home cracker over here! You should hear the son of a biscuit eater talk!"

And several folks laughed. It was all a joke. Only Howie failed to see the humor. He said nothing. What could he say? He was a stranger in a foreign land. People in the depot stared at him as if he had leeches on his face. He didn't open his mouth again while in Des Moines. He kept his thoughts to himself. Des Moines, he pronounced the name correctly in his head.

8

It had a distasteful ring to it when pronounced as it was supposed to be pronounced. A damn Yankee bastion. He and Indella wouldn't bring their kids here. They'd bypass Des Moines.

He suffered through the twelve-hour layover as best he could. His adventure had become redundant after Chattanooga and the mountains of Tennessee. Nashville and Memphis had looked the same. Then he crossed the Mississippi—he could hardly contain himself at the thought of crossing the greatest river on earth—and left his beloved South behind.

Cairo, Cape Giraudoux, St. Louis, Hannibal, Moline, Davenport, Iowa City, Des Moines. He had to be within spitting distance of the edge of the world or at least near Camp Iron Mountain and the fabled Black Hills.

He had considered Tennessee endless until he came to Illinois. And now Iowa. "Lord, deliver me from this heathen land," he whispered under his breath as he closed his eyes, hoping to ease on down the time road by way of sleep. His words were less a prayer than a conversation with a being he knew would hear him if his Poppa had anything to do with it and would most likely understand. He allowed such thoughts in his head, even though he hadn't been baptized into the fold.

Sleep didn't come easily. The depot was a beehive of people going and coming. When he slept, he dreamed of Momma's feather bed. He hadn't slept in it since he was eight years old and ill with pneumonia. To get sick at home was almost worth it, if it led to a night next to May Lou and Alexander Stevens in their soft and smelly feather bed.

His dream was comforting. In it Poppa told him: Steer clear of them Yankee folk. Never met a Yankee I could like and that's a fact. Pay them no mind. Trust who you are and let it be. Trust the lord. He'll take your hand on the asking. Promise you that. Promise. Promise."

Howie awoke, momentarily horrified on finding the hard concrete terminal floor underneath him.

Boarding announcements were made, and for the countless time, Howie climbed the steps onto another bus and felt the engine rev. Off he went, getting farther away from home but never any closer, seemingly, to the Black Hills and the promised C.C.C. camp.

Iowa was the ultimate of forever states. The towns were farther apart than any place he could imagine. Few trees, too. He couldn't remember when trees suddenly became rare. In fact, what trees there were had been planted; none of them were there by nature. So different from home where trees grew without being asked.

Bus stops were less often. Thank heavens the bus driver needed fuel every once in a while. Thank heavens there was only one more state to go.

A fella back in Davenport had shown him a map of the entire area and pointed out South Dakota. Judging distance as best he could from a piece of paper, he figured he had to be well past the state and bound at any moment to spy the Rocky Mountains out his bus window. Unless he was mistaken and Iowa was destined to go on and on without stopping. But then, maps don't lie. South Dakota had to be out there somewhere.

More and more folks wearing cowboy boots and hats got on and off the bus—more people with flat voices and clipped, sometimes unintelligible dialects.

He expected at some point to change from bus to stagecoach and maybe wagon train. He asked a fellow passenger about South Dakota stagecoaches, and the fella said, "Forget stage coaches, sonny. Once you get to the Dakotas you'll have to ride a damn horse!"

As his bus pulled away from the Sioux City depot, the vehicle was half filled with C.C.C. enrollees. He had traveled alone until Nashville. There three other teenagers, enrollees like himself, got on board. He didn't talk to them, and they didn't talk to him. More piled on in Memphis and Cape Giraudoux and East St. Louis and Springfield and Moline and

Des Moines. Even more in Council Bluffs, still more in Sioux City. Then the bus turned north. Howie could see a moderately large river out the west window.

"The Missouri," the C next to him said.

"You're kidding," Howie said.

"Next stop," the driver called, "Jefferson, South Dakota!"

Howie wanted to cheer, his first such urge since Chatanooga. South Dakota! He was nearly there.

He suddenly found himself thinking of Pierson. He was home where he was supposed to be, but still, it would have been nice to have the kid along. After all, it was his idea, this "seeing the world" Him with his happy feet, Pierson was cut out to be a traveler. After all, nobody could keep Pierson home. How many times had he disappeared, "Run off" was how Momma phrased it, only to drag home, stinking, dirty, and grinning from ear to ear.

South Dakota. That's what the sign beside the road said.

Howie felt a tinge of sadness. He was almost there, and he didn't deserve to be. He hadn't suffered enough. It had been too damn easy.

South Dakota was more forever than Iowa. At least Iowa had an occasional town. South Dakota had farms here and there, but mostly it was open, endless fields of grass. In South Dakota more than any place else he had ever been, there was what seemed to him too much sky. Once in a while, he saw a horse, maybe two, standing belly-deep in grass. Everywhere, in all directions, nothing. How do people live in a place like this? He left the question unasked. No trees, no shrubs, no water, no people, just wide open prairie, a sea of tan and green that moved like it had a life of its own.

"Something has to be wrong up here," he said to the C beside him.

"How come?"

"No trees."

"That's the prairie monster's doing."

"Say what?"

"Prairie monster. It lives in the Missouri River and comes out at night and eats all the trees."

Howie sat silent for a second, looking out over the bast plains. "Are you funning me?"

The C grinned. "Funning? Hell, what kind of word's that?"

Eight hours and thirty-nine minutes later, Howie stepped off the bus in Sturgis, four days, twenty-two hours, and fifty-five minutes from home. His body now told him he had suffered enough. It was time to sit still for a while. He stepped from the bus and was greeted by a sharp northwest wind that jerked his hat from his head and tumbled it down the street like a dancer gone berserk.

"Welcome to Fort Meade," the tall hawk-nosed fellow in a green Army uniform said to the enrollees who stood in a loose line outside a red brick building, fighting the wind just to stay upright. "You're gonna love it out here in the wild west," he said with a sad sort of smirk on his face.

"How far to camp?" Howie asked.

"Which camp's yours?"

"Iron Mountain."

"Only three, four hours up in the Hills," he answered with a shrug.

Howie groaned. His rear end throbbed with saddle sores. His back ached from lack of exercise. He stank from his own filth. And he was so homesick he could start wailing any minute.

The wind sliced at his eyes and tugged at his shirt and pants. The air was so dry it sucked the moisture out of his nose and left scaly flesh where it shouldn't been.

His skin felt like it might flake off his bones and leave him standing there, nothing but a skeleton, a damn misplaced Georgia homebody a long, long way from Momma's understanding touch.

Who would have thought this country could be so big? Too big.

He'd never get home again. He didn't know the way.

Confederate

Howie jumped off the tailgate of the bird cage when it stopped in the middle of Camp Iron Mountain. For the past three hours, switchback after switchback, bump upon bump, he would have sworn he was in the North Georgia Mountains, with all the twists and turns, tall straight pines, and good clean air. The Black Hills were almost like being home, but Camp Iron Mountain was depressing. It was just a bunch of tarpapered shanties, a far sight worse than what he left back home. He half expected to see the massive bulk of the cotton mill, where he worked since turning fourteen, with its imposing brick siding and barred windows sitting off to the edge of camp. Nope, nothing but woods and a spray of clapboard huts fanning out from a central building, all of them coated with a thin layer of mica dust.

He pulled his bag from the truck and tried to shake the stiffness of travel from his back. He felt as if he hadn't slept for two weeks and his muscles told him how much he needed to sit still for a while.

The two other Cs who had been with him on the trip to Iron Mountain wearily joined him: Manny Lakso and Stanley Frucostek. They were two homesick teenagers from small towns or farms not that far away. A gaunt fellow, whose eyes behind his glasses shone with intelligence and determination, met them in front of the mess.

"I'm Dolph DeSmet," the fella said with a cheerfulness that spoke of a comfortable time ahead. He carried himself

13

with an assurance that comes from knowing what was up. He wore Corps issue green and would have looked comfortable in Army drab. He glanced over the three young men with a quick eye and clicked his teeth as if to say, Gonna take some doing turning this bunch into Cs. "You guys'll be moving into Kensington Place and I'm your barrack leader. You're lucky, you know that, getting into the finest hotel in the Corps."

Howie had imagined better but would have settled for worse. The long, narrow building, Barrack No. 9, Kensington Place or Old K.P., was snug up against a steep rocky hill, shaded on the north side by the Ponderosa pines. Inside, the floor was bare timber, rough hewn but worn smooth by years of use.

Whatever else it might have been, it was clean. The walls were lined with enough bunks for thirty men. Three pot-bellied stoves, strategically spaced, sat on slabs of thick tin painted black. Through the open, bottom-hinged windows the high late May sun poured into the large room from both sides. The barrack was empty except for the four of them and echoed with the sound their shoes made on the wooden floor.

"Everybody's on crew," Dolph said. "You'll get to meet them soon enough." He patted a top bunk near the center stove. "There's enough empties, you can choose for yourselves. Top bunk gets the trunk at the foot of the bed, bottom gets the chest against the wall. Latrines up the hill, use the back door and follow the trail. Mess hall—well, you'll find the mess hall. Follow your nose. When you get unpacked, step up to the commissary for your stuff."

Dolph watched as the three new Cs eyed the empty bunks. "Do any of you know how to talk?"

"You bet," said Manny Lakso.

Stanley said, "Nice place you got here."

"You?" Dolph said and pointed at Howie.

Howie nodded.

"Then maybe you should say something now and again."

"Howdy," Howie said as he picked a bottom bunk near the far end of the room.

"That's more like it. The guys get back from the job around four. Mess at six. Rec hall's open till nine. Lights out at nine-thirty. You have a problem, bring it to me first. If I can't help you, then we'll go up a rung or two. Good to have all of you here. Questions?"

"Kensington Place?" Manny said.

"Why the hell not? You ever been to the other Kensington Place? You know if it's any better than this?"

"Never even heard of Kensington Place. What is it?"

"A hotel they tell me, somewhere in London. We also got the Hilton, the Waldorf—that's across the road for the regular Army—the Brown Palace, the Plaza, the Roosevelt, the Algonquin, a few others. Me, I'm partial to good Old K.P. This is the prime hotel, what with the north hill protecting us in winter. You'll love Old K.P. when the first blizzard hits."

"Never stayed in a hotel before," Howie said.

"You'll get used to it." Dolph looked at him closely, then grinned. "You the one from Georgia?"

Howie nodded. "Never seen a blizzard, either."

"Where's that? Georgia," Stanley asked.

"Long ways from here, right? I was through Georgia once," Dolph said. "On a train. I was nine, maybe ten. You ever been to Utah?"

"Nope," Howie said. "It near by?"

Dolph laughed. "I like the way you talk, Cracker," he said. "Utah's about two days from here. Not far."

Manny asked, "Hey, is it true what they say about Georgia Crackers?"

"I don't know," Howie said. "What do they say?"

"They don't wear drawers."

Howie grinned. "I wouldn't know. I never did it with a Cracker."

"I heard," Dolph said, "that most Crackers play a mean game of ball. You care anything about baseball?"

"You guys play baseball out here?"

"Just getting cranked up."

Howie was home. Did he know anything about baseball? Ha. He shrugged. "Maybe," he said. "Maybe not." He almost laughed out loud he was so happy. No place could be that bad if they played ball.

Dolph chuckled. "I guess we'll just have to wait to find out. Well, I got to get back to the crew. I only hung around to check you guys in. See you later."

After a visit to the commissary, the new enrollees headed back to K.P., decked out in their new standard issue clothes. Howie plopped down on his bunk. The mattress was lumpy and smelled of unwashed feet. He couldn't sleep, though every particle of his being told him of his need for a long, lingering undisturbed rest. His arm and leg muscles would not relax. They jerked this way and that as if he still rode a bus. When he closed his eyes, he felt swimmy-headed; he could almost hear the hum of the motor and the thump thump thump of the tires on the road bed.

He sat up and stretched. The other new Cs were already asleep. The flooring squeaked as he approached the door, but the sound didn't bother anyone. Outside, the warm May breeze invited him. The camp was empty and silent. It, too, was an invitation. Come see, it seemed to whisper to him, come see just what I am.

At best, Camp Iron Mountain was a temporary place. It was located in a little valley created by Squaw Creek. The long narrow huts had been built from rough hewn lumber milled right on the site from the Ponderosa pines removed to make room for the barracks, mess, rec hall, and other buildings. The eight "hotels" were identical, built in a fan around the mess and rec hall. Carved into the hill overlooking the valley and using natural granite for a floor was the latrine, with running water provided by the water truck parked above it and hoses fastened from the truck barrel to a pipe in the side of the building.

Down the hill near the creek was the hospital, a T-shaped construction with beds for five sick Cs and the camp doctor. Across the creek was the maintenance area where the moving machines, trucks, and tractors were kept in running order. Here, a bridge crossed Squaw Creek. The road that ran through camp continued over the bridge and down to the partially completed Center Lake dam.

Howie crossed Squaw Creek to an open field with just enough room to play a little ball. The diamond had been fashioned by use, not by design. Rags staked to the ground were the bases, and a couple of wheelbarrow-loads of dirt dumped in the middle of the field served as a pitching mound. A pine sapling had taken root just behind second base; home plate was a mud hole with a rock in the middle. He felt at home here. He hadn't dreamed there would be baseball in this part of the world. Everywhere else in camp he felt dislocated, out of place. He was a novice at such things as settling in, making himself comfortable. He recognized a little bit of Pierson in himself as he realized he missed the thrill of moving on, the joy of traveling. Why not just keep going, head on out to the ocean and see what they know out there. Then, maybe, freight-hop a while and find out if there really are people living in Tahiti or Bora Bora, places he'd heard of but had no notion where they might be.

He explored the mess hall, wandering through the kitchen area where a bed of hot coals glowed in the huge stove. Near the rear wall of the kitchen, Howie found a civilian asleep on a sack of flour, his head resting on a pile of unpeeled potatoes.

Howie was suddenly very hungry, hungrier than he had been since he could remember. When was the last time he had eaten, anyway? A slice of too salty ham back in Sioux City, a hunk of bread with some butter and a little sugar in Sturgis, and a chocolate bar, thanks to Stanley Frucostek, on the ride across the Black Hills. He leaned over the stacks of food, smelled the aroma of bread baking and gently lifted a raw potato from the top of the pile. His wrist was caught in something as strong as a vice grip and as intent on inflicting pain as anything Howie had ever known.

"What the hell you think you're doing, buddy?" a deep-throated voice said in a low whisper as Howie's wrist was squeezed ever more tightly.

"Let go," Howie howled. "I ain't done nothing."

"Drop the spud," the voice ordered. Howie obliged. "Okay now, you one of the new ones?"

Howie nodded.

"You hungry, you let me know, okay? None of this stealing stuff. You hearing me?"

"Yes, sir."

"Shit. Save the sir stuff for the officers. I used to be regular army, but now I'm just a damn civilian. Second class. Around here, there's three classes of people: military, civilian, and Cs, in that order. What's your name?"

"Howie Cobb," he answered.

"You sound like you're from—where the hell is it? Louisiana? You a Creole, boy?"

"Georgia."

"Be damned. You a real live Cracker?" The fella with the iron grip laughed. "Name's Meathook. Glad to meet you. You come a long way, right? I suspected you new recruits'd be hungry as flies at an Indian burial ground. Didn't suspect there'd be a Cracker in the bunch, though. Come on, I got just the thing for you."

Meathook led Howie to a cabinet in the store room of the mess hall. He pulled a cardboard box from a shelf and handed it to the newcomer. "Eat your heart out," he said.

Howie grabbed a handful of the soda crackers and slipped them into his pants pocket. He'd save them for when he really needed them and no telling when that might be.

Howie explored the recreation hall. It was bleak. The large open room, with the same kind of windows as the barracks, was furnished with several small tables. Chairs surrounded each table, and playing cards were out and ready for somebody to shuffle and deal. A pool table stood near one wall; the rack beside it containing three cue sticks, one broken. A pot-bellied stove in the center, a broken-down sofa. A bookcase with two dozen or so books in it completed the list of furnishings.

Near the camp's main entrance at the rec hall, a call board held the camp roster, a couple of pages of job assignments, a few announcements related to "educational opportunities for enrollees" from somebody called Professor Watkins, notes announcing rides to Custer, Rapid City, Keystone, or Hermosa, and a section labeled "Lost and Found" with nothing listed.

Howie studied the camp roster with its four columns. So many exotic names, most of which he couldn't pronounce, like none he had encountered back home. Yankee names. Antholtz, Brclosch, Christopherson, DeSmet, Grovun, Husenga, Kuszmaul, Pawlowski. So many new faces to put with such names. He checked under the "Cs" for Cobb. He wasn't listed.

The commissary was locked up now. Attached to the screen door was a note: "Gone to Hermosa, back in two days. G.F." Was that a town? a lake for fishing? a woman? Howie tried to see through the glass portion of the door, but it was too dirty. Mica dust coated just about everything.

He admired the stone work at the campe entrance. It took skill to mortar rough stones together, a skill he wouldn't mind picking up. Maybe he could request mortar work and get him a trade he could take with him back to Georgia. Anything would be better than going back to work in the mill. The mill trapped his Poppa, his Momma, and it was on the verge of taking his older brother Hev. Without the Cs, that was where he would have been right then, getting off work from the cotton-thread shift. That was something he wasn't going to miss.

The cotton-thread shift.

Back home.

Douglasville.

The small house with so many kids in it. That was what he missed. Hell, he hadn't thought of Hank and Martha, Annie and Horatio and Hev, Pierson and Brenda, May Lou and Alexander Stevens, none of them since stepping off the bus in Fort Meade. Now, here he was, already thinking about learning a skill and getting a job back in Douglasville, probably one worth a good solid living, getting his own place, maybe earning enough to get married on. Who knows...Indella.

"Put it from you, buddy boy," he said aloud, surprised to hear his own voice in that place so far from home. Just don't think about it. Keep yourself off what's back there, find the adventure you've dreamed of. It's here, all around you, the Black Hills, the Cs, the world you've chosen over what's back home.

The regular Army cabins were located across the road. They had a more permanent look than the C's. It wouldn't be bad, being in the army, if he could stay in places like these: genuine log cabins lost in the woods, a mountain stream nearby. Not bad for a country bumpkin.

He peered through a window of one cabin. Inside it looked a whole lot nicer than how he remembered back home: a fireplace, a bookcase filled with leather-backed books, a nice oak table with chairs around it, a cane loveseat with pillows tossed around for comfort—yeah, a hell of a lot better than back home.

Maybe that was what he should consider, a life in the service. A fella could do worse. All Camp Iron Mountain was missing was somebody he knew and cared about: Momma May Lou with her stern gaze that seemed to know everything; Poppa Alexander Stevens with his snuff cups, Bible, evening prayers, and gentle rock; his middle brother Hank, with his pestering; older brother Hev and his haughty silence and lovely Merle

Addams clinging to his arm; sister Martha with her mouth; baby sister Brenda with her silence; oldest sister Annie; even baby of the family Horatio and his screams for attention. And yeah, Pierson. God knows, Pierson would love a place like this. It was so unlike home he was bound to love it. Plenty of places to run off to and hide without getting into trouble. He should write his brother and tell him to join up just as soon as his age allowed. The Corps was definitely the place to be.

He wandered around the side of the cabin, past a lean-to with its pile of coal, and to the back yard.

He stopped.

Christ. There, lying on a blanket and naked as a rooster after a hurricane, her backside toward Howie, was the prettiest woman he had ever seen. She lay there on her side, unaware of his eyes, her body soaking up the midafternoon rays.

He felt frightened at first; she had to be the wife of one of the regular Army fellas. Maybe even the C.O. She looked so young. Or did she? He didn't know young from old when it came to naked women's bodies from the back. Secretly he wished he had accepted Indella's invitation, if that was what it had been, to explore her female secrets, if for no other reason than to prepare himself for a time like this. But Indella wasn't that kind of girl—he wasn't that kind of man. Something like that. Maybe he was just plain scared shitless and felt safest when he left such things alone.

He studied the woman in her nakedness, the way her rear end rounded itself into her thighs, the way her legs seemed to lure his eyes down and in between them, like magnets pulling him in, making him want to ease forward and put his hands on her soft white buns, maybe even kiss them lightly.

Are you out of your mind? This woman, whoever she was, was doing what she was doing because she was completely free to do it. His being there was an intrusion like none other. His better sense told him, best get out from here right now, just ease on back and leave, and never mention this to anybody. He wasn't a Peeping Tom, for God's sake. Get away, before you're found out.

He took a step backward. The stick under his shoe popped like an air rifle. Holy Jesus, you stupid fool, his adrenalin yelled to his body, get away from this now!

He ran. He had no idea if the woman saw him or not. He didn't care. Nor did he know where to run. He just ran, head down and boots clomping like the hooves of a workhorse on pavement, across the road, through the gate, down the hillside, across the creek, splashing himself with cold and comforting creek water, to the pitcher's mound. He sat in the middle of the ball diamond, pulled his knees into his chin, and tried as best he could to convince himself that what he had done, stumbling onto a woman's private sunning, wasn't a sin.

A sin. It had to be, considering how he felt. Lust in the heart. How many times had Alexander Stevens lectured him about lusting in his heart. A sin worse than lusting in the flesh, everybody knew that. Now he had done it. Lordy, he was sure to die and go to hell with so much sinning inside him.

Still, in a way he felt cheated; some of life's mystery was gone. Now, at least he knew that they, women, weren't all that different from men. In fact, except for women being a little rounder and less hairy and a heck of a lot more attractive, men and women were pretty much alike. At least from the butt side. He tried to raise images in his head of the woman's bare bottom. Nothing came. Instead, he imagined standing in the batter's box, bat cocked and ready to swing at anything anybody threw his way.

At five on the dot, the bird cages rolled into camp and stopped outside the commissary.

A hundred or so young men, a few actually younger than Howie, most a year or two older, piled out of the trucks amid a hubbub of sound and confusion, and filled the camp with a life the place had been missing since his arrival.

Howie stood on the threshold of K.P., with Stanley Frucostek and Manny Lakso beside him, watching the veteran enrollees act like getting back to camp was the most common thing in the world.

"Guess that's us come tomorrow," Howie said.

"Huh?" Stanley said.

"Never mind."

A squat, iron-jawed man in Army green, insignias that meant nothing to Howie attached to his collar and boots, coated with mica dust, and another uniformed Army man with stripes on his arm, stolled toward Kensington Place, chatting as they came.

The two halted near the stone steps. Dolph DeSmet rushed from the bird cages to K.P. and leaped to the top step before the two could enter.

"Sir," he said, "Captain, new recruits are present and assigned living quarters. Look sharp, gentlemen," he snapped at the three new enrollees.

Look sharp? Howie didn't know how.

Looking sharp meant, Howie figured out, step aside. The Captain and his underling entered K.P.

The Captain bellowed with a loud but pleasant voice, "Which ones are the new sonsawhores?" He looked at Howie and the others and grinned.

"Sound off," barked Dloph. The three stood as if dumbfounded. "Introduce yourselves."

Howie stood at attention as he had seen soldiers in movies stand. He made a ramrod of his spine, his breath caved inside himself.

"At ease, gentlemen. And welcome to Iron Mountain," the man with the iron jaw said and Howie breathed again. "I'm Clyde Munk, Captain, U.S. Army," he said. "This is my subaltern," and he patted the other military fella on the back,

"Liam O'Kelley. Don't let his name fool you. Not a drop of Irish in his blood." The Captain, O'Kelley, and even Dolph laughed loud and long at the little joke which the newcomers didn't understand. "Where you from, son?" the Captain asked Stanley.

"Wasta, South Dakota, sir," he answered.

"Uhn. Sorry little place, Wasta. Never been there, never hope to go." He stopped in front of Howie. "How about you?

"I'm from Douglasville."

"Where 'bouts in South Dakota's that?"

"Not, sir. It's in the proud state of Georgia."

The Captain turned to O'Kelley and said, "Be damned. He's a first, ain't he?"

"Far as I know," said O'Kelley.

"Well, I tell you this, O'Kelley. This kid from Georgia, he's a long way from home. He just might win the prize for most miles crossed getting to Iron Mountain. 'Spect we'll see his name on the AWOL list sooner than not. Damn rebels get homesick. That right, corpsman?"

"Ain't no rebel, General. Confederate maybe. But rebel— that's a different kettle of crawfish."

"My great granddaddy fought at Antietam," the Captain said. "Lost a leg and two fingers in a matter of fifteen minutes. He cried when McClelland got the axe. A great war, that one, right Confederate? And the right side won?"

"My great granddaddy's daddy sold moonshine during the war, sir."

"That right? To which side?"

"Both. Yes, sir, put two pearl-handled pistols on you and slap a red velvet sash around your chest, and you'd be the spitting image of my great-great granddaddy Morris, General."

The Captain laughed in a free and inviting way. He clapped Howie on the back and said to O'Kelley, "This son of a bitch just might fit in around here! He might know some secrets to make folks feel a little better on Saturday nights.

Tell Meathook to lay in a supply of corn mash." He turned to Manny, "How about you, son? Lakso, is it?"

"From Bismarck, sir."

"Good place for pheasant hunting. You like moonshine, Lakso?"

"Never had any. What is it?"

"Let our Confederate here tell you about it. Okay, you boys make yourselves right at home. Enjoy the day, what's left of it. Tomorrow, we'll teach you a few things. Don't kill them their first day out, Sergeant. Break them in real slow and easy. Camp Iron Mountain is your home now, boys, and will be for at least one calendar year. You'll find that we have just as much to offer as home, maybe more, so I'd appreciate your settling in, getting yourselves all fixed up, and leave the worry to us. There are rules you'll need to know, things you're supposed to do, not do, that sort of thing. Sergeant O'Kelley will fill you in on them. You have any questions, go to Dolph here first; he's the maitre 'd so to speak for this particular hotel. If he can't take care of you, he'll seek out the Sergeant here, and if he can't take care of you, he'll bring your problem to me. Try to remember, I don't like problems. They give me indigestion. Okay, boys, enjoy yourselves, have fun, and don't be putting it places it don't belong." He laughed again and punched O'Kelley in the side.

He left with the Sergeant trailing behind.

Howie watched as O'Kelley sauntered away. "What about those rules?" he asked.

Dolph slapped his hands together and rubbed them as if they were cold and needed warming. "There's only one rule, fellas, and we all abide by it: stay clear of the C.O. You attend to that, and you'll be just fine. Dinner's at six. Mess ain't much, but you'll get used to it. See you then."

"'Scuse me, DeSmet," Howie said. "What do we call you?"

"Shoot, I don't know. Anything you like, I guess."

"Sir?"

"Not on your life. Makes me sound as if I'm ready for the

worm. Or worse: makes me sound like an officer. I'm the same as you guys, only I'm in my second year. A re-upper. A foolish thing to be, but what can I say. Just call me Dolph and we'll get along fine.''

He started off toward the rec hall, but Howie had a question that needed an answer. "Do any of the regularArmy fellas have wives?" he wanted to know.

"The C.O., and O'Kelley's engaged, but she doesn't live here in camp, not yet. Why?''

"The C.O.'s wife—is she real pretty?''

"That woman's got the plainest face this side of Rushmore,'' Dolph said and laughed. "You tell anybody I said that, I'll make you out a liar. But I tell you, she'd scare ants off a picnic. You want to rid yourself of lice, just let them get an eye full of her. Still, she's the only woman in camp most of the time. She's always on Old Clyde's arm. Like she's stuck to him or something. What makes that woman so uncommonly plain ain't her looks, mister, it's the devotion she gets from the old man. He goes to church every night at that woman's feet. You'll know her when you see her. She'll be glued to the old man.''

"May already done seen her," Howie said, in nothing more than a whisper.

Howie joined the others as they made their way to the mess hall and was standing in line with his metal tray waiting to receive his portion when Meathook caught him by the sleeve and clanged a large spoon against the top of a table. An uneasy quiet settled over the place. Meathook announced, loud enough to be heard down at the hospital, "Yo gents. Look what we got here. One real live Confederate Cracker from the proud state of Georgia. What say we give him a welcome to Iron Mountain.''

The room filled with vulgar sounds, catcalls, whistles, boos, and even one, "Better get gone while you can, buddy, go back home to your mama!" Then laughter. Dolph led Howie to a table near the east end of the building.

Howie's first meal at Iron Mountain wasn't anything to write home about. Meathook served up an overcooked ham, some greasy green beans, and something that smelled like fried onions but had no taste at all. For dessert there was rice pudding with molasses poured over it, and to wash it all down was powdered milk, nothing more than creek water with chalk clouding it.

Howie missed May Lou's collards and cornbread, baked chicken, and mashed potatoes. Or yellow layer cake with pinto beans. Chocolate cake for dessert. If his first mess was what he had to look forward to for the coming year, Howie was already wondering if joining the Cs had been a wise move to make. Give it time, though, he told himself. Maybe Meathook just had a bad day.

After those around him had almost finished gulping their food, Dolph made formal introductions.

"Fellas," Dolph announced to the twenty or so enrollees at the table, "this is Cracker who says he knows a piddling about the game of baseball."

"You really from Georgia?" one of them asked.

"Guess so."

"You bet he's from Georgia. Listen to that accent!" another said.

Howie looked around, the grinning faces waiting to hear him talk. "What accent's that?" he asked. And the enrollees exploded with laughter. In less than a second his dander rose to attention. They were making fun of him, and that was something his Poppa would not allow. But their faces were full of good honest humor. After a moment, Howie grinned back. They were just like him, just kids away from home having a good time.

"These guys here, " Dolph said when he could be heard again, "make up the Cougars. The Iron Mountain Cougars. We're going to win it all this year, right guys?"

"What's a Cougar?" Howie wanted to know.

"Best damn baseball team in the Cs," somebody yelled and started a chant that was soon picked up by others in the hall until it filled the place. "Coo—Coo—Coo!" over and over again.

Captain Clyde entered the mess. He stood like a brick wall, hands on hips, his iron jaw set, glaring over the enrollees, his head nodding like a bobber on a lake.

Behind him came the Mrs. C.O., Antoinette Munk. She was a smallish woman, probably the same age as her husband, thirty-five, if not a bit older. She had bright yellow hair and wore too much make-up. She dressed in clothing more fitting for Chicago than the Black Hills. It was her clothes that fooled Howie and kept him from recognizing her right away. Another thing, too. She was much fatter than Howie would have imagined from having seen her from the back lying on her side. But she wasn't what Howie would call a usual fat. No. He realized, and it made him want to sink into the floorboards, that Antoinette Munk was nearing the final days of her time; that soon, probably sooner than any of the Cs could imagine, there would be the squall of a baby boy or girl filling the echoing valley.

When it dawned on Howie that he, that very afternoon, had been lusting over the nude backside of a pregnant woman, he flushed a bright rust, adding color to his already freckled face. He knew now he would definitely have to ask the Good Lord to forgive his sin, compounded now beyond all possible measure.

The C.O. wandered among the tables of silent men, his wife close behind him. They edged their way through, pushing some enrollees aside, nodding and sharing a few quick words with others.

Then Mrs. Munk stopped. She glared across the mess hall until she caught Howie's eye. She, too, flushed, in spite of her heavy make-up job. She held his gaze for only a moment before she raised her arm from her protruding belly and pointed a finger directly at Howie's nose.

"Him," she said. She turned on her heel, shoved Captain

Clyde aside, and marched out of the mess hall and up the mica dust road toward the comfort of her cabin.

Captain Clyde found O'Kelley at one of the tables, whispered something to him, took one last look at Howie's reddened face, and followed his wife back up the road. She was waiting for him outside the commissary, and the Cs could hear her railing at him, though not understanding what she said, as the two passed through the gate and across the road.

Sound returned to the mess, but no laughter. Other Cs glared at Howie as if he had ham grease for a mustache. Most conversations were now in whispers like everybody had suddenly realized they were at a wake.

Howie turned to Dolph and asked as quietly as he could and still be heard, "What's going on?"

"If you don't know, I sure don't." Dolph returned to his meal and finished it hurriedly and in silence.

As Howie dumped his food tray in the barrel near the kitchen, O'Kelley sidled up to him: "Meet me in the commissary in fifteen minutes, Confederate. Don't keep me waiting."

First day in camp and already in trouble, already drawing Captain Clyde's and his subaltern's attention. Howie didn't know where else to turn. He found Meathook taking a rest out back of the mess hall. He asked, "It normal for new enrollees to be singled out on their first day in camp?"

"No," Meathook said, offering no help or insights into the kind of trouble Howie might be in. "Fact is, Old Clyde doesn't usually show up at mess. Mrs. Clyde fixes him up special every night, orders stuff right out of the kitchen here and cooks it for him. I don't take it personal, though. Fact is I've never seen Old Clyde in the mess before. I don't know. Cracker, you're on your own I guess."

When Howie stepped into the commissary, Captain Clyde and Sergeant O'Kelley were waiting for him. They stared at him as if they were looking at the most hardened of criminals.

Their quiet made Howie sweat.

The inner office was nothing like Howie had imagined. On the walls were maps of the Black Hills with a bunch of spots highlighted with colored tabs. Work sites most likely. A photo of President Roosevelt was hooked to a nail under an American Flag. A photo of an older guy hung over a huge roll-top desk that was well oiled and littered with papers. The room also contained a work table, several chairs, and a coal burning pot-bellied stove, black as soot.

The C.O. stood at an open window, his back to the new enrollee. O'Kelley broke the silence and motioned to a chair by the wall. "Take a load off," he said.

"Just as soon stand if you don't mind, sir," Howie said.

O'Kelley cleared his throat and said, "Do you know why we've called you in here, Corpsman? What's your real name anyway? I forget."

"Howell Madison Cobb, sir."

"Well, do you?"

"Ain't got the foggiest, sir."

Old Clyde turned. His iron jaw seemed to have rusted closed. He had a scowl on his face as dense as any Howie had ever seen. A smile would have cracked his face into a hundred pieces, and he would have had to send his jaw out for repairs.

The Captain didn't mince words, but blurted out, "You're a goddamn voyeur, you no good piece of chicken shit. You know what that is: voyeru?"

"No, sir," Howie said, recognizing the word as representing what was most likely a particularly bad thing.

"Figures. He's stupid, O'Kelley. It means you're a goddamn Peeping Tom! You've been in camp less than a day, and you can't control yourself. You go spying on Mrs. Munk like she's some sort of pin-up, or worse, like she's a Rapid City whore. Get your fill of her, did you? I'd like to kick your ass out of here so fast it'd take a month for your head to catch it up."

"Take it easy, Captain."

"I know. I know. But the son of a bitch makes me sick. Look at him. Don't he make you sick, Sergeant?"

"I'm sorry, sir," Howie said. He couldn't keep his fear from showing. The irate man could shoot him, there on the spot, and nobody back home would ever know the difference. They could say it was an accident, his gun went off, if he had a gun, call it unfortunate, and May Lou and Alexander Stevens would put him six feet under and never know of his innocence, that it was all a mistake. In fact, he wouldn't be surprised to see the pistol come out of a desk drawer and empty itself into his chest and belly. Might make him feel better, Lord knows.

"Sorry?" The jaw was working now, loosened from its rust. "Hear that, Sergeant? He's sorry. That means you admit it, huh?" The C.O. came out of his chair and almost across the top of the desk, "Yeeeeeeeoooooooouuuu!" He settled back, winded, and whispered, a threat in the depth of his whisper, "I wish to God I could get you out of this camp tomorrow. No, tonight. Is there any way we can do that, O'Kelley?"

"No, sir, we're below quota as it is."

"You telling me we're stuck with this creep?"

"Commandant," Howie tried to say.

"Did anybody tell you you could talk, mister!"

"No, sir," Howie said.

O'Kelley edged between the teenager and the Army veteran. "What you want to know, boy?"

"You gonna shoot me or what?"

O'Kelley nodded, "Pretty good idea, but we'll hold off on that for awhile."

"Cause I had me an uncle on my Momma's side, name of Jonas Shedd, who got his ass caught spying on the mayor's daughter. This was a few years back..."

"Are you interested in this bullshit, Sergeant?"

"If he gets to his point, yes sir, I am."

"Then get to it for God's sake," the C.O. snapped.

"Well," Howie said, trying to raise a smile, "the mayor caught my Uncle Jonas with his eye sockets tingling you might say and took him out back, forced him to take off his right shoe and proceeded to shoot my uncle's big toe right off his foot. Uncle Jonas walked with a limp from that day to this. So I was wandering, you gonna shoot me like that, sir?"

"Sounds like a damn good idea to me. Sergeant?"

"Maybe next time, sir?"

"Yeah. Guess so." Captain Clyde was around the edge of the desk. "I'll be watching you, boy," the C.O. said, not taking his eyes off Howie, leaning toward him like a stick of dynamite ready to find a match. "You step one inch over the line, and I swear, I'll have your butt in so much trouble you'll wish you'd never left your mother's apron string. Maybe even shoot off your right big toe to boot!" He barked the next, "Do I make myself clear, C?"

Howie could only whisper, "Yes, sir."

"Let me hear you say it just a little louder."

"Yes, sir!"

"Good. Sergeant. See to it that our new friend gets a chance to learn how we clean the latrines here at Camp Iron Mountain. Make it a week's worth of lessons. Then, we'll see."

"Yes, sir," O'Kelley said, almost saluting, but restraining the urge.

But Old Clyde wasn't through. "Those civilians in Washington tell me you fellows gotta be treated with hugs and kisses, not like you're in the Army or anything. Well, I swear, Cobb or whatever your name is, I don't buy that shit. No, sir. You ask me, the Army's the right place to take care of scum like you. Now, get out of my sight before I throw up and embarrass myself."

Howie couldn't move. He was frozen, his muscles refused to budge. He wanted to run as far and as fast as he could, but his body wouldn't oblige. O'Kelley gave him a shove toward the door, "Go on, get out of here," he said.

Howie found his legs and staggered from the commissary, forgetting to close the door behind him.

"What the hell's wrong with you, C?" It was the Captain again, angry as ever. "You raised in a barn or what?" And the door slammed behind him.

Howie's stomach was doing all kinds of twists and turns; he had to force his legs to carry him toward Kensington Place. Halfway there, the greasy ham and vegetables he had eaten swam up his gullet and splashed in the mica dust. He covered his up-chuck as best he could, ashamed of what it said about him.

Finally, he sat on a rock and buried his head in his arms. Thank God it was pitch dark. Otherwise he would have been seen, shaking from fright and shame, unable to hold down his dinner. Silently, he wished he was home, a young boy again, cuddled up between May Lou and Alexander Stevens in their sweet-smelling bed.

He stayed outside until taps sounded. The night had turned more than chilly; it was cold. Downright frosty. His lightweight jacket was not up to the task of warding off the evening chill.

Still, he could not go inside. He was too ashamed. Nobody spoke to him when he slipped into K.P. just as the lights were turned out. It was as if he was contagious, as if he was in quarantine.

He kept to himself, slipped out of his clothes, and crawled, shivering, into bed.

Stanley Frucostek, in the bunk under him, whispered, "Hey, Cracker, you okay?"

"Yeah," he said. "Still got my big toe."

"Huh?"

"Nothing. Private joke."

Howie slept fitfully that night. His cotton mattress was lumpy. He couldn't find any place to lie flat. He felt like something was crawling on him, something coming from the covers, something that was hungry for his blood. Strange sounds kept waking him up, sounds like none he had ever heard before. Some sort of animal chewed outside the window, an animal that stood tall and breathed deep. A coyote in the distance yelled at the moon; another not quite so far away answered. He guessed the howling he heard was that of coyotes. He'd not heard anything like it back home. Something scurried across the barrack floor. Mice he could live with. But he wasn't certain these creatures were mice; the sound they made was too large. Whatever they were, they wouldn't bite would they?

There was so much he didn't know. And the opportunity to learn had been lost to him by his own stupidity. How do you figure? His mistake on the first day into camp had certainly put a taint on things, hadn't it.

He had to remind himself that he had asked for this assignment. Send him a long, long way from Georgia, some place where he could meet new people and learn new things and find out how other folks lived. Leave things alone and he'd be planting trees near Macon or digging ditches in Dalton or chopping cotton near Moultrie. No. He had to request an adventure.

He wasn't sure any more if adventure was what he wanted. This getting into trouble without even trying. Not knowing what was crawling on his body or what was grazing just outside the barrack window. Morning, he would be on latrine duty and follow that with other work detail. Maybe he was stupid after all, not knowing what the rules were and how he fit into things. God, he missed Momma and Alexander Stevens, Liberty Baptist Church and pasture ball, wildcat dens...He even missed Hank, the pest.

Martha, Annie, Brenda—even Pierson. Hev. Indella. He missed Indella even more than his Momma. Hev and his somber way of thinking, almost too old for his age—he had been born that way. Old. And knowing. Indella and her inability to keep tears inside her eyes and her sweetness, her innocence. Oh, sweet dear perfect Indella with those eyes of hers. What would she say about his first day in the Cs? What would he do if some blundering idiot like himself should happen up on Indella who might be sunbathing like the C.O.'s wife? And pregnant to boot. No way. Indella would never do such a thing as reveal her naked body to the sun. Would she? He didn't know.

Indella, the dearest person in the world, was nothing more than a stranger to him. He knew so little about her. They had met . . . He felt embarrassed now, lying there a lump of stupid Southern flesh, for what he had said to her that first time when they had met so casually. It had been less than a month before.

He, along with his brother Hev, eighteen months older and already a man of the world to hear him tell it, and the two Hembree boys, Mac and Ferd, were on their way home from a game of pasture ball when they passed the Shealy place. It took the oldest of the Hembree boys, Mac, the lankiest and most world-aware of the bunch, to notice the black-haired, black-eyed girl, skinny, not yet fully formed, sitting on the porch steps of her white-washed clapboard house reading a book.

It was hot that day. The girl had watched the four full-of-themselves ball players from behind the safety of her book as she fanned herself and pretended to read. She acted surprised when she heard the first whistle. It was lewd and sassy, the kind she had heard her daddy, Sylvester Shealy, use dozens of times when a good looking woman passed by the house. She straightened her jumper with the second whistle, an even sassier sound than the first. This was followed by a lewd laugh that her momma, Glory Bea Shealy, would have called, "Dirty minded. Typical of anything that wears pants."

The four teenagers had stopped near the fence that guarded the narrow path from the road to the Shealy place. Three of them leaned against the front fence post that had trouble sustaining the weight of its gate, and wasn't prepared to hold the leanings of the teenage boys from Douglasville. The fence creaked and sagged as the three of them gaped, open-mouthed, at the girl's long black hair and olive-toned skin. It didn't matter to them that the female they ogled was too young to be leered at in such a way. Howie felt ashamed.

He stood in the middle of the road, embarrassed, wanting to be somewhere else. He hated being around the Hembree brothers when they were in their sassy moods. Nor did he care for the sounds they made with the saliva in their mouths. He didn't consider making similar sounds with his own saliva. Seemed demeaning to himself and to the person the sounds were aimed at. It bothered him that his own brother joined in the way he did, slapping the boards of the front fence with his open palm and whistling through his teeth like some hick from Hapeville—and Hev, almost as good as engaged to Merle Addams, a fine catch of a woman if there ever was one. Howie wanted to keep going down the road, back to Douglasville where he could share the glory of his pasture-ball exploits with the Cobb clan. After all, two unassisted double plays and four-for-four were worth a lot of cockadoodling around the supper table.

"What do you all want?" the girl's eleven-year-old kid brother, Rudolph Shealy, shouted from the safety of the screen door. "Bunch of Douglasville hoods, ain'tcha," he said, his flip-staff in hand, already loaded with a smooth creek stone. He hadn't as yet used the staff against anything but birds and a rabbit or two, but he was practiced. He was ready to protect his sister, if need be, against all comers.

"You boys run on," the girl yelled.

Howie had tugged at the shirt sleeves of the others. "Let's get going," he said to the Hembree boys who were creating enough embarrassment to last till leap year.

"You don't go on, I'll call my papa," the girl threatened, clutching the book against her chest.

"You don't got a papa," Mac Hembree said and laughed. He was the brassy one of the bunch, not ashamed to say whatever popped in his head. "This is the Shealy place," he said to Howie. "I know old Sylvester Shealy. He's a sot if I ever saw one. He don't even live here anymore."

"Come on y'all," Howie urged. "Leave her alone."

"You got pretty hair," Ferd Hembree yelled and sniggered. Howie silently agreed. First thing he had noticed about this young woman was her hair, black and shiny, like it was made to be touched. She knew it was her best feature, judging from how she tossed it back with a twitch of her head. She must brush it ten times a day to get it shiny like that, Howie figured. Ferd insinuated more with the twist of his mouth than with his tone of voice as he shouted, "Where'd you buy such pretty hair?"

"God's gift," the girl answered. And she tossed it again, pride all over her face. Howie was even more embarrassed. She was feeding the fire by letting on that they were anywhere near. She should have ignored the bunch of them, and more than likely they would have been on their way. Instead, the taunting grew in racket and if they weren't careful, an adult was going to come out of that house and fill their butts with buckshot. Howie with such a possibility increasing each second they hung around the picket fence eased away to the center of the road. Somehow or other, the girl caught his eye and lifted a small hand in his direction, and he returned the tentative wave.

"One of these days, she's gonna be a looker," Ferd said loud enough for everyone to hear, even the girl. Then he turned, gave the fence a little side kick with his boot and the four of them sauntered down the road, Howie at the rear, keeping a distance from his friends he now thought of as the idiots they were. But for the fact that he needed the Hembree brothers for the pasture ball games, he would have said the hell with them and beat it back to the white-washed house and apologized to the young girl and maybe even found out what she was reading.

He separated himself from the group, his form of protest. Besides he wanted one last look at this girl he'd not seen before. She struck him as somebody he might like to get to know, give her a few years. Anybody who would sit around on a hot Saturday afternoon with her nose in a book had to have something going for her. To his way of thinking, being a bookworm and a female was not a bad combination. He hadn't really put the two things together before, but sure, if he ever got married, he hoped his wife'd be a reader, a reader of everything, somebody who could keep him informed so he wouldn't have to read anything himself. He kicked at the gravel in the road. His ideas were leap-frogging all inside him and he didn't know just what to make of it all.

She had followed as far as the gate, watching the boys, then into the road, watching them, then to the edge of the field. Howie stopped just before the bend in Big A Road where the screwball plum trees hid the Shealy place from the rest of the world. He paused, looked over his shoulder, and saw her there, standing on the edge of the ditch, her book dangling from her arm like a natural extension of her body. She roused a feeling inside him he had not confronted before and it had made the blood rush like a rivulet after a June gully-washer up past his collar and into his rusty-red face. All around him was the smell of honeysuckle, the sweetest aroma in the world. There seemed a connection somehow, his standing there smelling honeysuckle and looking back at the prettiest young girl he had seen probably ever. Then without willing it, his nose being led by honeysuckle, his hand rose from his side and sort of waved. He couldn't be sure, but his movement caused her to wave back.

"What's your name?" he yelled.

"Indella Cora Mae Shealy," she answered.

"Mine's Howie," he called back. "Howell Madison Cobb. Remember that cause I'm gonna be famous!"

Now as he lay in a strange bed with even stranger critters taking nibbles at his arms and legs, he felt ashamed of his words. "Gonna be famous." He banged his head against the hard mattress of the bunk until somebody in the darkened room groaned a complaint. Sure, he was stupid, just like the commandant had said. Stupid, stupid, stupid...

A coyote howled in the distance. It was the last thing he heard his first night in the Black Hills.

Latrine Officer

It was still dark when Dolph DeSmet shook him awake. Howie sat up with a start. What's wrong?

"O'Kelley's waiting for you," Dolph said.

"What time is it?"

"O'Kelley's time."

Howie shivered as he slipped on his pants, boots, shirt, and cap. It was colder now than when he went to bed. Colder than it got at home in January. He'd never get used to this place, not if he lived here a hundred years.

He put on his jacket and staggered toward the back door of K.P., his shoe strings making a clicking sound on the wooden barrack floor.

"Let's move it," O'Kelley barked. "You dawdle, and you'll hit work detail without chow."

The Sergeant rushed up the hill toward the latrine. If the man needed to go that bad, let him, Howie thought but didn't say as he dragged along behind, wishing he was still in bed.

Even that God-forsaken mattress he inherited from some former C was better than whatever O'Kelley had in mind so early in the morning.

As Howie entered the latrine with its line of doorless stalls, hard and cold concrete floor, trough of a urinal, and half-a-dozen shower heads, O'Kelley was pulling a huge mop, a pail, and a box of powder suds into the middle of the room. "I swear, Corpsman, you be lax in this and you'll go to the rock pile even on Saturdays."

39

Howie was still woozy with sleep. "Rock pile?" he asked.

"First things first. Now, this," O'Kelley continued, pointing to the mop and pail, "is to clean that," pointing to the floor. "Only you'll notice there's no water in it. Okay. You get water from this spigot," and he turned on a spigot that was dry. "Okay. Now the reason there's no water coming from the spigot is because it's hooked up to the water truck outside and the truck's empty. Now, to get water in the bucket, you got to have water in the tank on the truck. To get water in the tank on the truck, you have to crank up the truck, drive it down to the bridge, hook its top hose to the pump you'll find down there, crank up the pump, heh, heh, heh—good luck with that—and fill the tank from the creek. Then you pull the truck back up here, park it where you found it, and hitch it to the water system in here. Then you can fill your bucket from this spigot, mop the floor and clean the johns, urinal, and shower stalls. You with me so far?"

"Guess so," Howie said.

"Well, then, do it." O'Kelley emptied his bladder in the urinal as he said, "You get cold, you can cook up a fire in the Bell," and pointed at the potbellied stove near the shower heads. Then he left, going back down the hill, most likely to his warm comfortable bed.

Howie stood in the middle of the latrine, scratching at the numerous bites he had on his belly and back.

Without stopping, O'Kelley yelled over his shoulder when halfway back to the barracks, "You don't have long, Corpsman. Breakfast is in an hour and a half. See you then."

"One thing, though," Howie said mostly to himself since O'Kelley was too far away to hear, "I don't know how to drive."

Maneuvering the truck down the hill to the creek was no problem. Just get it rolling and guide it down the slope and stop it right in the center of the bridge. Nothing to it.

Hooking the hose from the pump to the top of the water tank wasn't a problem either. Piece of cake.

Getting the pump started with the piece of twine wrapped around the rotor was something else. Twenty pulls at the thing and it still sat silent.

But Howie didn't give up. It wasn't in his nature to give up on a thing once started.

On the twenty-eighth pull, the motor sputtered a bit. On the thirtieth, it burped and sputtered even more. On the fortieth, it spat alive and held. No problem.

Once the pump was working, the water flowed into the truck tank as easy as you please.

A grayish haze had settled over the hills and valley. The air was brisk but sweet, filled with scent of pine and clean earth. Pretty soon, the army bugle would blow and he wouldn't be the only C about. Oh, yeah, he almost said aloud, this ain't so bad.

He banged his arms against his sides trying to drive away the chill that lingered. He saw his problem right off. Sure it was simple enough letting the truck coast down the hill to the bridge, park it there and fill it with water. But it wasn't going to coast back up. No, he had to get the thing going, slip the truck into gear, drive it up the hill, and park it in its place above the latrine, next to the hose that led to the toilets, shower heads, and urinal. Well, he figured, what comes down a hill has to go up.

He cranked the truck, easier than getting the pump underway, ground the gears, let the clutch out too soon, and flooded the motor, causing it to choke to death. The smell of gas oozed into the cab. Only thing was, Howie didn't know what flooding meant to a machine like the water truck. He didn't know that to flood a unit such as this meant it would take a good twenty minutes of sitting idle before the extra gas would evaporate and the truck would crank again. If he had known that, he wouldn't have ground the starter on and on, impatiently waiting for the motor to leap to life.

Which it didn't. Just keep trying, he said to himself, it's bound to catch. After all, on the fortieth pull the pump started.

The sound of the grinding starter echoed through the valley of Squaw Creek, popping consciousness into the eyes of most in camp, sending shivers of disgust through most bodies now awake. A huge cry of "Don't treat a motor like that!" came from the Plaza.

But Howie didn't hear it. All he heard was the whine, whine, whine of the truck engine refusing to turn over.

When it did, it lurched forward with a surge, sloshing water over the edges of the tank and dousing Howie's back and neck, sending sparklers of cold to every particle of his body.

"Well, goddamn it to hell!" he hollered as the front end of the truck crashed through the guardrail of the bridge, splintering the wood into the creek below, and leaving the right front wheel hanging over the creek bed.

The engine died one more time. He jumped to the bridge and kicked the tire that hung in mid-air and whispered, "Shit, shit, shit..." so soft his Momma couldn't hear. Wasn't he already in enough trouble with the C.O. without bringing additional wrath down on his head through his cussing?

He didn't care. "Shitfire and hellstones, you goddamn stupid vehicle, don't you know nothing?" and he banged his fist against the truck's right fender.

O'Kelley had told him to do a thing, and by God he was going to do it, and no damned water truck was gonna keep him from doing it. He slammed his butt in the seat behind the steering column and ground the starter on and on, a sound that could cause strong men to weep. He ground it until it was little more than a tinny rasp, an even worse sound to the handful of Cs who had begun to gather near the back of the Mess, staring down at the truck. But the starter ground on and on.

One of the Cs yelled, "Why doesn't somebody stop the fool idiot?" But nobody did.

Nobody approached the bridge and the truck with Howie sitting alone and determined inside it.

After a tireless effort that brought over half the Cs from the barracks and left them standing in a dozen or so groups, huddled together for warmth, a miracle occurred: the motor caught once again. One or two of the groups raised a little cheer.

But Howie had the vehicle in forward gear.

The truck leaped forward one more time, splintering more of the railing, popping a board or two of the bridge flooring, and taking the left front wheel off the bridge entirely.

The cab was now sitting on its chassis, it's two front wheels spinning ten feet above the swirling water of the creek. Water from the tank cascaded into the cab, soaking Howie completely, sending shards of cold all through him.

Somebody among the Cs began to clap in a sarcastic staccato until Captain Clyde stepped out of one of the groups and strolled to the bridge and yelled above the sound of the rushing creek, "What in God's name is going on here?!"

Howie recognized the voice. "Not now," he said. "Leave me alone, I'll fix it, just don't give me a hassle, okay?"

Captain Clyde stood beside the truck, surveying the damage it had caused his bridge, and the repairs it would take to get the water truck back on all wheels. "You got things under control, do you?" he said.

"Everything's just fine," Howie said with a quaking voice, shaking this time from both fear and cold. The early morning chill was turning his wet clothes into ice blocks.

"Oh, yeah, I can see that, Cobb, fine as can be." Captain Clyde merely shook his head. "Just fine as apple pie and ice cream. My, my, my."

It took the Cs most of the morning's prebreakfast exercise period, but the truck was righted, the tank refilled, and the vehicle parked in its prescribed place on the upside of the latrine, pouring water through the spigots for whatever purpose anybody needed.

Howie stood at the far end of the bridge and watched as those who knew how did his work for him. His pride was in a shambles as the enrollees and regular Army filed down the hill to the mess hall, leaving the latrines to him.

"Gonna be famous."

He had found him some fame all right. He quickly swabbed down the latrine floor, sloshed some water into the urinal and metal toilets, and rushed to breakfast which was all but finished by the time he entered the mess.

All eyes watched him as he took his bowl of oatmeal with brown sugar and cup of milk to a corner table. He felt totally embarrassed. Why did it take coming to the Hills for him to find humiliation?

The oatmeal was lumpy and half-cooked. Even brown sugar couldn't make it edible.

He sat alone and stared at his glass of watered-down milk with granules of undesolved powder on the edges. Hell, don't they know milk is supposed to come from cows out here?

Dolph, a fella named Marv Drexler, and a couple of others sat down around him, and chatted among themselves, treating Howie as though he wasn't there. They punched each other and joked about the unusual morning's activities, especially about missing out on O'Kelley's calisthenics on the grass in front of the mess. Pulling a water truck out of the drink was a much better start to any day.

They laughed about this or that, speculated on how the truck wound up half on, half off the bridge, and things like that.

Finally, Dolph slapped Howie on the back and said with something of a grin on his face. "Where in blazes did you learn to drive so good, Cracker?"

"Just leave me the hell alone," Howie said as he tried to eat his oatmeal.

They left him the hell alone.

The rock pile was four miles or so outside camp up the Needles Highway. Howie and a crew of fourteen others under the charge of a re-upper named Doubleside, enjoyed the ride through the Ponderosa pines.

The work site was a pile of granite stones, some as big as a house, all part of a natural outcropping like so many others he had seen in the Hills. Nothing unusual at all about the rock pile. It was just the same as all the others. This pile, though, was for construction use, and the Cs had the job of quarrying it out, loading it on flatbeds, and transporting it to a construction site fifteen miles away in the park.

"Wanna drive?" Doubleside asked Howie as they were leaving the grounds of Camp Iron Mountain. Everybody on the work detail thought that was the funniest thing they had ever heard.

The taunts continued through the morning until finally, Howie figured there was nothing left for him but to join in. Swallow his pride. Hard thing to swallow, pride. But he tried.

Howie hopped from the bird cage when it reached the quarry site and shouted to Doubleside, "How about letting me drive this contraption home?"

Nobody thought he was a bit funny.

Work started and the taunts were put aside. It felt good, this sun. He felt good, too, like if he stuck with it long enough, he'd learn not only what to do but how to do it, when to do it, and for how long.

The granite, as much quartz and sandstone as anything else, was rough and brittle, making getting it into workable sizes with sledge hammers and stone chisels no big chore. In fact, once into the work, Howie found himself enjoying himself, using his shoulders and back, legs, and belly in ways he'd never used them before.

Get the stone the right size, then drag it using an ancient-looking tractor with a chain for a tail to the ginnylift, attach the stone to the cradle on one end, then hoist the stone off the ground with the weight of four or five bodies, swing it around, and plant it gently onto the waiting flatbed.

The work went well. The task warmed him with sweat. By noon his shirt was on a nearby rock and his back was soaking up unobstructed rays of sun. It felt great, better than any work he had ever done before. It was his work, work for himself, done because he chose to do it, not like the slavery of the mill back home where he worked because he was told to and stopped when they said he could. Never did anything but hateful work, day in day out. This, he could learn to love this, give him time.

Lunch was divvied out from the back of a bird cage. Pork sandwiches, tepid tea, fried potato strips, cold and greasy, and fried apple pies. After doing this type of work, even Meathook's lousy food tasted good.

Howie wanted to laugh out loud he felt so full and free; he had never had it so good.

Back at work, Howie asked the C he was working beside, "Where're they taking these rocks?"

"Damned if I know," the fella said, stopping to wipe sweat from his eyes. "I just do what I'm told. They say, split this rock, I split this rock. They say roll in the mud, I roll in the mud. No skin off my behind." He was a big fella, over six feet tall, probably two hundred pounds, with bulging shoulders and a neck thick as a twenty-year-old tree. He had been doing this kind of work for a long time. He was practiced. And he didn't care a whit what he did it for or who he did it with.

"Don't you get curious?" Howie asked.

"'Bout what?"

"What they're building with rocks like these."

"Why should I? All I want is out of this rat hole." The re-upper spotted their break and yelled, "Keep it going over there, Bull. Keep at it, Cracker, let's go."

They worked.

"Your name's Bull?" Howie asked.

"Yeah?"

"Nothing."

After a minute or so, Bull tossed a piece of quartz at Howie and said, "What's a Cracker anyway?"

"Be damned if I know."

Mid-afternoon, a string of jalopies and beat-up Ford pick-ups pulled into the work site beside Squaw Creek. The way the men sat like silent crows in their vehicles, not moving, reminded Howie of that time, back home, when the Klan in their cars and trucks and dumpsters drove past his house, car after car, an endless string of empty eyes. Bull crossed his arms and sat on the slab of stone they were honing. He sighed, "Gonna rest a while, you bet."

"What—" Howie started to ask, but Bull rammed his elbow in the new-comer's side.

"Just keep your trap shut, Cracker," he whispered. "This is no joke." Bull lit a cigarette and offered one to Howie. He took it and smoked like it was second nature, though the acid taste stung his tongue.

Twenty men, maybe more, came out of the parked vehicles. At least twenty more stayed put. The men sauntered through the work site and greeted a couple of the local Cs, there weren't many, most of the teenagers came from East River or Nebraska, and of course there was Howie, the lone alien from so far away nobody knew where it was.

"What's going—" Bull's glare stopped Howie in mid-question.

The men, some armed with shotguns, others with rifles or walking sticks, passed the statue-like boys and collected the tools for working the stone. Sledge hammers, chisels and picks, axes and work gloves, a stray boot or two, first aid kits and empty lunch containers were gathered and pitched into the back of the truck. What the hell, Howie wanted to say but didn't. Strangest sort of help he'd ever seen offered. How were the Cs going to manage the stone if all the cutting tools were stored in somebody else's pickup truck?

A red-bearded fella with hollows under his eyes and skin as pale as a Halloween skull stopped in front of Howie and stared, then held his hand toward the sledge hammer Howie had been using to break open the stone:

"You want this old thing? Shoot. It's the only one I got," Howie grinned.

"Give it to him," Bull said.

"How come? Ain't I been using it right?"

Then he was skidding across the rough-edged stones butt first. The local shouldered the hammer and slipped the chisels into his dungarees' pocket, taking Bull's pick axe as well.

Bull held Howie on the ground as the fellow with the red beard moved through the work site and collected all the hammers and chisels and picks and tools and tossed them in the back of the pickup truck.

"Let me up," Howie said much too loud. "I'll skin that old geyser and have his lights for supper."

Another fellow drew near. He held a double-barrel twelve gauge shotgun in the crook of his arm. He stood over the pissed off Howie, still in Bull's bear hug and said, "You got you a problem, son?"

Howie eyed the ends of the shotgun. He caught the mean looking glint in the fellow's eye. He smelled the liquor that oozed off him like so much pollen off a Georgia pine and he knew there was nothing but hurt to be gained by messing with this fellow, no matter how much effort it took to swallow his Southern pride. So he said, "None I can't take care of on my own," and smiled.

"'Cause," said the fellow, meanness dripping off his lips like saliva from a mad dog's grin, "you got a problem, I got a problem. That right?"

Howie called on his biggest smile. "I'm just tickled pink to be done with work for the day, mister. I thank you for that."

The fellow spat a stream of tobacco juice at Howie's feet, missing his boots by less than an inch, and said, "Shit."

"Back home," Howie said when the fellow was out of hearing, "we'd call that bastard a hillbilly. What you call him out here?"

And Bull answered, "Sir."

Howie could understand that.

Then a smallish fellow, the one with the cane and wearing a black four-in-hand tie hanging down from his once-upon-a-time white collar, stepped up on the fulcrum of the ginnylift and said with a voice so full it could be heard all across the work site, "Why don't you babies do everybody a favor and go on home. You hear what I'm saying? Just go on home, and every last one of us'll die happy. That okay by you?"

His question was met with silence. He stared over the heads of the teenage Cs and said, as soft as the breeze across Center Lake, "Yeah, that's what you do, you bet. Just go on back where you came from and make every last one of us joyful."

He stepped down, got into the lead jalopy, and drove off, followed by the other cars and trucks and last by the pickup, now loaded so heavy with the workers' tools it dipped in the rear end, leaving the Cs in a cloud of mica dust hanging thick in the hot afternoon air.

Howie stood up on the rough stone, his rear-end stinging from the treatment it had received. "Well, hell!" he said, but nobody paid him any mind.

Doubleside sat like a lump on the slab of granite attached to the hoisting end of the ginnylift. The Cs sidled his way, since it was Doubleside who told them when to work and when to stop, when to eat lunch and when to pile onto the flat bed for the trip back to camp. It was clear to Howie that Doubleside didn't know what to do. He sat and scratched the mosquito bites that red-dotted his ankles and shins.

It was Bull who broke the silence. "We going back to base camp or what?"

Doubleside said, "Suppose so."

"How come?" It was Howie asking the stupid question. It was Howie who took the moans and the pokes and the cold stares from the rest of the Cs.

Doubleside said, "Well, they took all our tools just now or didn't you notice."

Howie didn't know when to leave well enough alone. "How come?" he asked again.

"Don't you know nothing?" one of the Cs said. "What they feed you back there in Georgia, loco weed?" another said.

Howie grinned. "Fed me grits and string beans. Brain food." And that brought a laugh. Everybody laughed, even Doubleside. It felt good to laugh, so Howie joined in, though he didn't know what was so funny.

When quiet came back to the work site and the Cs relaxed themselves among the quarried stones, Howie said, "I'm just wondering who them people were, what they wanted, you know? Shoot. They didn't seem all that happy to me."

Bull, who had grown up in Spearfish, not so far away from where they stood, said, "Who says they've gotta be happy? All they want is work. And what little work there is, we take it from them." And he spat into the dust, his final commentary on the discussion, if discussion it really was.

"Well, shoot," Howie said. "We got us half a dozen or so rocks ready for the flatbed. Let's get 'em loaded and down to the construction site, what say?"

The Cs looked one to the other. Even their breathing went unnoticed. It was Doubleside who put their fears into words.

"They find out we're still working, they come back out here and do more than take our tools."

Bull said, "I know a couple of those guys. They ain't mean. Just hungry and need work."

"Looked mean enough to me," one of the Cs said.

Howie was like a dog after a lone flea: he couldn't leave it alone. "What they gonna do, Doubleside, shoot our balls off?"

"You bet," was the reply.

"Well, I don't believe it." Howie's muscles needed something to do. He wasn't used to sitting around counting the number of bumblebees stumbling over dandelions looking for pollen. He said, "Doubleside, you're the boss, but it seems we got us some more work to do.'' And after a bit of reflection, the rest of the Cs agreed.

The flatbed was pulled into place, the stones were dragged to the lift and fastened to the cradle end, and the truck was loaded with two medium-sized chunks of unfinished granite. Howie hopped onto the flatbed and sat with his back against the cab of the truck, legs crossed, and picked his teeth with a sliver he found on the flatbed flooring.

Doubleside yelled at him, "Where do you think you're going?"

"Well," Howie yelled back, "Ain't nothing we can do around here till this truck gets unloaded. Might as well go see what it is we're building."

The rest of the guys piled on.

The truck with Doubleside at the wheel jerked forward, finding it difficult but not impossible to transport the stones as well as the fifteen Cs down the road, around the curves, through the woods and over the Hills to the site in Custer State Park.

Riding the openbed truck was better than the annual Liberty Baptist Young People's hay ride to the Dog River and Sinner's Hole—except there were no girls along. Girls might have helped everybody's mood a little on this trip, but for Howie it didn't matter. It was just as well his girlfriend was safe inside her clapboard and whitewashed house back home in Douglasville and not here, not right now.

After his long and seemingly endless journey out of Georgia and across the wide expanse of this great country, Howie was wide awake for the first time and beJesus if the Hills didn't make up about the most beautiful hunk of landscape he had ever seen. Better than the Blue Ridge back home and he had sworn to his older brother Hev that nothing, not here, not nowhere, could possibly match the spectacle of the Blue Ridge. He tried penning his impressions to Indella, practicing writing in his head, but he had too few words to meet the task of sharing his impressions of the Hills. He determined to try writing home when he got back to Kensington Place and sacked out on his bunk with the sunlight pouring through the northern window. Though better in every way, the Hills still reminded him of the Blue Ridge and filled him with a homesickness unlike any other he had felt so far. He wasn't sick to be home like before; these deep woods that rolled past said to him that he was home. If facts be known, he felt better just then than he had ever felt in his life. It was damn good just being alive. He wanted to hug somebody, but there was nobody there who would understand. So he kicked the nearest stone with the flat of his boot and knew exactly what he meant.

The trip into the park was too short. The flatbed was waved into a ditch as a local with a double-barrel shotgun blocked the road. The tires of the vehicle sank deep into the loose mud of the ditch, and there it would sit until a tractor came along to help it break free of the muck.

Howie sat atop the cab with Bull; Doubleside climbed on top from behind the steering column to get a better look. They took everything in. A quarter of a mile up the slope in the middle of a lush meadow was the purpose behind the quarried stone: a good-sized building being constructed entirely of rough, unrefined granite and mortar. The building was only a third finished, mostly foundation and a back wall maybe ten feet high. Howie counted twenty-five non-government vehicles parked ahead of them and more than fifty locals standing around, some armed with guns, others with picks, hammers, and an axe or two. Not far from the granite foundation in the middle of the meadow was Captain Clyde Munk, dressed in his khaki work clothes, listening to a handful of locals who gestured this way and that with an animation that denied the Captain the pride of his rank. Old Clyde pointed repeatedly to the pile of stones beside the building yet to be put into place and at the building itself, saying something of obvious importance to himself if not the others in his easily recognized iron-jaw way. The locals listened to him, or least some of them did.

Howie poked Bull in the side. "You folks always have this much fun on work crews?" Bull shrugged and offered cigarettes to those around him. The Cs sat, and listened, and smoked, and listened some more.

Howie pointed to the unfinished building. "What's that supposed to be?" he asked.

Doubleside blew a stream of smoke in the direction of Old Clyde. "This here's a park," he said, "and that is to be the visitors center. The rate we're going, we might get the thing done by the winter of 1945."

Howie looked around him. "So this is a park. Never been to a park before." Bull grunted. "What do folks do in parks anyway?"

"Eat picnics," Doubleside said.

Howie nodded. "Sounds. . . nice I guess." He blew a stream of smoke toward the small group of locals who had gathered around the flatbed. "These folks live around here, that right?"

"Can't you keep quiet?" Doubleside whispered.

More locals approached the truck. One of them pulled a C off the back and pushed him toward the road, saying, "Why don't you delinquents go back where you came from!"

Another of the locals yelled to the rest of the Cs on the truck, "Get off and none of you'll get hurt."

Bull said as he lifted his bulk from the top of the cab, "Guess we better be getting off."

"How come?" Howie asked.

"Cause they said to, that's how come."

"I ain't heard the C.O. tell us to do nothing," Howie said with a gaping smile. "Ain't he the one who gives the orders?"

Bull glared at him in disbelief. "What are you, some sort of idiot? Get off the damn truck!" Then Bull, Doubleside, and the rest of them hopped to the ground.

Howie stayed. He had no idea why, but he stayed. From the edge of the meadow, Doubleside called, "Come on Cracker, for Pete's sake."

Howie grinned, waved, and sprawled his shirtless torso across the warm top of the cab. The sun felt good. It was too nice a day to get all bent out of shape over a make-believe squabble.

One of the locals, the one from before with the red beard but now toting a twelve gauge shotgun, tossed a small chunk of sod at Howie's head. "What's the matter, boy, you deaf or what? We said off the truck."

Howie waved at him and said, "I'm right comfortable, thank you. Nice day, ain't it."

He heard a loud angry shout coming from the construction site: "Get the scabs off the truck, Hubert!"

Howie noticed the rest of the Cs gathering behind the C.O., and he wished he'd gone along and done the same. But now, how could he get off and still keep his pride? No way. He was stuck. It was ridiculous, he realized, but he was stuck. Besides, the way the Cs were dragging themselves along wasn't a pretty sight. Tucking tail was not a desirable thing to do. He realized that something was not right, but he wasn't sure what it was. And he had no desire to be party to anything that wasn't right.

The red beard, looking meaner than before, yelled up to him, "You gonna get off the truck, sonny, or what? One way or the other, you bet your britches you're coming off that truck."

And Howie said, "You gonna unload all this stone by yourself?"

The man was growing more angry. "Nobody's unloading any more rock today."

It was amazing. The way the man's nose quivered, the way the sun glinted off the blond fibers in his red beard, the way his eyes squinted. Howie couldn't help it. "You know, mister, if you were missing your front two teeth, you'd be the spitting image of my Uncle Jeb Stuart Cobb. Old Jeb Stuart was known all over Douglas County as the best Saturday night drinker God ever created. One time, he took it on himself to relocate Stone Mountain by his lonesome. He would of done it, too, if the mule pulling the wagon hadn't broke its two back legs giving the old wagon one mighty hefty tug.''

"Huh?" the red beard said.

"Yeah, you would of liked old Uncle Jeb Stuart Cobb. He had a wise crack a minute and never met a man he couldn't drink under the table. Played poker, too, but he cheated. I wouldn't recommend you get into a card game with my Uncle Jeb. One time, he just about got his nose cut off in a knife fight with a fella from the Hembree clan. Them Hembrees, meanest sonsabitches you ever laid eyes on.''

Red beard growled, the shotgun coming out of the crook in his arm, "Get off the damn truck, buddy!" By now twenty or more locals had circled the truck, and the other Cs along with Captain Clyde were edging down the hill, curious about what was going on with this newest member to their corps, what this newcomer was thinking as he seemed content marching to his early grave.

Howie thought the sun felt better than it had ever felt before, the breeze as comforting as any breeze could be. "You know, this is a pretty damn good truck. Made it over some tough roads with this here load. Oh, man, let me tell you, this granite ain't worth shit, too much sandstone and quartz. You need some good solid Georgia granite for fitting stone work. Hey, hop on up here, one of you and give me a hand. We'll dump this no good rock right here in the ditch and make everybody happy.''

Nobody breathed. The red beard cocked the hammers on both barrels of his shotgun and leveled it at Howie's feet. "I said off the truck, you smart aleck juvenile delinquent!"

"Cobb!!" The word echoed through the woods, back and forth, back and forth, like it was on a yo-yo with too short a string to do the rock-a-bye-baby. Howie recognized the voice, and turned and caught his Captain's eye. He waved.

The explosion from both barrels of the gun took out most of the window in the back of the cab. Glass and buckshot splinters splashed as everybody, even Howie, ducked. Howie covered his face and cowered on top of the truck. He clutched his feet, miraculously untouched from the buckshot blast, to his chest and huddled as small as he could make himself on top of the cab. Still, he made no move to crawl down. He figured the fellow with the shotgun either was a lousy shot or missed his feet on purpose. Either way, he was staying put. Safest thing he could think to do.

Red beard breeched his gun, the spent shells flying into the ditch, and reloaded. The sound the gun made as the barrels were clicked back into place was the scariest thing Howie had ever heard. Still, he could not force his body off the truck. The man with the walking stick, the man who seemed to know what was what and how to get things done, the man with the black four-in-hand tie dangling from what once had been a white collar, came up to the flatbed, placed a hand on one of the granite slabs and said, "Nobody wants anybody to get hurt, son. So come on down and do like we're telling you. Work's finished for the day, your captain knows that, so you and your friends can go on back where you came from and all of us'll die happy. That okay by you?"

Howie was amazed. People were just damn people, it didn't matter where they came from. And he couldn't help his smile of recognition as he dangled his legs over the edge of the cab.

"You know, mister," he said with a smile, "if you had on a dress and had enough hair to pull up in a bun, you'd look just like my Great Granny Roper. She walked with a cane, too, and was so skinny. Lord help her, you turn her sideways and she don't stop the breeze. But could that woman cook pinto beans? Lordee could that woman—"

"Cobb!" It was the iron jaw again, closer than before. "Get your butt off my damn truck! Now!"

"Yes, sir," Howie said resisting the impulse to salute. He hopped to the ground, turned to the red beard, doffed his hat and said, "Pleasure meeting you fellas. Y'all come back and see us again, ye hear?"

"We will," the red beard hissed.

The locals cleared a path so Howie could make his way to Old Clyde and the rest of the Cs. None of them said a thing. After a silence of stand-off, Captain Clyde cleared his throat and said to the fellow with the cane, "See you."

The fellow said with no emotion in his voice, "You bet."

Old Clyde and his troop of Cs turned toward the woods and said, "Looks like we walk home, boys. Nice day for a hike."

They began the long traipse back to camp.

Bull tagged along beside Howie and whispered, "You got balls, Cracker, you know that?"

"Balls is stupid," Howie said. "I just didn't want to walk back to camp. You see how much good it did me."

"Just another stroll in the woods, Cracker, just another stroll in the woods."

Captain Clyde hung back and fell into place beside his new C from far away Georgia. Now what, Howie wondered but didn't ask. It seemed he was attracting an awful lot of attention from the C.O. for being so new in camp. Bull surged on ahead, putting distance between himself and what he figured to be a major chewing out. But Old Clyde simply strolled along, adapting his stride to Howie's, turning the retreat into a casual meander, the rest of the crew pulling ahead and eventually disappearing.

Finally, the Captain broke his silence. "So, tell me, son, what was that all about back there? Uncle Jeb Stuart Cobb?"

"Just having a good time, sir," Howie said, trying to laugh it off, but the Captain's mood was too severe.

"Yeah, having a good time." After a second or two, he said, "I guess I'm just not cut out for this kind of work, babysitting a bunch of kids, C.O. to a bunch of sugarteats. What do you think?"

"Well, shoot, I ain't been around much."

"You know, me and the missus ain't had us a baby before this. Our first. Gonna be the first Army brat born in Camp Iron

Mountain. Maybe the last. I don't know. And I wonder, do I want my baby to grow up and do what you just did. Makes me want to head home, tell my missus, let's get as far away from all this as we can. You know what I'm talking about?"

Howie didn't know what to say. The Missus Clyde Munk, the only female in camp, was so large she could have her baby any day now, and it had the Cs all in a lather about whether there'd be another female in camp or yet another boy. He hadn't thought about this thing of the baby growing up and becoming a man—or a woman—and what sort of man—or woman—he—or she—would be. He thought of his brothers and sisters back home, about how he had watched them grow and become people, like Horace the youngest, how he had come into the world hardly big enough to fill a hand, yet when he had left home, how Horace had actually cried, understanding that his older brother might not come back at all. Howie hadn't thought about any of this back there with his feet forming target practice for a stranger with a red beard. Shoot, he wanted to say, let me go back there and redo everything. Let me fix it. But he couldn't find the words, so he stayed silent as he and the C.O. strolled through the woods.

"Sometimes," Old Clyde was saying, "I can't help but feel something close to pride, though. Watching you fellas come into my camp and start learning about things. Most of the boys from the Dakotas never met a tree before, you know. Hell, they have no idea what a stump is much less a forest like we have here. Then, there're days like this, days when I watch one of my boys almost get his head blown off, and I wonder, yeah, can't help but wonder if it's such a good thing, bringing another kid into this damn world. It makes me feel awful sad, son, how you behaved back there just now."

Howie felt his words slip out of his mouth. He didn't want to say them, but he couldn't keep them inside. "That man weren't gonna shoot me, sir."

"That right? Just how do you know that, Cobb? What instinct you got that I don't?"

"Well, it wasn't in his eyes."

Old Clyde gruffed under his breath. "It was in his belly, though. And the bellies of his kids back home, going to bed hungry and him not able to do anything about it. You ever been hungry, son?"

"Couple of times, I guess."

"But not every morning when you wake up and every night when you go to bed. That's these people, Corpsman, and we're taking away work that might rightfully have gone to them if we hadn't come along. So, how can you say for sure that man didn't have the belly to blow your brains out?"

Howie was silent. He couldn't answer. He didn't know the answer.

"Yeah, makes me wonder, the missus and me, bringing another kid into this damn world."

The two strolled their way back to camp, Howie confused by the chewing out he had just received.

That night, Howie didn't eat dinner with the rest of the Cs. Breakfast the next morning either. He was testing his belly, whether or not what was or wasn't in his belly could cause him to pull the trigger, to put a double load of buckshot in another person's chest. Back home, he'd gone to bed without supper lots of times. But had he ever been hungry? It seemed there was always some cornbread or biscuits or homemade grits or pinto beans somewhere around the house. It hadn't been easy, but then he'd never really been hungry.

Noon next day he downed a couple of ham sandwiches, unable to resist the hunger he was feeling. So he didn't get his answer. Maybe there was no answer. So it seemed. Still, he was a long, long way from home and he felt, for the first time in his life, uncommonly vulnerable to things in other people's bellies. You never know, do you. You never know.

The Cs didn't go back to the rock pile. Instead, the quarry

crews stayed in camp and took care of a list of little tasks, cutting weeds along the creek, building a new trail between the latrine and the C.O.'s cabin across the road, repairing leaks in the Algonquin and Plaza roofs, reinforcing the mud dam across Squaw Creek, clearing a flat area near the hospital for horseshoe stakes, and putting up a couple of basketball hoops.

The C.O. stayed in camp, too.

Parked outside his office in the commissary was a local's pickup truck. The guy with the cane and the limp stayed through dinner, conferring with Old Clyde about things most Cs knew and cared nothing about.

"They're probably playing poker," Manny Lakso said and meant it.

"They're probably hugging and kissing and making babies, too," Bull said.

"You're full of it, Bull," Manny said, and before Manny knew it, he was sprawled on the ground, nose pouring blood.

Bull stood over him. "You watch your lip or I'll watch it for you buddy," he said and after a momentary glaring match with a handful of Cs, Bull returned to swinging his scythe through the tall grass beside the creek.

"You know what happens to mean sons of bitches, don't you, Bull?" Howie asked as he helped get Manny's bleeding under control.

"No. What?"

"That's funny," Howie said. "I felt sure you'd know."

The following day, the local didn't return. And the Cs seemed to put the visitor center project behind them and turn attention to a new task: clearing the underbrush from alongside the now-under-construction Iron Mountain Highway.

Cutting trees. This wasn't what Howie'd joined the Cs to do. He could cut trees back home. He wanted to plant them.

Oh, well, at least here he was getting paid. And he wasn't going to bed hungry nights, either. He had a great deal to be thankful for.

Cracker

Saturday, his first in the Hills, Howie sat on the floor at his footlocker carving his name into the underside of the locker lid with his pocket knife. Cold Steam Stanley perched on his bunk, watching, mouth cocked open like it always was, his right forefinger twisting the laces on his boot.

Sounds from across Squaw Creek filtered through the barrack door. The Cougars were taking on the Golden Eagles from Camp Pactola in the big event of the week.

Howie tried to throw all his attention into his carving, but the cheers from across the creek and the crack of ball hitting bat kept his mind switching back and forth from the task at hand and what he really wanted to be doing.

"You don't like baseball?" Cold Steam asked.

"Love the game," Howie answered. Without his willing it, a deep sigh slipped loose from his chest. "Just can't stand to watch it."

"Me neither," said Cold Steam slipping to the floor from his bunk. "I can't follow it."

"Huh?"

"You know. I just don't get what it's all about. Seems stupid to me."

"What's baseball all about? You gotta be kidding."

Howie finished the "C" he was working on. Done. The trunk was now officially his.

He turned his attention to the enrollee beside him on the floor. The two of them were assigned to work as a team on road

61

clearing detail. Howie knew that Cold Steam, though a nuisance, was harmless. Not good for much except chopping saplings from beside the road.

Their fourth day on Iron Mountain road crew, Cold Steam had flailed away at two pine trees. Somebody asked him why he was cutting at two trees at once. Cold Stream responded coolly, "Well, I figure you're supposed to take down two trees at a time. Else, why would the axe have two blades on it?"

Cold Steam now gaped at Howie's carving.

"What's the matter with you?" Howie said.

"Huh?"

"You want my knife, that it? It's not for sale."

"I got a knife."

"Then, go do your own whittling."

But Cold Steam still sat there, saying nothing.

Howie's patience with him had reached its limit. "Okay, what is it? What do you want!"

Cold Steam Stanley eased to the floor and reached toward the trunk.

Howie slammed the lid, almost taking one of Cold Steam's fingers off at the nub. Howie was in a rotten mood. He couldn't remember the last time a baseball game had been played without him being on the field. He could smell the oiled leather and it made him ache deep inside.

Cold Steam Stanley brushed Howie aside. He lifted the lid, lifted it like he was opening a genie's box. Then, he pointed at the letters Howie had been carving. "What's that?" he asked.

"Well, be damned," Howie said, his anger flaring. "I know it ain't much, but it's the best I can do. Lemme alone."

Somebody across the creek just hit a homerun. No way a ball could make a bat sound like that without it leaving the playing field. He squirmed with anticipation and deep seated longing.

Cold Steam wouldn't leave him alone. "No, Howie, what is it?"

"It's carving."

There were only a few faint cheers. A Golden Eagle must have been the lucky batter to hit a ball so hard. He didn't know how much longer he could resist the urge to wander toward the playing field.

"I mean the figure," Cold Steam persisted. "What's it for?"

"It's a damn 'C' for God's sake."

"A 'C'." Cold Steam fingered the lines of the figure like he was touching a woman's breast. "What's it stand for?"

"What do you mean, 'What's it stand for?!' You stupid idiot, can't you read?"

"No."

Was the fellow setting him up? Was this some sort of April's Fool at the end of May? "You serious?"

"Yeah. Never learned any book reading and that sort of thing. Never had time. Never missed it, either."

Not read? Why, you had to be a total dolt not to read. That or a simpleton. Cold Steam was neither.

Not read.

Howie had been reading since he couldn't remember when. He learned at Alexander Stevens' chair, looking over his Poppa's shoulder as they both pondered the Bible.

Not read.

Christ, that must be really something.

"The 'C' stands for me, my last name, Cobb."

"Your mark, huh."

"Well, sure, in a way. 'H.M.C.' That's me. Howell Madison Cobb."

Cold Steam thought about it for a minute longer. "My mark's the same as my dad's." He spat on the floor and with his forefinger drew an 'X' in the gob of spit.

"It may be your mark, but it don't stand for your name," Howie said. "My great uncle Bulldog Cobb used an 'X' to sign his name, too. And it got him sent up river for fourteen years.

Hard labor on the gang. Shoot, Steam, use your 'X' and you just asking for problems.''

"What's the figures for my name then?''

Howie spat on the floor and with the wetness drew an "S" on the floor. "You have a middle name?''

"Steam.''

"I mean a God-given name. Stanley something Frucostek. What goes in the middle?''

"Don't tell nobody.''

"For God's sake—''

"Jerome.''

"Stanley Jerome Frucostek. S.J.F.'' And he drew the letters in the spit. "That's you.''

"That?''

"Bigger than life.''

Cold Steam studied the letters and traced over them with his finger. "You suppose I should put that on my trunk?''

"Up to you.''

"If you'll help me.''

The Cougars were up four to two in the top half of the eighth when Howie finally wandered down to the creek to watch.

Dolph was pitching. All week he had heard about Dolph's ability on the mound, the envy of every C.C.C. camp in the Hills. Even the guys over at Pine Creek wanted "The Speed of DeSmet.''

But Dolph was first and last an Iron Mountain Cougar. On first was Cage Swanson, a potato farmer from north of Fargo. Could hit the ball a country mile when he put bat on it, which wasn't all that often. At the keystone was Roy Martin, a city slicker from Sioux Falls with something of an asshole's attitude. Pretty good range but no arm—that's why he was second sacker. At short was Arnie "The Boot" Carrington. Arnie hated baseball. He played because his Poppa bought him a glove on his ninth birthday and because he bunked in K.P. along with most of the other players. When your arm gets twisted enough by the rest of the guys, you'll play for the Cougars, Dolph had told Howie over breakfast that morning. That was "The Boot." His arm got twisted and not a game passed without him living up to his name. At the hot corner was "The Glove." Nothing got past Grover Cleveland Blaine. If it was gettable, he got it. It would have been nice if he could do more at the plate, like hitting a few out of the infield, but when a body could field like Ty Cobb, a bat didn't really matter. In left was "Fleet." Fleance Schmidt could have played for any double-A team in the country if he wanted. He could hit, field, run, everything. His problem—he wasn't all that bright. He would try to steal second with two out in the bottom of the ninth when the Cougars were six runs behind. Or, he'd make a perfect throw to first while a run scored from third. Other than his mental lapses Fleet Schmidt was a natural. Woody Woodsley claimed center. He was the field captain. He commanded respect when little was due. Woody was steady; not pretty to watch, but he got the job done. In right was JoJo Pietrzak. When JoJo took his position, everybody on the team prayed no one hit a ball to him. He couldn't run, couldn't field, could hit pretty good, couldn't throw. He played because he loved the game and had the best memory on the team. He was good to keep around if only for his ability as team historian. Behind the plate was Marv Drexler. Good ole Marv. Everybody's pal. The Joker. The backstop. What he didn't catch, he blocked with his body, which stayed black and blue throughout baseball season.

Howie studied the team. He watched them play. The Pactola catcher led off the eighth with a sharp grounder to short. The ball careened off The Boot's glove into center field. The next batter, a husky fellow with more belly than he needed, slapped a come-backer to Dolph. He gloved it, whirled and threw to second—but The Boot was nowhere near the bag. The ball sailed into center field putting runners at first and third, no outs.

Howie could sense Dolph's frustration. He dug deep. The next batter went down swinging. The next took a fastball down the center of the plate for a called strike three.

The Golden Eagle power hitter, Franklin Farmer, stepped to the plate. Howie had heard talk of him at the breakfast table and how if there was an all star on the Pactola squad, Frank Farmer was him. He took a few practice swings and stepped to the plate. He carried the hopes for a Pactola victory on his bat and he knew it.

Dolph went into his wind and hurled the sphere toward the plate. It was a perfect curve, breaking down and in. Frank swung as hard as he could, but the ball wasn't where he thought it would be. The ball tipped the end of the bat and squirted feebly toward short. The runners were off with the crack of the bat. And The Boot just stood there, shocked that a squibbler was heading his way.

Then there came The Glove, slashing out of position and across The Boot's path. He stretched for the ball, picked it with his bare hand and threw in one motion. Cage stretched at first. The ball found his mitt a fraction of a second before Frank's foot touched the bag. Inning over. Howie could feel the deep sigh of relief escaping every Iron Mountain C in the camp, and he decided: Arnie "The Boot" Carrington had to retire.

He had the gall to mention as much to Dolph at dinner: "I'd like to be your shortstop," he said. "What do you say?"

"I say we already got us a shortstop."

"What you've got is a deadhead," Howie said.

"Well, let's go see."

There was still an hour of daylight left. The baseball field was empty. The ball was the same color as the dirt. That didn't bother Howie. It was no different from back home.

He bragged to Dolph, "Where I come from, the ball's usually more black tape and loose string than leather."

"Season's young," Dolph said. "We got plenty of tape." Dolph was as good with the bat as he was with a curve ball. He peppered some sharp grounders to Howie who fielded most of them and threw strikes to Dolph at home. The stones in the playing field didn't bother him. Bad bounce or true, he stayed down, snagged the sphere either with his glove or chest and threw it home. After all, the playing field at Iron Mountain was much better than the pasture ball he was used to back home.

"Not bad for a Cracker," Dolph said, all smiles. Then "The Boot" Carrington showed up along with JoJo, Marv, and a couple others.

"What the hell's going on?" Boot asked.

"Finding us a shortstop," Dolph said.

"That's my position."

"Was," said Dolph.

"Now, wait a cotton-picking minute—" Howie tried to protest, but not too hard or too loud.

The Boot was hot inside his C.C.C. issue shirt. "Who gives you the right to make that kind of decision? Hell, we don't know if the guy can hit or not."

"Well, let's find out." Dolph called Howie in and handed him a bat. "Know what this thing's for?"

"Fanning the ump to keep him cool, right?"

"Some folks use it for that." Dolph said, looking at Boot. Dolph strolled to the mound. Marv pulled his catcher's mitt from inside his shirt. JoJo trotted out to the field along with Fleet, Woody, and a couple other guys. Boot said he'd call them and took his place behind Marv at the plate.

Dolph finished his warm-up tosses.

"Okay, Cracker, show us what for."

Howie stepped to the plate.

"You left-handed?" Marv asked.

"Nope."

"Then how come you're swinging from the left side?"

"Cause he's throwing from the right."

"Which side's your power?"

"Neither."

"Which side's your best?"

"Both."

"You ain't cocky are you, Cracker?"

"Nope. Just cock-sure."

Dolph pitched his best but Marv didn't need his mitt. Howie hit everything. Liners to center, bloopers to shallow left, hot grounders through the hole to right and up the middle, long deep ones to right, and Texas Leaguers every which way.

"Man, where have you been?" Marv asked and pounded Howie on the back.

Howie stepped across the plate and bade Dolph to give him some more. He did and Howie sprayed the playing field with one ball after another. Nothing got past him, not even pitches that should have been left alone. The bat was an extension of Howie's arm and the ball went wherever he wanted, like he was throwing it there.

The Boot sat down on the players bench halfway through the exhibition, and when Dolph finally called a halt to the try-out, Arnie walked up the hill to K.P.

"Ah, come on Arnie," Marv yelled. "You're still our starting shortstop."

"Like hell," Arnie answered and continued up the hill. Woody and Fleet, JoJo and Dolph slapped Howie on the back and welcomed him to the Cougars.

Dolph said, "Not bad for a rookie."

Woody said, "I heard you Crackers were something else."

"Is it true what they say about Crackers?" JoJo asked. Howie just laughed.

The second weekend in camp, Howie, Dolph, and JoJo managed a trip into Rapid City with the government delivery truck. Rapid was off limits to Cs, but Dolph's importance to camp life as barrack leader of K.P. and star hurler of the Cougars manipulated things in his favor.

Rapid City was off limits for a reason. The last three times groups of Iron Mountain Cs went to town, brawls had broken out between the enrollees and the flatfoots from Fort Meade.

Dolph himself had been involved in the last one, not more than a month ago, and to hear him tell it, the fight was the greatest thing since Brigham Young sat on a rock and said, "This is the Place."

The delivery truck dumped them at the depot.

The three wandered down Phillips Avenue with something of a strut in their walk. They passed shop after shop but didn't have much money to spend. The people they passed stared at them and didn't speak.

"Not much of a town, huh?" Dolph smirked. "Look at the squatters, would you? My Lord, you'd think they'd get the drunks off the streets."

Two male Indians sprawled against the side of a building, empty bottles on the ground beside them.

"You ever seen a drunk Indian before, Cracker?" JoJo asked.

"Never seen any kind of Indian before," he said.

"Don't get too close to them," Dolph said. "You're not careful, you'll pick up their stink and carry it back with you to Iron Mountain. It's impossible to wash off."

"You have niggers where you come from, right, Cracker?" JoJo asked.

"None I know of."

"You're shitting us. No niggers?"

"No Indians, no coloreds. Just us white folks with the friendly smiles."

"I thought you said you was from Georgia," JoJo said.

"You got that much right."

"Well, I heard that's all you got down there, a bunch of niggers who rape your white women."

"Not where I come from. Had no doings with colored people in my life. Heard of them, of course. Who ain't? But never met one."

"What'd you do," Dolph asked, "shoot them in the head after the Civil War? Bury them out back with the potato plants?"

"Never thought about it much. Them people just don't live in my part of Georgia."

"Got no niggers, got no Injuns. Who the hell you got to hate?" JoJo asked.

"Rich folk," Howie said. "Never learned to abide no rich sonofabitches."

Dolph said, "I told you I liked Georgia better than out here. Heaven, as far as I'm concerned, would be here and now if the drunken Injuns were all dead and in the ground."

"You don't mean that," Howie said.

"Hell, yeah. You don't know. You don't have them where you come from, so you don't know."

Howie wanted to argue the point but didn't know how. He didn't understand the first thing about Indians or about life in Rapid City or any place outside Iron Mountain. He kept his mouth shut. He determined to keep it shut until he couldn't keep it that way any longer.

What he heard Dolph say wasn't all that new to him. The same words had been uttered time and again back home, only not about Indians. The color line worked. He'd heard the phrase, "Don't let the sun set on your back, nigger." And he knew it was meant for any colored who ventured over the county line. His Poppa Alexander Stevens had never talked that much about his feelings on the matter. So, Howie had no thoughts he could share.

They passed the Indians, with Dolph stopping long enough to spit in their direction.

"You got a nickel, mister?" one of them asked.

"Goddamn waste of time" Dolph said and continued down the street.

"My Momma's momma's momma was a full-blood Cherokee," Howie said once the drunks were behind him.

"So what's that make you?" JoJo asked.

"An all-American, I guess."

"Makes you a goddamn breed," Dolph said. And Howie figured he should let the subject drop.

The three located a bar that looked seedy enough and went inside. "You guys C.C.C., right?" The barkeep had tattoos on both arms.

"Hell, no," JoJo said.

"Out," the barkeep said and pointed at the door.

"Say, listen, friend, with your two front teeth missing, you'd be the spitting image—" Howie started.

"Out!" the barkeep said.

The next bar was less friendly than the first. "Mother of sweet Jesus," the second barkeep said, "you punks gotta stay out of my joint, you hear me?"

The third, fourth, and fifth were no different. It didn't look like the Cs were going to get drunk after all.

Dolph sat on the curb and puffed on a cigarette, "What's the use in twisting a ride into town if you can't get boozed up? Might as well stay in camp and be on Meathook's kitchen duty." He offered his cigarette to Howie who took a deep draw.

Howie saw her first. She was waiting at the next corner. Maybe expecting a ride, or perhaps she had noticed them and was waiting for them to sidle up to her and strike up a chit-chat. No, he decided, she looked like too nice a girl for that, pretty as she was, dressed in a long coat that tried to hide her figure but didn't quite succeed.

"Maybe she'd takeus to her house and you know what," JoJo siad. He laughed a dirty laugh.

Dolph said, "Betcha the baby doll's lost or something."

JoJo drooled, "Look at those ankles. Don't have ankles like that in camp, do we guys."

Howie was suddenly aware of the cigarette in his hand. It was Indella shaming him for eyeing the woman at the next corner and thinking sinful thoughts. It was Indella in his head who said over and over, "You're saving it for me, remember, you're saving it for me." For God's sake, guys, he wanted to say, she's an upright young woman with a family and probably goes to church every Sunday...and more than likely detests smokers. He crushed the cigarette under his heel.

"She's coming our way!" JoJo whispered. And Lord if she wasn't. She crossed the street, heading directly toward them.

Dolph found a spot of grease on his sleeve and rubbed it with vigor. JoJo picked at the sole of his shoe where there was gum stuck to the bottom. Howie stuffed his hands deep in his pockets and twisted on his heels as the girl passed them on the sidewalk, almost brushing against his arm.

She moved away, obviously waiting for somebody. She glanced over her shoulder, caught Howie's eye, and smiled. The prettiest smile he had seen since he took Indella in his arms that day in the Wildcat Den. And what she had given him then could hardly be called a smile. "Christ," he whispered.

"Talk to her," Dolph said, poking him in the side.

"Chance of a lifetime, pal," JoJo said, "so go for it. She's waiting for you."

"She's not that kind of girl," Howie whispered. His heart was whamming away inside his chest. His hands in spite of the brisk northwest wind were damp and clammy.

"What does it matter what kind of girl she is? Talk to her."

"What do you say to a nice girl out here in this country?"

"Nice things. Go on."

"I swear," Howie said, "you guys are gonna get me whacked."

"She's not going to wait forever, fool!" And Dolph gave him a little push in her direction.

It's like poker, Howie said to himself. He had played the game a couple of times back in camp and lost most of his money. You play the hand you're dealt— Jesus, Joseph, and Mary, she's coming this way.

"Excuse me," the girl said—she was talking to Howie. Sweat oozed from under his cap and into his ear. He wanted to swipe it away but was afraid to move.

"Ma'm?" he said hardly above a whisper.

"I couldn't help but notice you fellas. You're from one of the camps, aren't you."

"Yes, ma'm. Iron Mountain."

Dolph poked him again and whispered, "Fool!"

"Is that so. Weren't you fellas talking about me just now?"

Howie almost gagged on his spit. "Well."

"What were you saying?"

Howie looked to Dolph for help. Dolph was all grin. JoJo was still fiddling with whatever it was on the bottom of his shoe. "Well, ma'm, I was remarking as how you're not that kind of girl."

JoJo snorted and Dolph whispered, "Christ almighty."

"That kind of girl?"

"You know... that kind."

"No, I don't know what kind. You'll have to tell me the kind you have in mind."

JoJo hugged his shoe tight to his chest, and Dolph leaned against the side of the building and slid to the ground.

"Well," Howie tried, he was obviously not going to get any help from his friends. "The kind of girl that a person like me's tempted to talk to."

"I'm here to tell you," she flirted—her eyes danced from Howie to JoJo to Dolph and then back to Howie— "that I'm exactly the kind of girl you came to town looking for. It'll be five dollars a piece, up front. And you pay for the room."

Howie nearly dumped in his britches. Momma had said there were such women in this world, and if he wasn't careful when they were around, he'd find himself in a peck of trouble without even trying. Here he was, first time out on the streets of Rapid City, his first adventure among the natives so to speak, and he was being propositioned. He, Howell Madison Cobb, aged seventeen in the year of our Lord, nineteen hundred and thirty-six, was standing on the curb of life on the verge of losing the one thing he was absolutely certain was his. She was so lovely, so wholesome, so like the kind of girl he wanted to have his children.

Dolph grabbed his arm and pulled at it like it was a rope tied to a lifesaver, and JoJo still picked at his shoe with blackened fingernails.

"Right cold for June, don't you think?" Howie said. He could feel Dolph collapse with disgust and JoJo turn away in disbelief.

"No, it's always like this," the girl said. "Didn't you hear me just now?"

"I heard you," he said. "Five dollars is a right smart amount of money, ma'm."

"How much do you fellas earn a week anyway?"

"Twenty-five dollars," Dolph lied.

Howie felt relief. Finally, one of his buddies was in this thing with him.

"It's early yet," she said, looking around as if she expected somebody else to come strolling by. "Let's make it four dollars a piece, only thing is I'll have to take you all at the same time."

"Holy cow," JoJo said and started digging in his pocket.

Howie cleared his throat. "You mind if we discuss this for a bit, ma'm? I mean, me and my buddies?"

"Discuss? What do you mean, discuss?"

"Oh, you know." He gestured lamely. "Talk about it."

"Just don't take all night." She turned her back to them and dug a cigarette out of her purse and lit up.

The three Cs huddled. "Well?" Howie started.

"Let's do it," JoJo said, holding out a wad of dollar bills.

"She's not much older than my sister," Dolph said.

"Sister blisters, we gonna let this chance slip by us?"

"Well," Howie didn't know what to say.

"How much you got?" Dolph asked. And all three of them emptied their pockets into Howie's cap. Dolph counted. Twenty-eight dollars.Twelve to her, leaving them sixteen. Gotta rent the room.

"Excuse me, miss," he said. She turned to them. "You know how much it's gonna cost us for the room?"

"Five dollars plus tip."

"Whew," he said in response and rejoined the huddle. "She wants us all at once. I don't know if I'm up to that, JoJo," Howie said.

"Me," JoJo said, "I don't give a shit. I can get it up for any damn broad. Forget the room. Let's take her right here."

Howie felt his head shake. He didn't mean for it to, but it was shaking "No."

"Why the hell not?" Dolph said. "This is why we came into Rapid, isn't it? Well?"

"I don't know why I came to town," Howie answered. He couldn't get his Momma out of his head. She sat there, right behind his eyes and scolded him for allowing lustful thoughts to linger. She didn't say anything to him, she didn't have to.

Instead, he turned to the girl and said before his buddies could stop him, "I'm not interested. No thank you, ma'm, but I'm just in town for a bit, here for the sights. Thank you kindly."

"Thank you kindly?" she repeated. "Would you believe it? A hick. So, how about the rest of you."

JoJo said, "You bet, miss—"

Dolph said, "Well..."

"Now come on, Dolph, for God's sake. Don't you go getting sanctified on me."

"I just don't know about this."

"Well, shit!"

The girl took JoJo's arm. "Guess it's just you and me, sugar."

"Guys—,"JoJo whined. But the other two had moved away. "We don't really need a room, you know, sugar," she said.

Then JoJo pushed her away. "We gotta get back to Camp, miss. Sorry about that."

"Hey," she snapped, all sweetness gone. "Just fuck you fellas. You hear me? Fuck you!"

She moved on, taking her scent of fresh peaches with her. Dolph whammed Howie across the back. "You idiot! We had the money. Jesus H. Christ, if you don't take the cake."

"You want her, go get her. I swear, Dolph DeSmet, you hit me again, I'll stuff your teeth down your throat one at a time."

"A damn hooker," JoJo said.

"And we lost her!" Dolph crumbled beside JoJo on the curb. "I'll be damned, we lost her. Thanks a lot, Cracker." And he chuckled lightly as if he'd just heard a joke. He looked at his new buddy from Georgia and laughed out loud.

JoJo joined in, though he didn't know why.

"What's so funny?" Howie wanted to know.

"She's not that kind of girl," Dolph sneered. "You're miss Sweet Sixteen. I'll be goddamned but do you know how to pick 'em!"

JoJo laughed so hard tears ran down his cheeks. Howie joined in. The three of them laughed until their faces hurt. And then they sat in silence until their ride came along and hauled them back to Iron Mountain, their money and their virtue still intact.

"Next time, okay?" Dolph said.

"Sure thing," JoJo said. "Next time we'll screw the whole stinking town."

Baseball fever infected Camp Iron Mountain.

Against the Camp Narrows Lame Johnnys, Howie went three for four, scored two times, and drove in one run. He started three double plays and snagged several grounders that could have been hits, took a hot liner with a belly-flop and tossed the ball to The Glove to double off the only Lame Johnny to get to third. Dolph pitched a five-hit shut out. The Lame Johnnys of the Narrows limped home wondering what had hit them and warned the Legion Lake Sioux to look out when they took on the Cougars.

Camp Galena was tough. They came to Iron Mountain with three straight victories in the young season and a cockiness the Cougars took issue with. Cracker was only two for five but drove in four runs and scored twice. And Dolph, resting his pitching arm, turned in a solid center field as Woody held the Mountain Lions to just enough runs for Iron Mountain to edge by them nine to seven.

"This is better than cow patty ball," Howie said at mess that night after the game.

"Cow patty?"

"You play in a pasture and hope the ball don't land in a pile of fresh cow shit," he said.

"For crying out loud," Marv said as he spooned soggy mashed potatoes into his mouth. "You crackers are strange."

"You ever cut your foot, Marv?"

"Sure, dozens of times."

"No. I mean—in pasture ball." Howie was enjoying himself.

"Never played pasture ball."

"What the hell you think we're playing out here? Sandlot? Take it from me, you don't want to cut your foot. You play with shoes on, else you'll step in a fresh pile and the stuff oozes up between your toes—that's called 'cutting your foot.'"

Howie laughed at the expression on Marv's face.

Then everybody at the table started "cutting feet" with

mashed potatoes. The mess they made didn't please Meathook in the least. Mashed potatoes became a rare item at Camp Iron Mountain after that.

The clearing of the forest and underbrush along the Iron Mountain Highway continued, bseball or not. Swinging an axe helped Howie with upper body strength, and long balls off his bat were becoming a near certaintly.

Cold Steam Stanley knew nothing of felling trees. He and Howie worked as a team on most occasions, mainly because nobody else had the patience for Cold Steam's ignorance.

"Never put axe to a stressed tree," Howie told him.

"How come?"

"Come on, Stanley, use your brains."

"What's a stressed tree?"

"Look. The safest thing is to fell the tree exactly where you want it to go. Notch it deep," Howie told him. "Notch it past center so you can control where it falls."

Cold Steam Stanley nodded. "Easy as pie," he said, and proceeded to fell trees in all directions.

"You're a danger in the woods, Stan," Howie said. "Why don't you sit down over there and let me do the felling. You can trim."

"I can do it," Cold Steam siad. "Don't worry about me."

"I'm worried about myself," Howie said. "Just let me get far enough away. If you cut your foot off, yell out."

Day after day, they felled trees, limbed them, and left them where they fell. Howie tried reasoning things like waste. To clear the Iron Mountain roadway, they had to cut the trees, clean the trunks, and roll them into stream beds or off mountain sides and leave them to rot.

To cut a tree, denude it, and leave it to turn back to top soil seemed to Howie almost a sacrilege. Especially since coal was shipped into camp from Rapid City, piled in giant funnels outside the kitchen, and used as the sole fuel for all the potbellied stoves. Why not burn wood instead? he asked of nobody in particular. Save the coal, leave it in Rapid. Use the wood. Make something useful out of obvious waste.

Cold Steam, out of sight in the deep woods, screamed out. He had been cutting on his own. Oh, Jesus, he's probably lost half his foot, Howie thought as he rushed through the trees.

Should never have put an axe in the fella's hands.

Howie found Stanley twenty feet from his axe which had fallen where he had last put it to use.

Howie recoiled from what he saw. Cold Steam's right arm hung limp and useless inside his long-sleeve shirt. The sapling had caught him at the elbow and hurled him backward through the forest, ripping the right arm from its socket snapping it and leaving it dangling, like so much wasted flesh.,

Howie knew the forest had its way of gaining revenge, making waste of its own.

Howie bent over his unconscious friend. "Christ, Steam, how many times do I have to tell you? Never touch a blade to a stressed tree. Oh, you've done it now, man."

Cold Steam was sent home to Wasta, right arm in a cast up to his neck. The doctors had saved it, but all doubted if it would be of any use to him again.

Strapped to his suitcase, a silent memento of Iron Mountain and his salad days in the woods, was a double-bladed axe.

The Cougars electrified the camp. Iron Mountain had a winner. Even the C.O. decided to attend the Rockerville game. He and his wife drove over with the team for the Saturday outing.

The Rockerville Red Sox were no match for the Cougars as the Iron Mountain team pounded them to a pulp. Cracker led the way with six hits in six at bats, seven RBIs, and some hot dog fielding that made the Red Sox wonder where he came from.

The C.O. and his wife led the Iron Mountain cheering section. There was talk of hiring a bunch of girls from Custer to come over and be cheerleaders for the big games ahead, but the C.O. put such talk as that down as quickly as it came up.

Even Meathook got Cougar fever. On Sunday, he put T-bone steaks on the table to celebrate four wins in a row, a Cougar all-time record.

Talk was starting that maybe, just maybe, this Cougar team could challenge the old timers, the best, the almost semi-pro Treetoppers from Pine Creek.

"Tell me about the Treetoppers," Howie said to Dolph.

Dolph was busy hacking away at a Ponderosa pine, but he stopped, leaned on his axe handle, grinned a little, and said, "Pine Creek has a team that's a little different, a little bit older, probably the best bunch of players this side of the minor leagues. Their C.O. recruits, you see. He goes out and finds the best ball players coming out of the service, gets them to sign up and... Well, you'll see," Dolph said.

The Cougars squeaked by the D-Lays from Roubaix, crushed the Slickers from Doran, dodged a bullet aimed at them by the Legion Lake Sioux and used the Hill City Mountain Men and the Hazelroot Nutcrackers for batting practice.

With the C.O.'s wife as head cheerleader assisted by Meathook, Manny Lakso, The Boot and others from camp, the Iron Mountain nine eased to the end of the season only one game out of first place. One more victory, and they would claim a share of the championship of the Hills.

That victory had to come against the veterans, the Pine Creek Treetoppers.

Iron Mountain had played the Treetoppers earlier in the season and had been humiliated on their home field. But on that particular early May day, Dolph had been hampered by a head cold and "The Boot" waved a white flag of surrender from short. Plus, the Treetopper ace, left-hander Speedball Gibson, the only southpaw in the C.C.C. league, made mincemeat of the Cougar batting order, allowing only two hits all day and both of those to Fleet.

As the final game of the summer, the Cougars had to take their act into the belly of the beast and play the Toppers in the half-finished Mount Rushmore parking lot.

The hype began early in the week. Saturday couldn't come soon enough. The team was pumped tighter than a helium balloon on the Fourth of July.

There was no escaping the excitement. On work detail in the woods, guys took turns giving Howie a rest from stripping downed Ponderosa pines. "You might pull a muscle," they said. "Why don't you rest a spell."

They treated Dolph, Fleet, Marv, Woody, The Glove, Cage, JoJo, and the rest the same way. Rest yourselves, save your strength, you'll need all you've got against the Toppers come Saturday afternoon.

On Wednesday after lunch, the team was sent back to camp early by the C.O. "Go to the field and put in some practice, men," he said. "I don't want to see you back in the woods until you whip those Toppers' hineys good and proper."

"If you need anything, just let me know," he told Woody. "If there's anything at all, just anything, all you need do is ask."

They got five new bats, a catcher's mask for Marv (it was about time, the poor guy had knots on his forehead from a dozen or more foul tips), a couple of new balls so white and slick Dolph didn't know how to grip them, and an actual rubber for the pitcher's mound.

"Should ask him for a fence around the field," The Glove suggested. "Keep the ball out of the creek." But Woody didn't want to push the old man too far. Marv's mask was a little extravagant as it was.

Howie and Roy Martin, second sacker, worked on their combination. Cage at first got to the point where he could actually turn the double-play from his end by learning to drop to his knees as soon as he loosed the ball to Howie at second and trust Roy to cover first. "You guys are slick," Fleet said from left field. And Howie tipped his hat. He had visions of playing short for the Detroit Tigers. Just another in the long line of Georgia Crackers finding their way to Motor Town, another Cobb in the Big Leagues. It was a dream worth keeping. It was even possible it could come true.

Friday came and there were T-bones once again on their plates.

That night, the C.O. brought a friend into the rec hall where the guys were lounging around and introduced him: Hank Snowden. "Used to play for the Cardinals back before most of you men were born," he said. "Hank's here to see what you guys can do tomorrow, so don't let me down."

For once, the chatter in the hall was gone. In its place was a dense, almost touchable silence. Hank Snowden. Could he be an honest-to-God big league scout?

"Hell, it's just a game," Howie whispered.

But nobody believed him.

Saturday brought rain. It rained enough to remind Howie of Georgia and make him a little homesick. It would have taken fins and goggles to play ball that day.

Mid-morning, the C.O.s from Iron Mountain and Pine Creek conferred. Wait till after lunch. Then, we'll see, they decided.

Lunch came and went, but not the rain. It stayed constant.

At two in the afternoon, the C.O.s again conferred. The earth was sodden. The creek ran at maximum. Though the sky was clear at Iron Mountain, rain continued to fall at Pine Creek, sixteen miles away. The playing field was one huge puddle. Time to postpone, they decided.

The news spread. Postponement of one day. No problem everyone agreed. No problem at all.

"Mormons don't play ball on Sundays," Dolph said.

"So?" Howie said.

They sat around the center pot bellied stove in Old K.P. A small fire was going, just enough to cut the chill of rain.

"I'm a Mormon."

"Well, I'm a foot-washing Baptist, but I'm willing to overlook it. Shame the devil and take the hindmost," Howie said.

But Dolph was more than a Mormon. He was a devout Mormon. A more devout Mormon than Howie would have guessed.

"What are you saying, Cracker? That I put my religion aside, for convenience sake?"

"No, not convenience. Baseball, maybe, but not convenience."

"I can't."

"There's a bit more involved here than your convenience," Howie said.

"Yeah. The C.O.'s pride."

"Try Cougar pride."

"You know where pride takes you."

"Yeah. To the Big Leagues."

"You're a cocky bastard, Howie Cobb. Somebody's gonna come along one of these days and take you down a peg or two."

"Without you in the line-up, it's gonna be the Treetoppers and that's a fact, buddy. A live-long honest-to-God fact."

"We'll see," said Dolph.

Conversation closed.

Old Clyde heard: Dolph DeSmet, a veteran, a re-upper, a barrack leader no less, was on the verge of embarrassing the entire camp. Not only that, with Hank Snowden around, watching over everything like some sort of hawk, word that the best pitcher in the Hills, maybe in the entire Corps, was threatening not to play ball on Sunday was doubly problematic for the C.O.

Maybe there was more at stake here than just another game. Maybe Snowden really was somebody special and was in the Hills because he had heard about the super-charged Cou-

gars and the upcoming confrontation with the Pine Creek
Toppers.

Regardless of his motives, Old Clyde was upset when he
called Dolph into his office in the Commissary.

Howie tagged along but the C.O. kicked him out. Still,
Howie lingered outside the door and heard everything that
went on.

"We're counting on you, Dolph," the C.O. said. "The
whole camp's counting on you. The pride of Iron Mountain is
on your right arm!"

"Pride goeth before the fall," Dolph said.

"Pride be damned. This ain't no Sunday School picnic,
you know."

"Get them to postpone until next Saturday."

"I can't do that. I'm sorry."

"Why not, sir?"

"Next Saturday starts the regional play-off in Cheyenne.
Besides, Hank won't be able to hang around here another
week. We gotta play this thing on Sunday. You're playing, is
that understood?!"

"You don't seem to understand sir. I can't play ball on
Sunday. My folks'll kill me if I do."

"Your folks aren't here, son. I am. And I promise you, if
you don't suit up tomorrow, I'll kill you myself, and that's no
lame threat, either."

There was a silence.

Howie figured Dolph had been convinced, that he was
shaking the C.O.'s hand and settling the matter once and for all.

That wasn't what was happening at all. Dolph must have
done something, God knows what. There was a huge crash, like
a bookshelf collapsing, and then Old Clyde's most irritated
voice, the one he reserved as a last resort. "Christ almighty,
then, get out of my sight."

When Dolph left the commissary, he wandered toward
Center Lake.

Howie didn't follow. He figured his friend needed to be alone.

Sunday. A beautiful day. Not a cloud in the sky. Howie sat on his foot locker. His baseball knickers were stained green at the knees. His tunic was unbuttoned so the "Cou" was on one side and the "gars" on the other. He whammed his cleats against the floor. There was no mud to unclot; he simply needed the noise.

"Guess we'll just have to kick some Treetopper butt without you," Howie said.

"Guess so," Dolph said.

"Don't think we can do it, though."

"Sure you can."

"You're our backbone, Dolph."

"And Christ is mine."

Howie didn't have an argument to that. He knew what his friend was saying. It didn't make sense, but he understood. His own Poppa, Alexander Stevens, would have done the same, if he'd been a ball player. So would his Momma and probably Hev and Hank and everybody else in the clan. Indella, too. Everybody but him. Why should a baseball game on Sunday be any more a devilment than one on Saturday?

He must have put his thoughts into words readable off his face for Dolph said, "If you believe something, you believe it. You don't not believe it when it's convenient or when you feel like it. I believe that the Sabbath is holy and that it should be treated as such, you know, like it's holy. You can't change what you believe just because it happens to rain on Saturday or because your pals need you to play a game. If you believe something, that's all there is to it. I don't ask you or anybody to believe the same as me, though I'd really like it if you did. So I guess I'll just have to stay here and leave the gaming to you and Marv and JoJo and the rest of the guys."

"You know, Dolph, it really doesn't matter."

"It does to me. Are you a Christian?"

"No."

"I thought you said you're a foot-washing Baptist."

"My Poppa's a Baptist preacher. I go to a Baptist church sometimes. I guess that makes me something of a Baptist. But it don't make me a Christian. I never been baptized."

"I thought all you Georgia boys were in the fold."

"Never been baptized. Least, none that counts. I don't have to believe in it."

"What do you believe in?"

"Not much. Baseball. My family. Indella. Maggots."

"I'll pray for you."

"And for our victory?"

"I wouldn't ask the Lord to waste his time."

"Then, I suppose we're on our own." Howie stood. He could see the sky out the door. Not a cloud in it. Dolph had his hands between his legs. Howie knew his friend loved baseball as much as he did, and missing the game was hurting him, but that didn't matter. Let Dolph hurt. Let him know he was letting down a whole bunch of others.

Howie stalked to the door and stood with the cool mountain breeze inviting him outside. "Thanks a lot, friend," he said without turning.

"You're welcome."

The entire camp was loading into bird cages for the trip over Iron Mountain to Mount Rushmore. The truck with the team pulled up outside Kensington Place. The horn sounded like a celibate goose. Howie waited a second longer, his cleats strung around his neck and his hat reversed and the bill cocked upward.

"You're sure about this, Dolph?"

"Are you sure about maggots, Cracker?"

"No."

"May you go six for six and return home the conquering heroes."

"Fat chance."

Howie ran down the steps and jumped onto the tailgate of the bird cage.

"Dolph coming?" Woody asked.

Every eye focused on Howie. He glanced around the small covey of quail-like boys. He saw them for the first time as what they were, himself included: a hoverless passle of scared chicks about to face a bunch of hawks and they didn't have their leader along.

"Nope," he said. "Who needs him, right?"

Fleet rammed his open palm against the corrugated iron of the cage. "Me," he said.

"Guess you'll have to pitch, Woody," Howie said. "I'll play center if we can get Arnie to be 'The Boot' one last game."

"Goddamnit," said The Glove.

"Hey, watch your mouth, Glove," JoJo said.

"Give me one good reason before I pop you one."

"Well," JoJo said, "it's Sunday. Sunday's a holy day, so watch your mouth."

Howie stuffed his mitt between his teeth to keep from laughing. The oiled leather tasted good.

The parking lot at Mount Rushmore was mostly mud. That was enough of an excuse for the Cougars. They slogged their way through five innings of the biggest game of the decade before conceding the contest, the season, and the trophy as "Best of the Hills" to the Toppers.

Hank Snowden left before the Toppers finished batting in the first inning.

Though they played under the same conditions, nobody heard a Topper complain about mud or slush or soggy balls, and it didn't keep them from scoring runs, a round dozen before the end of the second inning. By then it didn't matter anyway.

Howie decided it was too much fun, playing ball, not to enjoy himself. It didn't matter what the field was like. He had played on worse. It didn't matter about the score. He had lost by more. He took off his shoes and let the mud slide between his toes, and he laughed at the goo he carried with him to home plate or out to his position in center field.

"It feels good," he said, pointing to his toes, "almost better than getting my feet cut!"

With that off came all the Cougar shoes, and the team sloshed through the mud puddles with glee. It didn't matter that they lost the game eighteen to two. It didn't matter that the disaster was called after five due to a sudden thunderstorm. What mattered was that everybody had a good time and went home happy.

Even the C.O. and his wife, so full she looked like she might burst any minute, had a slap-happy good time in spite of it all. The C.O. didn't expect to beat the Toppers anyway.

And once Snowden made his departure from the field of battle, the day was changed to a frolic. In fact, Old Clyde decided he could do better than Woody on the mound, took off his shoes, waded through the mud, and pitched an inning and a half of scoreless ball.

Howie couldn't help feeling that Dolph would have enjoyed himself that afternoon regardless of his religion. Though the Cougars got smeared, the game they lost was by far the best of the season, the one the Cs of Iron Mountain would remember as long as time itself.

That night a new sound was heard in Iron Mountain. First it was a single startled cry, then a continuous stream of baby screams. The good camp doctor delivered unto the Munks an eight pound, two ounce baby girl, and the Momma was doing just fine.

Squawman

Bert "The Bull" van Dorst was a good two inches taller than any other C. He weighed just at two hundred pounds, and thanks to Meatloaf's high carbohydrate meals and the number of servings Bert took, his bulk was growing.

Bert treasured his size. It gave him certain privileges, like being first in line at mess, having the first game of pool in the rec hall, and occupying the first chair at the nightly poker game. It also made him a shoo-in for the annual inner-camp double elimination Iron Mountain Boxing Championship.

The announcement was posted. Each hotel could enter its best man. Three rounds in the preliminaries, six in the finals. If a barrack couldn't decide on its best man, then inner-barrack tournaments would be scheduled with the winner moving into the center ring. The ultimate winner from the camp would then represent Iron Mountain in the Black Hills C.C.C. Boxing championships at Fort Meade in September.

Bull, the pride of Iron Mountain, was the reigning Black Hills champion, an honor he received the year before by whipping a seasoned veteran from Pine Creek. The opportunity to defend his title was the primary reason he re-upped for a second year of the Cs.

Kensington Place selected its best man in a democratic fashion. "Okay, chumps," JoJo said, holding a handful of sage brush stems, "draw. Short stick goes into the ring."

"How short's short?" Woody said.

"We'll know when they're all out."

Howie closed his eyes when he drew his straw. He had no desire to take up boxing. It was a big man's sport. At five-eight when he was stretching and one hundred thirty pounds on a good day, he didn't qualify.

"Ah, shoot," Marv Drexler moaned as the others breathed a sigh of relief. It was fitting that Marv represent Old K.P. He was the burliest C in the barrack, and his time behind the plate for the Cougars had toughened him up, or so Howie liked to remind everyone. JoJo would be Marv's second, just in case, and Woody volunteered to take charge of training.

Howie settled back on his bunk. He was feeling good. The inner-camp ping-pong tournament was coming up next, and he was going for that. He was actually getting pretty good at the game, winning more often than losing. He was working on his horseshoes, too, thanks to the new pitching area behind the hospital, and he had heard rumors of a track meet in the spring.

Life couldn't be better he decided. If he wasn't in heaven, he didn't know where to go looking for it. He wrote home urging the rest of his brothers to join the Cs. It was the best life in the universe.

Saturdays were the highlight day of the C's week. Not only was there no work scheduled, but now with the boxing preliminaries and the weekly dance in Custer on Saturday night, the day was what all Cs lived for.

On the first Saturday of the inner-camp tournament, a makeshift boxing ring was constructed between the mess hall and the hospital. A single rope was strung between four fence posts in a ring that wasn't quite square. Liam O'Kelley served as referee; the C.O. and Professor Watkins, education director, were judges; and Meatloaf clanged a couple of pots together to start and end each round.

With Meatloaf's whamming of tin pot against iron skillet, the first bout began. The enrollees crowded around the ring, pushing for a better view as the Waldorf representative slugged it out with the fellow from the Plaza. Waldorf ground his opponent into the dirt with a series of wicked rights to the jaw and temple. Two minutes into the first round O'Kelley stopped the match and raised Waldorf's right hand into the air. Plaza slumped through the crowd, looking for a place to hide as cheers rose for the tournament's first conquering hero.

The contests continued throughout the afternoon, with the crowd growing hoarse from excessive cheering. Marv went the distance with his first opponent and could have taken the match if he had been able to keep his footing. Twice he slipped to the ground and both times received a mandatory nine count. At least he distinguished himself. Going three rounds in the mica dust of the Hills was something of an accomplishment, and the guys from Kensington Place were pleased with his showing. Next week, he promised, next week in the consolation round, he'd get him.

Bull had drawn a bye. He sat on the sidelines, looking on. Nobody talked to him. He seemed content to sit and watch, nod his head, and spit. His time was coming. His body posture said better look out when it's here.

Howie didn't know how to dance, but that didn't stop him from getting on the bird cage late Saturday after mess with most of the other Cs to ride into Custer for the weekly youth social sponsored by the local merchants.

He didn't care much for the socials held in Rockerville, Hill City, or Pactola Valley. The locals there were still pissed at the Cs for taking work away from them. Besides, just the name, Rockerville, made Howie feel old. Hill City was too tame, not enough to do. Pactola Valley was too rough. The workers from Mount Rushmore and the older guys from Pine Creek made Pactola Valley the perfect place to secure time in the clink, and when that happened, the C was sent packing, dishonorable discharge from the Corps.

Custer was another matter. In Custer booze was kept to a minimum; fights were rare. They had to be since the jailhouse was just across the street from the Community Building. The girls came out in droves. So did their boyfriends, but the Cs didn't mind that. In Custer the Cs could count on a swinging good time.

"This is gonna be Custer's Last Stand," one of the Cs yelled from atop the bird cage that Saturday night.

As they neared the Custer city limit, someone started up a Cougar chant used to spur the baseball team on to victory. Out of context it seemed vulgar to Howie.

"Rip 'em up, tear 'em up, Coooooouuuu-gaaaars. Rip 'em up, eat 'em up, Coooooouuuugaaaaaars!!!"

Custer was as small as Douglasville back home, maybe even smaller. Main Street was wide enough to allow parking down the middle. Stores, bars, and restaurants lined both sides of the street. On the west end of town was the huge brick courthouse with clock in its tower that chimed the hour.

On the east end was the Community Building, built out of civic pride and dedicated ten years prior by President Coolidge's wife. The so-called largest log construction in the world, the building was ideal for Saturday night dances. The sharp scent of pine inside the unpaneled walls and the warmth created by the huge open hearth fireplace urged everyone into a dancing mood. The first time Howie entered the place, he was awed by its beauty. After his first Saturday night in Custer, he was certain the aroma of pine could bring dancing to mind faster than any music.

Girls with and without boyfriends planned their weeks around the socials on Saturday nights. They could count on at least three bird cages from Iron Mountain every week and smaller numbers from camps Custer, Lightning Creek, Tigerville, the Narrows, Legion Lake, and occasionally Pine Creek.

Howie attended all the dances he could. He was determined to learn the art of the slow dance and surprise Indella with his new-found ability when he returned home.

The girls were pleasant enough. Few of them had the qualities necessary to teach a klutz like Howie the fineries of the waltz or the sexiness of the rumba. The one or two who could were already claimed. There was little chance for a C in such competition except among the weekly wallflowers, and in Custer there were always plenty of them.

One wallflower in particular this Saturday night caught Howie's eye. She was small and seemingly timid with straight shoulder-length black hair, high cheekbones, and coal black eyes set in a deep brown complexion that had to be nurtured by some secret oil. Howie saw semblances of Indella in her. He looked at the girl from Custer and felt homesick.

Howie hesitated to approach her, though no one else was asking her to dance. He admired her from across the shiny floor and daydreamed of dancing with her. Others not as good looking as she danced every dance, while she stayed on the sidelines, studying her shoe tops.

He tried to ignore Indella even though she sat in his head right behind his eyeballs. What would one spin around the floor do, spoil their relationship? Indella wouldn't care if he asked the girl for one brief dance, would she? More than likely Indella was out with friends at a similar party back home. After all, it was Saturday night. And if she was, he would hate to think of her being overlooked and left with nothing but her own shoe tops to look at. Some nice young man, like himself, would surely ask her for a dance or two. No more than two, though, and not as nice as him, nor as handsome. Maybe a great deal homelier. Maybe less cocky. Come to think of it, she ought to stay home where she belonged.

The country band, a makeshift group of Cs from the Narrows, began "Let Me Call You Sweetheart" for the third time. It was one of the few numbers they knew. The rhythm was easy enough to follow. Even if he didn't know how to dance, he could fake it.

He approached the girl, who stood with hands clasped in front of her. Sweat poured from his arm pits and stained his C-issue shirt.

"Care to dance?" he asked after clearing his throat and wetting his lips.

She seemed startled. He glimpsed a brief panic in her eyes. He was afraid she might bolt from the building. He prayed she would accept his invitation. It had taken most of his energy to generate those three words. He wasn't at all certain he would be able to speak them again if she refused.

"I don't know how to dance like this," she said. Her voice was as soft as he had expected it to be, as soft or softer than Indella's. She glanced at him, but couldn't hold his gaze. Instead, she stared at a pine knot in the flooring.

"Well, neither do I," he said. "Don't seem like we have much to lose, huh?" He tried to laugh, but he was too nervous.

She looked about the room as if hoping no one saw her talking with him. "All right," she said.

Her hand was cool to his touch as he led her away from the wall. He looked for a dark section of the dance floor, a place where they might hide their inexperience, but there wasn't one. The huge room was awash with light.

He slipped his free arm about her waist, and they began to sway tentatively to the music. She kept her eyes down and away. He could feel the tenseness of her back muscles and the warmth of her body through her lightweight summer dress.

"What's your name?" he asked. Noise in the building made quiet talk impossible.

"Tilda."

"Tilda what?"

She didn't reply.

"Howie Cobb. That's me. Folks around here call me Cracker. You know why?"

She was silent.

"Cause I come from Georgia. You ever been there?"

Silence.

"A long way from here. I'm out at Iron Mountain, a C. You?"

Nothing.

"Tell you what," he shouted, "put you in a pretty print jumper and a pair of saddle oxfords, and be damned if you wouldn't be the spitting image of my first cousin Marcelle."

She didn't smile. She didn't even look at him. He thought for a second he was dancing with a life-size cardboard poster.

"Yeah, ole Marcelle's the prettiest looking female in the whole Cobb clan. And you're her spitting image."

She didn't say a word.

It wasn't as romantic as he wanted, having to yell over the din and getting nothing back. He wanted to get to know her, find out who she was, where she came from, what she wanted from life. But she obviously didn't care to converse.

The song came to an end, leaving them on the dance floor, both unsure of what to do next. The band rescued them as it swung into a lively rendition of "Apple Blossom Time."

Howie looked at Tilda, the question of "Want to try another?" in his gesture. She nodded. They danced again, this time a little closer.

He felt conspicuous as a dancing partner, but she didn't seem to notice his stepping on her toes. In fact, she did not look at him the entire time. Her movements were as jerky as his.

"Having fun?" he yelled over the noise.

"Yes," she said. She didn't smile, not once.

"I tell you, Miss Tilda, we don't have this kind of dance very often where I come from. In Georgia, it's all square dancing, that sort of thing. You like square dancing?"

Before she could answer, a hand grasped Howie by the shoulder and whirled him around. Howie looked up into Bull's angry eyes.

Bull, backed by two other Cs from Iron Mountain, pulled him close to whisper-shout in his ear, "Get that squaw off the dance floor."

"What?" Howie yelled.

"Get her off the floor or we'll do it for you," he said.

Tilda, head lowered, eyes on the floor, looking for a possible crack to crawl into, returned to her spot against the wall where she stood, arms folded across her chest.

"Take your hands off me," Howie said. His anger was growing as he realized what Bull was saying.

But Bull's strong grasp stayed. "We don't take kindly to Indian lovers in these parts."

"What the hell're you talking about?" Howie tried to brush the huge hand off his shoulder.

Liam O'Kelley was on his way across the floor.

Bull let his hand drop. "We keep Indian trash where it belongs," he said, and with a twitch of his head, he left Howie alone without a dance partner.

He looked for her, but she was gone. Be damned, he said to himself.

He saw Bull in the middle of the dance floor with his partner, a natural blond with deep blue eyes. He rubbed his shoulder where the man's hand had come down on him like a claw. It hurt a little from the pressure Bull had used, but it was nothing compared to how his pride felt.

"Be goddammned," he said out loud. "Bull van Dorst, you're a goddamned son of a bitch."

The noise was too great. Nobody heard him.

Monday, Howie's crew hauled rocks to the new bridge being built across Squaw Creek on the Iron Mountain Highway. Bull passed him with pick and shovel in hand. "How's the squawman today?" He said with a sneer and a chuckle.

"Hey, you bastard," Howie yelled, "choose which one of these you want to sit on!" And he held up the middle finger on both hands.

Bert tossed aside his tools and charged in his lumbering fashion toward where Howie had been.

Howie darted away and kicked the larger man squarely on the rearend as he passed. "Hey, fat man, you better leave alone what you can't handle."

Bert would have killed Howie on the spot, but he couldn't catch him. Howie was gone through the woods as fast as his legs would carry him.

The next morning at mess, a couple of Bull's friends shoved Dolph and Marv aside as they sat on either side of Howie. Then Bull himself sat across the table from him. "Here's what I've got to say to squawmen," he said. "You can run, but you can't hide."

"I've got no time for you, Bull," Howie said.

"You're damned stupid, fella. You don't know what you're getting into."

"You wouldn't know stupid if it bit your ass."

"The squawman's got a mouth on him, boys. And such a little mouth, too. A puny little mouth, 'bout the size of his pecker, don't you think? But it don't take much mouth to do a squaw." He laughed and twisted Howie's tray of food around.

"Enjoying this manure?" he said. "Needs more flavoring, right?" He spat on the scrambled eggs and stirred them around. "Come on, now, eat it."

Howie tried to get up, but strong hands on either side of him held him in place.

"Lay off, guys," Dolph said but he was pushed away. He didn't press it, knowing that if he did an explosion would surely occur.

"I said—eat it," Bert said.

"Not hungry," Howie said.

"Hold his nose, Mo," Bert ordered. One of the guys pinched Howie's nose closed as the other two pinned his arms to his side. When his mouth came open for air, Bull crammed it with scrambled eggs and whispered, "You mess with me, I'll bust you into twenty small pieces, squawman."

Howie sprayed the unchewed eggs in Bert's face.

The table flew aside as Bull, a raging mass of muscle, crashed his belly into Howie, ramming him backward into the mess hall wall. Howie tried to respond, but arms held him back.

Marv, Woody, JoJo, The Glove, and Dolph leapt between the two, holding the bigger man off.

Woody did his best, "Come on, settle down, Bull."

"I'll kill you, you damn little Indian fucker," Bert yelled. "I'll kill the fucker—"

A heavily buttered biscuit flew across the mess hall and splatted against the wall near Howie's head. It was followed from the other direction by a handful of eggs, then some bacon, and a saucer of cereal. Flying food filled the air. Dishes shattered against the floor, the ceiling, and people's heads. The din grew. Some balled fists were thrown at neighbors. A couple of tables were overturned.

In the midst of it all, Howie and Bull glared at one another, sizing the other up. Bert was a good five inches taller, his arms half a foot longer, his body eighty pounds heavier, but Howie didn't consider all that. He knew the time of direct confrontation was somewhere ahead of them both. The question he faced was how to survive it.

With the blast from a drill whistle, the food fight stopped as suddenly as it began. Three regular Army camp supervisors led by Sergeant O'Kelley stood in the door of the mess. "All right, what the hell's going on here!" O'Kelley demanded.

Someone cracked a joke about Meatloaf's sausage not being dead, and laughter followed by a muffled "Mooooo" rippled though the crowd of Cs.

O'Kelley yelled, "Nobody leaves this joint until this mess is cleaned up. Now, move!"

The C.O. entered the hall as clean-up began. He shook his head as if disappointed in the character of his boys. He surveyed the damage, whispered something to his second in command, who whispered something in return, and left. Old Clyde slammed the screen door behind him.

Bert gave Howie a shove and marched away.

O'Kelley's whistle again brought quiet to the hall. "Van Dorst!" he yelled. "You and Cobb report to the C.O.'s office on the double. Now!!"

"I don't care to know what's wrong between the two of you," Old Clyde said to the two Cs standing across his desk from him. "That's your business and I expect you to handle it. When things like shoving matches and food fights start happening, then you've made it my business. I promise you, I won't put up with it. This organization's already got the reputation of being just a bunch of hoodlums, social outcasts and delinquents. You two make me think the rumors might be true." He took a second and beat out a rhythm on his desk with a pencil. "Another outbreak like this morning and I'll pack you both in a bird cage and let you bust each other apart. Then I'll ship you to Fort Meade where you'll spend three months in close confinement, probably in the same cell. Do I make myself clear?"

Howie nodded. Bull merely grunted.

"Starting tomorrow, van Dorst, you're on K.P. for a month. Cobb, you're on latrine."

"Again, sir?"

"Yes! Again. Pretty soon, the word'll be still, Cobb, if you're not careful. You so much as grumble at one another while you're in my command, I'll have you both in Fort Meade quicker than you can count your toe nails. Now get out of my office. You're fouling my air."

That night, Howie found an eagle feather in his foot locker. It was broken in half. On his pillow was a piece of rawhide with a black cross painted on one side.

He glanced around the barrack. No one was paying him any attention.

He showed the items to Dolph who merely shook his head.

"I've seen this before. I'd keep my eyes open if I was you," Dolph said.

"I don't need this kind of stuff," Howie said.

"So who does?"

Howie shook his head.

Dolph clinched his mouth. Since the Sunday baseball game, he had been shunned by everybody in Old K.P. Only Howie remained his friend. Now, with the attack aimed at Howie's head, the two of them felt together again. They were both Cs on the outs.

"We could leave," Dolph whispered.

"Say what?"

"You know, leave. Pack our bags and be out of here when the sun comes up."

"You're full of shit, Dolph."

"Others are doing it. Every day, there's somebody else not showing up for roll call. Seems to me there're more gone AWOL than left in camp—and it's not even winter yet."

"Quitting ain't a word the Cobb family knows."

"One way or another, Cracker, you're going home. Walking or riding in a pine box. You're in charge of the walking. Bull's in charge of the box. It's your choice."

"I don't know what you're talking about."

"What else you think those things mean? They're gonna snap you in two."

"But I didn't do anything."

"You're not that stupid, Crack."

Howie listened to the wind moaning through the pine trees. It had started turning a little colder in the Hills. Every night a little colder. And here it was, the middle of August. Howie didn't understand things at all.

Howie got a chance to see Bull in the ring. He was aggressive but slow. His right was a powerful weapon; if it landed, his opponent would more than likely not get up for a week. His left clung to his body like a parasite, of little use except to hold an opponent at a distance or keep him close while the right did its damage. No matter the opponent, Bull made quick decisive work of him. No man came out of the ring after a bout with Bert van Dorst on his own two feet.

Howie studied the big man's style: lean in and wham away, right after right. Each time the right began its crushing descent, the left would drop to his side. A lazy left. Easy prey for a savvy combatant. And Bull didn't move. He couldn't. He was flat-footed and swung his right from the heels, leaving him slightly off balance on the follow through. A slasher would have a hey-day with this fellow.

Howie was surprised no one picked up on the little things Bert did. Nobody seemed to notice that a left hook could damage Bull's jaw each time Bull cut loose with a right smash. Maybe, if you're in the ring scared peeless, you don't have time to think about silly things like strategy. Surviving, that was on all opponents' minds.

Bull won both his matches with ease as the two Cs he went up against were too intimidated by the big man's size to be effective. One threw in the towel after the first round and had to be helped from the ring, the other was knocked cold less than a minute into the match.

Howie admired Bull's power. When his punches connected, he was awesome. Howie could feel the jarring blow in his own body when it landed on someone else. The secret to beating Bull was simple: don't let him connect.

Marv did well for Kensington Place in the consolation

bracket. He took out his three opponents with ease and moved into the semi-finals the following Saturday. His opponent in the semi's was Bert "The Bull" van Dorst. If anybody could beat the bigger man, it would be Marv, but nobody believed he could do it.

All of Kensington Place piled into the bird cage heading for Custer that Saturday night. Spirits were high and Marv Drexler was everyone's hero. He had come out of the consolation round with a black eye, a swollen neck, and a loose tooth. But he was feeling good. And he had a full week to get himself ready for the battle against Bull van Dorst.

With that in his future, he was determined to have a slambam night in Custer, and he led the whooping and hollering all the way into town.

That night the light that poured out of the Community Building was golden. It was full of romance and promise.

Howie searched the line of wallflowers for Tilda. She wasn't there. Maybe Bert and his bruisers had scared her off the week before. He hoped not; he wanted to know her last name so he could think about her and give her a complete name.

The band from Camp Narrows was just warming up when he spotted her. She was serving punch with the Methodist minister.

"Well, howdy," Howie said.

She was dressed in a white summer frock that made her dark skin, hair, and eyes seem even darker, richer, more enticing. "How are you tonight?" he asked, not knowing what else to say.

"All right," she said and poured him a cup of fruit punch. She sloshed some of it on his trouser leg. She didn't look at him at first and when she did it was with apology.

"I'll get a cloth," she volunteered.

"Don't worry about it," Howie said.

He smiled at her; she didn't smile back. "I've had worse things than fruit punch spilled on these pants legs. You gonna save a couple of dances for me?"

"I don't think so," she said. She glanced about the mass of boys and girls, locals, Cs, loggers from Nemo, and miners from Lead. There were even a few regular army from Fort Meade.

"Then how about a walk? Let's you and me go for a walk, okay? You can show me the fair city of Custer. I love a good walk. Don't you?"

She looked at the minister. He nodded as if to say "Go ahead, there's no harm in walking." She smiled, the first time Howie had seen her smile. It warmed her face and made her the most beautiful girl in the Hills, the most beautiful girl this side of Indella.

Outside, the smell of the forest was everywhere, mixed with the odor of burning wood coming from the sawmill not too far away.

It was cool. Howie buttoned his lightweight jacket. She wore a white sweater over her summer frock. Delicate lines of bead work outlined the collar and front of the sweater.

They stopped first at the small rock-walled well. He drew a bucket up from below using the windlas. She dipped her hands into the water and drank. He did the same. He dumped the remaining water onto the ground and lowered the bucket for the next thirsty dancer.

"What's your last name?" Howie asked as they crossed Harney Street heading north on 8th.

"Does it matter?"

"Sure. A last name makes a person complete. Mine's Cobb."

"Like in corn on the—?"

"Actually, like Cobb County, not too far from where I grew up. They say my ancestors were the namesakes for Cobb

County. Makes a good story anyway. You ever heard of Ty Cobb?"

"No."

"You kidding?"

"Why would I kid?"

"Well, shoot then, you must be about the only person in the world who don't know of Ty Cobb."

"Doubt it. Is he a relative of yours, too?"

He thought about lying but stopped himself. "Wish he was."

"Why?"

"Cause he's the greatest."

"At what?"

"Baseball."

"Ah."

They walked for a block before she said, "Eaglewing."

"Where?" he said and looked around on the ground.

"My last name is Eaglewing."

"Oh, yeah. Tilda Eaglewing," he repeated her name several times. There was a nice sound to it. It fit her as neatly as the white beaded sweater.

"Howie Cobb." She repeated his name as well and they laughed.

"You see? It finishes a person. You really are an Indian, then?"

"Indian's the name you people use. I'm Lakota. I live with my mother in Rosebud during the school year. I visit my father in the summer. I could use his last name, I suppose, Lanchester. There's so little in a name like Lanchester. I prefer Eaglewing. That's the name of my grandfather on my mother's side."

"Rosebud?"

"South and east of here. A hundred miles or so. The reservation's where I live."

"I've never been on a reservation. What's it like?"

She didn't answer.

The full moon was a spotlight of blue and orange. It made her white dress shine as if worn by a ghost.

They reached the top of the hill and looked over the sleepy little town.

"This place you live—Cobb County?"

"Douglasville's my home town. That's in Georgia. Way down south. Warm year round."

"Really? Warm all the time?"

"Well, sometimes it turns a bit nippy."

"You have reservations down there?"

"Naw."

"Indians?"

"Naw."

"What do you have?"

"Trees, cotton fields, cotton mills. Lots of little towns real close together. Whole bunch of nice folks."

"Custer's a nice place to spend the summers," she said.

"Some of the Cs from around here say that when there's a full moon like tonight, you can climb to the top of the Needles and, if you're in the right frame of mind, you can actually carry on a conversation with the Great Spirit. Do you believe that?"

She hesitated a moment. "No," she said.

"I haven't seen any other Indians—Lakotas—around here, except in Rapid City. Why not?"

"Paha Sapa is holy ground."

"Paha Sapa?"

"The Black Hills. They're sacred. For the Lakota Paha Sapa is for reverence, not living."

"You're here."

"I'm only half Lakota."

"I have Cherokee blood in me," Howie said.

She smiled a second time. "I'm not impressed," she said.

"My great-great-grandmomma on my Momma's side was a full-blooded Cherokee Indian princess."

"Princess," she said.

They strolled on, their clothes brushing.

He slipped his arm around her waist. She didn't protest. He edged closer to her, she made no move away.

He pulled her chin toward his and bent to kiss her. Their lips touched. He smelled apple cider on her breath and he wondered if his mouth had a similar aroma about it or if maybe he smelled of cigarettes or something worse, Meatloaf's cooking. He pressed himself against her and felt the rise between his legs. It felt good, being so close to a female once again and having his organ rise to the occasion.

She shoved him away and grabbed his now-erect penis through his pants and squeezed—hard. He winced in pain as her grip tightened.

"You white boys are all the same. A piece of Indian squaw and thank you kindly, My Injun Maid. Princess. You want to mess around, I'm your princess. After the messing around, I'm just another smelly squaw. You make me sick, make me want to empty my innards on your shirt. Put this pole of yours someplace else, Easy-Tongue, but not in this squaw's tipi."

She half ran, half walked down the hill. Her head was up, her spirits high.

Lord Jesus, Howie wanted to shout after her, that's not what he wanted. She thought he had wanted to make love. Didn't she know? All he wanted was to be close, for heaven's sake. He was saving that part of himself for Indella. He simply wanted to kiss her and dream of Indella and home and the future the two of them would have together.

"Hey," he called after her, "It's not like that!"

"Bullshit!" she yelled back, her stride filled with accomplishment.

He could have kicked himself. All he had wanted was to be close, to smell her skin and explore her mouth. Why?! he wanted to yell but had nobody to yell it to, Why does everybody in this part of the world insist on misunderstanding things?

He straightened his crotch. He could still feel her fingers squeezing his now limp penis. It made him feel strange, the pressure still being felt down there. Nobody had ever touched him down there before, and it worried him that the sensation of her fingers on his privates wouldn't go away.

He rammed his hands deep into his trousers, and strolled nonchalantly down the hill. Nobody, not even Dolph, especially Dolph, was to know about this. He whistled a tune as he strolled down the hill back to the dance hall. He took in the beauty of a full-moon night in the Black Hills and wondered if the rumors of visiting with the Great Spirit in the Needles were true.

On work detail two days later, Howie found his favorite axe with handle broken and the two blades dulled from being driven into a slab of granite.

He showed the tool to Marv. "That damn Bert," Marv said.

The latrine was befouled. Such things hadn't happened before his reassignment by the C.O. to latrine duty! Now that Howie was more or less alone on permanent latrine patrol, somebody peed in a corner away from the urinals and left piles of human waste in the shower stalls. The toilets were stuffed with pine needles four or five times a day, causing them to overflow.

Howie didn't complain to the C.O. or Sergeant O'Kelley or even to his fellow enrollees. The latrine was his problem and he would deal with it.

One night he found dog shit between his sheets.

The next day he came in from work detail to discover a dead rabbit hanging from the end of his bunk. Its underside had been slit open and its guts hung almost to the floor. Howie didn't complain. He took the rabbit to Meatloaf and suggested he make rabbit stew. Which he did. Which he and Meatloaf enjoyed.

His photo of Indella was taken from his foot locker. It was the only one he had. Later he found it stuck in the middle of the dart board in the rec hall with a dart through Indella's forehead and a note beneath that said: "The squawman's squaw."

Howie tore the damaged photo into shreds and decided he had taken enough. He was willing to put up with a lot, but when they drew his girl into it, they had gone too far.

He wrote Indella asking for another photo and telling her if he came home in twenty pieces she should look up a fellow named Delbert van Dorst from Winner, South Dakota, and shoot his balls off with a twelve gauge shotgun. He didn't put it so crudely in his letter, but he was certain she would get the idea.

"Let me take your place this Saturday," Howie said to Marv after the photograph incident.

Marv looked at Howie as if his buddy had gone crazy. "You want in the ring with that dumb ox?"

"Why don't you get sick or something so I can take your place."

"But JoJo's my second."

"I know. JoJo can get sick too if you want."

"What for? You worried about me? Thanks, Cracker, but I can take the guy."

"No, you can't. You fight the way Bull does. You swing from the heel and you hope for a lucky punch. Bull is bigger and stronger. You don't have a chance, Marv."

"What makes you think you can do better?"

"Cause I'm smarter than he is. Besides, him and me have a score to settle. After I've beat him, you can get well again. I don't care. Just get sick this coming Saturday, okay?"

"I think you're crazy. With his reach you won't get within two feet of the man. You sure you want to do this?"

"Positive."

"What have you got planned for him?"

"Total humiliation."

Saturday brought word that Howie "Cracker" Cobb was replacing the regular Kensington Place boxing representative in order to do battle with Bert "The Bull" van Dorst.

The bad blood between the two was well-known. Bert bragged about how he was going to squash the Squawman like he was a tick on a mangy dog. He was going to chew him up and spit him into the urinals Howie obviously loved to scrub. Bull was going to send Cracker home to his momma in a tow sack with a lock of his hair in a separate envelope. They would need the hair to identify the contents of the sack. Besides, it was the closest the Bull could come to taking the Squawman's scalp.

Howie took all the talk with a grin. He nodded each time a new threat came his way and went on with his business. He made a few threats of his own, but in a calm, almost sermon-like manner. He said to the guys at the poker table one night, "Bull's as good as beat." Nobody believed him, including Howie himself. Dolph, JoJo, The Glove, and even Fleet got into the fracas. All of Kensington Place were ready to enter the ring against all of Brown Palace.

Fleet started a shoving match at Center Lake when some Brown Palace folk taunted him about living in the same barrack as an Indian fucker.

JoJo knocked two teeth out of Mo's mouth when Mo urinated in Howie's water jug. Howie watched, nodded, and grinned and offered Mo a rag to catch the blood flowing like creek water out of his mouth.

Dolph led an egg attack against Brown Palace on Thursday before the big match. Meatloaf, not caring much for the Brown Palace people, turned the other way so Dolph could pilfer the eggs.

The Brown Palace gang retaliated by catching two horned owls and setting them loose in Kensington Place at one in the morning. The guys in K.P. considered keeping the owls as mascots, but they escaped the next day.

Somebody mixed firecrackers in Meatloaf's coal so that the stove at mealtime on Friday nearly exploded. That trick almost got Old Clyde mixed up in the feud.

Somebody put a handful of live earthworms in Meatloaf's spaghetti and meatballs. Only trouble was, none of the Cs noticed.

Everybody, whether they wanted to admit it or not, was having a grand time as Saturday's challenge match drew nearer. All the C.O. could do was watch and hope the uneasiness in his camp would soon peter out. Secretly he hoped that Howie would be taken out in the first round and let that be that. After all, since Howie was K.P.'s representative, he was in the loser's bracket. If he won, he would have to go against Bull a second time, probably a week later, and the C.O. wasn't sure Camp Iron Mountain could survive another week like the one just past.

Marv helped Howie prepare. He began with Texas dirt. Howie found a tin of the red stuff stored with the trappings of the Camp dramatic troupe which wouldn't be active again until around Thanksgiving time. He resurrected the broken eagle feather and piece of rawhide with the black cross painted on it that Howie had found on his bunk and used them as part of Howie's costume. Then he borrowed some make-up from the C.O.'s wife. She knew all about the coming match and was more than eager to be of assistance, especially if it required such a little thing as make-up, she being the only expert in camp on its application. Finally, Howie found a hooded parka stored in the commissary, waiting for colder weather, and his costume was complete.

Marv laced the gloves for his friend and showed him how to hold his hands to get the best effect from his blows. "Keep low," Marv advised. "Make him have to reach for you. Stay away from him. Watch his eyes, and remember his lazy left hand."

Howie grinned. He didn't know why, but he was looking

forward to this, his first fight ever. It made him feel alive from toe to nose. All he needed was Indella in the crowd to watch him take Bull down a notch or two. He would write her about it afterward—if he could.

It was hot that Saturday, made so by a direct sun and a cloudless sky. For once, the wind was still and the heat sat over Camp Iron Mountain like a canopy.

Meatloaf watered down the boxing ring several times before the two o'clock match, but it did little good. Within minutes, the mica dust was thick as ever. The dust was so bad the C.O. suggested laying down a tarp, but there wasn't time to do it and still hold the match as scheduled.

Betting began early that morning with odds makers taking ten-to-one odds in favor of Bull. By lunch, they were down to four to one. Everybody knew what Bull could do and probably would do, but Howie was an unknown.

By one-thirty, every C in the camp, every civilian, every member of the regular Army, and even the C.O.'s wife and two-month-old daughter as well as a few visitors who had gotten wind of the so-called grudge match, crowded around the ring.

The talk was low, expectations high, and the cloud of mica dust thick as fog.

At two, Bull stepped out of the rec hall and marched down the hill toward the ring. He was dressed in regular shoes, pants and shirt. When he stepped into the ring, he removed the shirt and allowed Mo to strap his fists inside two huge gloves. He whammed them together, causing more dust to fly into the air. He was ready.

Somebody started a chant, "Cracker! Cracker," that was taken up by residents of K.P. and echoed through the Ponderosa pines. That was soon joined by Bull's buddies from Brown Palace with "Squawman! Squawman!"

The C.O. looked at his education director and said, "What's this all about?"

Professor Watkins said, "Heck if I know."

Howie stepped out of K.P., wearing the hooded parka, a headband that held the broken eagle feather, and a pair of boxer shorts. He was barefoot. He stepped into the ring.

The parka made him look much larger than he was.

Marv tied his gloves on as the chanting grew to impressive proportions, the "Squawman" version taking over.

Bull sidled up to Howie, leaned down and whispered, "I'm gonna knock your head from here to Center Lake." He sneered his special way.

Howie didn't say a thing, keeping his face deep inside the hood of the parka. Meatloaf clanged his pots. O'Kelley announced the combatants. An unequal mixture of boos and cheers greeted the boxers as O'Kelley called out names.

O'Kelley drew the two men into the center of the ring and whispered something. Howie wasn't listening. The ref touched their gloves together and said, "Go to your corners and come out fighting."

Howie took off the parka.

There he stood, face, arms, chest, and back red as a Texas mudbank. Streaks of war paint on his face gave him a strange, comical appearance. The broken feather, weighed down too long by the hood, drooped down his back, looking more like a tail than a headdress. And the black patch of rawhide hung around his neck like an amulet. Howie had painted over the black cross and drawn a large bull's eye in its place.

O'Kelley, at first dumb-struck and then a little pissed, waved his hands as he crossed to Howie's corner.

"Get that crap off your face, Cobb. What do you think this is, a circus act?"

Marv threw water on him and wiped off as much as he could with a towel. The rest smeared. "At least if you start to bleed," Marv whispered, "we won't know if it's you or your war paint running."

Bull was already panting like he had run a mile.

"I think I made him mad," Howie said. He watched Bull

kick up a cloud of mica dust, pound his gloves together, and respond to a piece of advice from Mo by pushing him away, sending him into the crowd and upsetting several rows of seats and the Cs in them.

It was easy to see, O'Kelley was going to have a difficult time keeping control of this particular match.

Meatloaf clanged his pots again.

Bull charged into the center of the ring with murderous intent.

But Howie wasn't there. He was highstepping, Indian fashion, around the edge of the rope enclosure, whooping and getting the crowd to clap in rhythm. He continued to dance his war dance, even as Bull rushed him with a wild right uppercut. Howie danced aside and planted a sharp left hook in Bert's ribs.

He flitted away, still whooping. He stopped, aimed an imaginary bow in Bull's direction and mimed an arrow sent into his opponent's midsection.

Bull came for him, but Howie danced away.

Bull stopped. "You interested in boxing or what?!" he yelled.

Howie kissed both his gloves in Bull's direction and continued his squawman's routine.

In blind anger, Bull lowered his shoulder and charged his challenger. But Howie wasn't there when he arrived. He had stepped lightly aside.

Bull's weight threw him over the single strand of rope and into the seated Cs, all of whom hooted and hollered.

Howie took four bows as O'Kelley counted up to five. Bull returned to the ring.

Howie held up an open-palmed glove. He struggled momentarily with the headband that held the broken eagle feather in place. He removed it, threw it deliberately into the dust and trampled on it. Next, he removed the amulet from around his neck and threw it into the dust as well. He indicated for Bull to trample on that item.

Bull did.

Then Howie waved Bert in, assumed the position, gloves raised as if he knew what he was doing, and lowered his head behind the protective mitts on his hands.

Bull closed in and blows began to flow like neither man knew they were only boxing.

Third round.

Howie had whipped Bull's bulk with his quickness and his well-aimed left hook. At the end of the second round when Bert stumbled into the dirt like a poorly cut pine tree, there were doubts he would get up. But the clanging of Meatloaf's pots sent the match to its final two minutes.

"You're doin' great," Marv whispered to Howie as he wiped away the accumulated mica and sweat. "You've got this thing won. So stay away from him. Stay out of the corners and on your toes. Cracker, you're the greatest!"

"I don't want to win," Howie said through labored breathing.

"Huh?"

"Hell, if I win today, I'll have to fight him again next week, and I don't think I want to do that, Marv. This is damn hard work."

"You want me to throw in the towel?"

"Do that and you die." Howie was standing, ready for the final round. "I ain't a quitter," and Marv knew he meant it.

He had it won, yes. But somewhere in the back of his mind, Howie knew, winning wasn't enough. The guy opposite him had pinned his precious Indella's photograph to the dart board and called her a squaw. Just to win wasn't enough. No. He had to make Bert feel more than physical pain. He had to crush the bigger man. He had to humiliate him. There was the pride of the Cobb clan to uphold, and simply winning wasn't enough.

He knew he could win. What he didn't know was how big his victory could be.

The pots clanged.

Howie moved into the center of the ring.

Bull eased around the edge of the rope, eyes glued to Howie. Howie could see the energy flowing out of his opponent's huge body with each step. His enemy was finished and Howie was the man to make him pay. Yes, he could do it. But if he did, there was next week and the boxing ring all over again. Still, this wasn't for himself, was it? Indella was at stake as well as the Cobb pride. Forget Cobb pride. It was Confederate Pride. It was the damn Civil War all over again, and this time the South was winning!

Besides, he had worked hard to get this far. No opponent had made it to the third round with Bert "The Bull" in two years.

Yet there he was. And Bert in reality was no longer a Bull. At this moment he was more like a mole.

A swift combination to chin and temple and the bigger man would crumble into the dust like a house of cards. The image of Bull sprawled at his feet and O'Kelley counting down to the magic number of ten played momentarily in front of Howie's eyes. He liked the look of what he saw. Forget next week. He'd cross that bridge when he got to it. He wanted to enjoy the feel of this, his moment of victory. To revel in it. To send it home to Indella with a note saying, "Look what I did!" He lowered his head and charged.

Bert's long left arm enveloped Howie's neck and shoulders and pulled him close.

Howie hammered at the protruding stomach, but nothing seemed to phase the bigger man.

The Bull's powerful right arched for one final, one massive, one deciding downward plunge.

Howie saw it coming and tried to cover up, but the blow was too swift and too strong. He didn't feel it land. He didn't hear the pop of the laces of his gloves as they gave way under the power of the blow. He saw stars for a brief moment and a sudden rush of blood past his clinched eyes. He felt as if his head was bursting from inside out as his knees buckled and he thudded like a meager little pine sapling into the center of the ring.

He didn't get to see O'Kelley swing his arm ten times over his prone body. He didn't know that Bert van Dorst picked him off the ground and held his hand high in the air and then carried him like a half-empty potato sack to the infirmary where he was cleaned and dressed in a gown and left to wake of his own accord.

He had to be told all this the next day when he woke up with a headache like none he had ever had before. And two darkened eyes. And a swollen, broken nose.

When he finally woke, he found Bert sitting by his bed, sleeping like an overgrown child of ten.

Pulaski Medalist

The piece of string almost sliced off Howie's nose. He was taking the short cut behind the mess hall on his way to the latrine when the tight and unforgiving piece of hemp scraped up his nose, across his brow, and knocked his ball cap to the ground. The string twanged like it had just sent an arrow flying.

"Jesus Christ," Howie exclaimed. "Who's the damn son of a whoring bitch who tried to take my head off!"

He had his pocket knife to the twine when he heard Meatloaf say, "Leave it be." Meatloaf stood in the back door of the mess, empty pot in one hand, cleaver in the other. "It ain't hurting you."

"It near about took the nose off my face, man."

"Well, you've got no call wandering around back here with your eyes shut. Stay where you belong and your nose'll be just fine."

Howie picked his cap from the ground. He knocked the dust from it before replacing it on his head. "What's it for, Meatloaf? Clothesline?"

"Fire predicting if you've got to know. And let me tell you, we're in for some bad doings not too far down the line. The fiddle string don't lie." Meatloaf twanged the string with his forefinger, then wet the finger and twanged it again. "Damn, tight as I've ever seen it this time of year."

117

"I could piss on it if you want me to," Howie said and laughed.

"Sure. Laugh your fool head off, but you'll see. How long's it been since we had any moisture here in the Hills? And I ain't talking about what you carry in your pants. You tell me that?"

Howie shrugged his shoulders. He didn't keep up with when and how much it rained. "Week or two, I don't know. A week ago Thursday, it rained a little."

"I'm not talking about rain." Meatloaf stuck his cleaver into the back step and sat down beside it, pulled out his tobacco pouch and rolled a cigarette. "I mean moisture—I mean dew, fog, things like that. It can rain and not do squat. The dew's what matters out here."

He struck a match and held it to the tip of his cigarette, drew a long draw in his mouth and watched the glow eat its way toward his fingers. He offered the cigarette to Howie, who took it.

Meatloaf rolled another. "I tell you, Cracker, it's been a while since that kind of moisture's found its way to the Hills. We're on a tinder box, buddy, and nobody seems to be concerned about it." He sat with the new cigarette, unlit, hanging from his lips. "I've lived in these Hills all my life. There's no such thing as moderation. When it rains, it floods for months. When it's dry, well . . . "

"You told the C.O. about this? What'd you call it, fiddle string?"

"You'd think he'd already know, wouldn't you? I mean, when the insides of a person's nose start to crackle up like a dry river bed, you'd expect somebody like him would notice. This, my Southern friend, is prime firefighting weather. Seems like every August it's the same. And what else're you fellas doing out here if not to fight off fires? A Civie from the Narrows was through here just last week and said they've been in firefighting training for the past month and a half over there.

Damn smart of their C.O. if you ask me. What's Old Clyde doing here? Not a damn thing."

Howie noticed for the first time that Squaw Creek not more than ten feet away was hardly moving, little water in it to move. He kicked at the dirt near the mess hall door and dust boiled up. Maybe Meatloaf was right. Maybe there was something to what he was saying about dew and fog. Back home, hardly a day passed without dew on the ground. In Douglasville, fiddle strings weren't possible; they'd never tighten up. No such thing, not that he recalled, as prime firefighting weather, as Meatloaf named it, in his north Georgia hills. Howie looked at the graying man whose gaze was on the cloudless sky.

"Wait and see, Cracker. All it'll take is a storm or two, a storm with the dry heaves, and these Hills'll go up like so much kindling. We'll be cooking each other, sending boys back home in canvas bags, and the Old Man'll never know it was all his doings."

Howie tried to imagine what a forest fire might be like. It gave him shivers of excitement to consider such things.

He secretly hoped that the storm Meatloaf talked about, the one with dry heaves, would make itself known. After all, that's why he came out here, wasn't it? To have adventures?

When he stepped outside Kensington Place, he gazed into the woods and tried to imagine what they might be like if they should be overwhelmed by a blaze. He shared his thoughts with Dolph who merely shook his head. "You want to be a hundred miles from a forest fire," Dolph told him. "Meatloaf's right. These are prime fire days. Any fool who's been in this part of the world knows that."

"You ever seen one? A forest fire?"

"I've seen where they've been," Dolph said. "They're not very pretty. We have fires all the time up in the Wasatch and Uintas. Usually they don't amount to much. But every once in a while, they get carried away. Then...well..."

Their next Saturday, free of all obligations, Howie talked Dolph and Marv and Cheater Evans into hiking up Harney Peak with him. One of his "constitutionals." His purpose was to visit the fire tower there.

Word was that Reliance Panott, the fire ranger atop the mountain, was a strange sort who lived the life of a hermit, yet welcomed all visitors by serving them samples of his specially made homebrew. It had been months since Howie had drunk any shine, and a twelve mile walk was nothing if the shine was as good as folks said. Besides from the lookout tower atop the highest mountain east of the Rockies, a body could see the edge of the world. Howie wanted more than anything to see the edge of the world before he died.

"Do you know how far away Harney Peak is, Cracker?" Cheater said more than asked as they strapped canteens of water to their belts and put extra pairs of socks in their pockets.

"Six miles."

"Yeah, from Sylvan Lake. And guess what, we're nowhere near Sylvan Lake."

"We'll hitch us a ride."

They hitched a ride with the Pactola coal delivery truck up the Needle's Highway and down past Little Devil's Tower to Sylvan Lake.

The lake was nestled among huge chunks of granite that jutted into the water and made for challenging rock climbs, but the granite boulders weren't the lure for the Cs on this day. It was only seven in the morning and too cool for a dip in the water anyway, even if they had time. Howie stored the site in his memory as a place worth a visit if for no other reason than to scale the cliffs there abouts.

"Howie, how're we gonna get back to camp?" Marv wanted to know when they jumped off the back of the coal truck.

"Hitch back, I guess. Or walk. Not so far that we can't walk it."

"You and your damn happy feet," Marv complained.

The lake had a hazy mist rising from it. They could hear the trout breaking water and the buzz of insects feeding on the cattails.

They stopped for a moment at the charred ruins of the old Sylvan Lake Lodge and tried to imagine the kind of blaze it would take to destroy such a fabled place. On the hill above them they could see where the trees had been removed and the new lodge was being built.

"Wonder if this new place is gonna be fireproof?" Marv said.

Dolph answered, "No such thing, fireproof. Ain't a thing in this world that won't burn if you get it hot enough."

As they started up the old logging trail toward the top of Harney Peak, Howie was feeling fit to burst. The air was just right, clean as rain, and dry as a cactus ranch.

Dolph said, "I've heard Reliance Panott's crazy as a cow in loco weed. He casts spells."

"I heard he's a witch," Marv added.

"Let's go home," Cheater said. But they kept going.

Howie laughed aloud at his friends' ideas about a maker of spirits. If nothing else, it was the ranger's fabled spirits called shine that drew him on.

The hike wasn't as bad as they expected. No difficult grades, just gentle slopes always up. Whoever cut the logging road knew what they were doing. The grade never drew the guys' hard wind.

Woods flanked them all the way. There were no vistas, no chances to look out over the Hills and admire God's handiwork. Instead, they were forced to enjoy the denseness of the forest and the life it supported and wonder at the lack of water this high up.

By the time they neared the end of the logging road, they were glad they had brought extra canteens with them.

Howie puzzled over how the forest ranger got his food and water up this far.

"He's a witch, I tell you," Marv repeated. "He makes his food the same way he makes his moonshine. He casts spells."

"You keep on saying things like that and you'll soon be believing them," Howie said.

"Do believe them." They didn't say a word the rest of the way.

Near the top, the climb was more difficult. Loose rocks and huge boulders became more plentiful until near the end where the road gave way to granite outcroppings and dwarfed pine trees.

Finally, from a distance, they spied the stone tower that sat astride the pinnacle some two hundred feet or more above their heads.

Dolph saw it first and pointed. "Looks like C stone work," he said. They could recognize the C.C.C. trademark a mile away.

The Hills opened up before the three of them. "God," Howie whispered. If he wasn't seeing the edge of the world it was because the world didn't have one. Otherwise, he was convinced, it could be seen from where he stood. The entire Black Hills and the deserts beyond spread out in a panorama like none he had ever seen. Peaks and rock heaps and even the backside of Mount Rushmore were below his feet and he knew, by the nature of the vastness of it all, he would some day, perhaps soon, have to come to grips with his notions of a godless world. It just didn't seem logical, standing where he stood, that there wasn't a god somewhere, having a say in things.

The stone steps up the side of the tower were pretty intimidating. What if the rumors they'd heard about Reliance Panott being a dealer with spirits were true? Would the ranger lure them to the top of the tower and cast them over the side like happened in fairy tales? Would he drain out their blood and make them drink it? Would he put them in a cage and use them for evil experiments? It was Cheater who said, "Maybe we'd better head back."

"The man's a forest ranger, Cheater. Come on," and Dolph led the way.

Halfway up the eighty-foot-high tower, they stopped to catch their breath and be awed by the vast world around them.

"Hey, look at that," Marv said and pointed.

There, not far below them, tucked in between slabs of granite was a pool of crystal clear water. The rocks formed a natural cistern so that when it rained, water was held in it until it rained again. Now the pond was nowhere near full. White lines on the granite several feet above the water level told how much water had once-upon-a-time been held by the pond.

"I heard that Reliance Panott sunbathes in the nude up here," Marv said.

"That's in July," Dolph answered, "not in late August. Nobody in their right mind sunbathes in late August."

They shared a look. Though they didn't say it, they knew anybody who chose to live alone in this particular spot year round most probably wasn't in his right mind to begin with.

"What do you boys want?" The voice came from above them. It was so near and strong they had to rely on the stone work around them to keep their legs from crumbling and dumping them like jelly on the rocks below.

Gazing at them from the last level of the tower still twenty feet above was a grizzled old head, eyes full of fire, and beard plastered tightly against his face by the wind.

None of the Cs could find a voice to answer him.

"I say—who told you you could trespass on my front porch!"

Howie gulped and said, "Excuse us, sir. We've come hoping to see Mr. Reliance Panott."

"Well... You're looking at him. You coming up, then come up for God's sake. I've got work to do."

If living the life of a hermit was anything akin to how Reliance Panott went about it, then Howie could almost embrace the idea, as long as he could bring Indella along.

The fire tower that squatted with the solidity of a medieval castle atop Harney Peak was filled with every comfort, a good deal more inviting than old K.P. back in camp. Windows opening on all sides gave the forest ranger a clear view of the Hills in every direction. On a clear day, and most of the days were crystalline, he could see a campfire twenty miles away and pinpoint it on his huge topographic map that was spread across the top of a long table. From his vantage point, he could see forever, since there were no other mountain tops nearly so high as Harney between him and the Rocky Mountains one way and the Great Smokey's the other.

"This is the life," Howie whispered to nobody in particular as he tried to take everything in, store it for sharing with Indella and Momma, Hev and Hank, maybe even Pierson. There was nothing like this back home in Douglasville, Georgia, and he wanted to make certain that when he got back there, he could share everything in detail.

Howie was amazed at how much ranger stuff could be made to fit inside such a small space. There was a comfortable-looking bunk, an easy chair, a writing table with a plentiful supply of paper, ink, and pens, a generator for electricity which Reliance said he used only for the short-wave radios, one as backup, just in case, a couple of hurricane lamps, and a bookcase filled with mystery novels and stories of the Old West.

Reliance, a portly man with more belly than he needed and a nest of hair he called a beard, invited them in and pulled a couple of folding chairs from the wall. "I belong to Thoreau's school of community," he said. "I keep one chair for solitude, a second for company, and a third for society. Looks to me like you fellows done out people the whole of my social order, so a couple of you'll have to squat on the floor over there."

He took a pull off his tobacco plug, offered it around, took up an empty can for his spittle, and said, "What brings C.C.C.'s to my front door?"

"How do you know we're Cs?" Cheater asked.

"Cause that's what you smell like."

"We've heard about you," Howie said.

"That so? In what light?"

Howie continued, "We heard you're the one who'll spot the great fire that's coming our way. That right, fellows?"

They all agreed.

"We also heard you brew your own liquor up here and it's the best this side of the Missouri River."

"You might be right about that." He pulled a jug from beneath his bedding. "Are you fellows old enough to drink?"

"Sure," Howie said for all of them. "We get drunk every Saturday night. Besides, the climb up here'll give anybody a thirst."

Reliance poured out four small shots of whiskey into tin mugs. He didn't have a fifth, so he drank directly from the jug. "Not as fine as it sometimes is. Too dry this past year to get good grain. Still, it ain't bad."

They sipped at the biting liquid. Howie grimaced as the whiskey pricked his tongue and throat. "Good stuff, Mr. Panott," he said.

"Yep, among the best, they say. Hear they're building a new fire tower over on Mount Coolidge a bit further south. I 'spect the fellow they put over there will challenge me in liquor making. Well, that's okay, too. And what smoke I don't spy, guess that fellow'll do it for me." He spat into his can. "You know you guys are so high up here you'll get yourselves nosebleeds." He seemed to think a second, then said, "Yep, conditions ain't ever been better for one hell of a blow up. You guys know how to handle yourselves, don't ya, when one comes along?"

"Sure," Marv said.

"Sure, hell, Marv," Howie said. "Our C.O.'s kept us on Iron Mountain Highway so long we've had no time for firefighting stuff."

"All most of us know to do is pull out our peters," Cheater said, "and piss a fire out."

"Yep," said the forest ranger, "that's one way to do her. Assuming you've got enough storage," and he cackled at his joke.

Howie said, "Meatloaf's fiddle string says there's something coming, that's sure."

"Goes in cycles, you know. More?" he asked as he held up the jug.

All nodded and the jug passed around a second time.

"Mankind thinks he's on top of things. All these new fangled ideas about fighting nature. Sure, they work for Mother Nature's little temper tantrums now and then, spot fires here and there. I tell you, boys, what man puts out, nature'd put out just as quick if we'd let her. Best thing for fires is let 'em burn. They'll burn themselves out. This modern firefighting stuff comes from our need for heroes. We use heroes like cows use hay. But regardless, you fellas keep out of the fire's road. Just steer clear, that's the best advice I know."

"You ever fought fire?" Marv wanted to know.

"When I was twenty-two, a bit older than you fellows. I was into hero-making myself back then," the ranger said, spitting again, his spittle clinking against the side of his can like it contained metal. Then, he took a draw off the jug. "I tell you, that one time was enough for me. Taught me something about 'heroic action.' Taught me to stay up here spotting fires, not down there spitting on them."

"What was it like?"

"Like?" He chuckled. "Everybody wants to know what it was like," He pondered the question for a bit, then said, "Like hell on earth, like the Devil's own kingdom opened up around us and make Shadracks, Meshacks, and Abed-We-

Goes out of all of us. Like... No way on earth to tell you what it's like. You gotta be there."

He pulled his shirt out of his pants and unbuttoned it from the bottom up and held it open. On his chest was a large red patch of flesh that appeared blistered and inflamed. He leaned toward Cheater.

"Touch it."

Cheater sidled away.

"No, go on, son, touch it."

Cheater reached out a hand and ran a finger down the center of the scar. "Like leather," he said.

"My medal, my Pulaski medal." He rebuttoned his shirt and then rolled up his right pants leg. There, just below his knee was another old and sinister-looking scar. He slapped it tenderly, like it was an old friend. "See the redness of it, fellows? Proof. We're in prime fire season. My Pulaski medals don't lie."

Dolph was sitting forward. His eyes were big as copper buttons. He was awed so his voice was hardly a whisper. "You were with Pulaski, Mr. Panott?"

"That's right, son. You know your history."

"My granddad told me about the Big Blow-Up. 1913?"

"August, 1910. Wallace, Idaho. You fellows should of been there. I swear, if you'd seen what I seen those two weeks, you'd gladly freeze to death in a jiffy before you'd go close to another forest fire. They're fickle as a woman's heart and twice as deadly."

Cheater turned to Dolph. "What—"

Dolph answered with a hiss that caused even Cheater to pay attention.

Panott continued, "You guys know about firebrands, right? Hell, the hot spot was six miles out in the mountains and firebrands were setting awnings ablaze in downtown Wallace. I was just a private then, stationed at Fort Meade, and we got the call. Rushed two thousand miles to watch a town melt before our eyes. Taft, Tuscore, Deborgia, Haugan. Only thing that saved Wallace was the volunteer fire department. Don't know how they did it but they bested the beast in the middle of town. Lost two men doing it, but saved most of the buildings.

"I was up in the hills, then, sent with a bunch of kids to take on the flames face front. I remember the spade I was using to dig a firebreak caught fire right in my hands. The handle just burst into flames like so much kindling. One of the last trains out of Avery, not much of a town, over a thousand people on it, had to take the only line left open, right through the mountains. The engineer just made it to the tunnel outside town when the firestorm swept right over them. He stopped the train inside the tunnel and kept it there till the storm passed them over. Some folks claim that the two end cars, those closest to the tunnel opening melted on the tracks. Only thing that saved them people's lives, they tell me, was huddling in the middle of the tunnel and pouring water from the engine tanks over tarps and covering themselves with them."

The four Cs sat spellbound as the old ranger gazed out over the hills, looking for any sign of fire, spitting in his can and chugging from his jug.

Their cups were empty now, but they didn't dare ask for more.

"Yep, I truly love company, but everybody wants to know about the Big Blow-up and old man Pulaski, and I'm alive to tell you fellows about it because of that foolish man's courage. Hell, I had no courage at all. None of us did. They give me a real medal, you know, but I threw it in the trash. If I could throw these scars in the trash, I'd do that too. Throw them out and start over again."

"Who was Pulaski?" Cheater asked.

Dolph spoke up, full of pride. "Greatest ranger of them all."

"You don't know anything, boy. Pulaski bought into the notion of hero-worship. His great granddaddy or somebody was a grand hero from the Revolutionary War. Old Eddie Pulaski figgered he was meant for the hero thing, too, and he was determined to get it, no matter what. We were up there near St. Joe River in the Bitterroots. August 20. I'll never forget it. Dark as pitch at mid-day, air so thick you couldn't breathe. Wind came up like nothing I'd ever seen before, wind so strong it was pulling pine trees out of the ground, roots and all. Caused by the fire's appetite for more air, they say. Oxygen. Just sucked it all in. That's when we knew we were up against something stronger than us.

"Old Pulaski looked at at us, forty-five in all, and said, 'Fellows, looks like we better get us back to Wallace. Ain't no good us hanging around here much longer.'

"So we started back to Wallace, wind blowing so hard it was all we could do to stay afoot and the fire roaring down on us like twenty freight trains. I tell you, there was only a couple of us regular Army guys along, the rest were volunteers, pick-ups. They knew enough about fighting fires to fill a thimble. There was fire raging on three sides of us, trees crashing, exploding, exploding like sticks of dynamite. Pow, you know, and splinters were flying every way but down. We were doing pretty good, until we looked up and what do you know? There's fire in front of us, too. Must of come from Wallace, one of their backfires. So what do you expect? Couldn't breathe, couldn't go back, forward, sideways. We panicked, me right along with the rest of them. One fellow, name of Kjos, went right out of his head and rushed into the fire headlong. I don't guess he made it, never heard from him again.

"Old Pulaski pulled out his revolver and said, 'Anybody else want to make a run for it will get a bullet between the eyes,' and somebody hollered at him, 'Go ahead, Eddie, it'd be better than dying like this.' Then Pulaski said, 'Come on, follow me.'

"Well, we didn't have anything else to do, so we followed him. Seems he remembered an old mining shaft somewhere nearby. The old deserted War Eagle mine. 'Can't be too far away,' he said. We came to a steep hillside already half ablaze and there it was. Pulaski sent us all inside that old shaft.

"At the far end of it was a seepage, not much water, but enough to soak our shirts and pants and things. So, we did it and covered our heads with our soaked shirts. I tell you, most of us were out of our minds by this time. We knew the heat would blaze the studding around us, the wood beams that held the roof of the shaft up, and if that happened, we'd all be burned alive. A handful of fellows started screaming as loud as they could, trying to out yell the fire, I guess, and they would of dashed out of the mine and back into the firestorm, me right along with them, if Old Pulaski and his trusty revolver hadn't put himself near the mouth of the tunnel and held us all at bay.

"The tunnel filled with the hottest air I've ever pulled inside my lungs. I must of passed out, figgering if I died and went to hell it'd be a relief. I don't know how long I was out. It don't matter. I came to with an inch of ash all over my body. Some of my shirt was burned away, here, where my medal is, and some of my pants leg. I didn't have any hair left on my body. It'd all been singed off. I'll never forget the smell in that mine shaft. It was almost sweet, almost pleasant, like crushed cane that's too hot mixed with that phosphorous smell you get when you set off firecrackers. A couple of other fellows were already sitting up, just sitting there, staring at the walls of the tunnel, surprised, I guess, that they were still alive even though most of the timbering had melted away. And it was so quiet. Like inside a coffin.

"Somebody behind me started laughing, and I figgered, what the hell, we're alive, maybe that was enough to laugh about, so I laughed, too. I crawled through the layer of ash toward the mouth of the mine shaft. Off to one side I saw what was left of Old Eddie Pulaski, curled up in a ball like he was expecting to be reborn. Somebody asked if Pulaski was dead or not and another answered, 'Yep, the boss is dead,' and you may not believe me, but out of that curled up ball of charred flesh came a voice clear as a bell, 'Like hell he is.' Pulaski was blind as a bat, but he could still breathe. Thank God, every last one of us could still breathe."

"Pulaski was a hero," Dolph said.

Reliance laughed. "Pulaski was a fool. He should never have taken us out there in the first place. That's why I threw away the medal they gave me. Sure, I thank him for saving my life. But I also blame him for putting my life in such danger, and giving me other medals I can't cast off. There's no cause to ever march like idiots into the direct path of a firestorm. The Devil himself is in charge of them things, and he's one hell of a fast runner. Faster than a hundred men. So, take it from a vet: pray for rain, boys." He cleaned his mouth from a bucket of fresh water and spat his residue tobacco into the bottom of the can, then took a deep swig of whiskey from the jug. "Okay, fellows, care to see my putting green?"

"Putting green?"

"Sure. A fella's got to do something with his time. So I built me a putting green. My stroke's coming right along. Bobby Jones better watch his rear cause Reliance Panott's gaining on him. Or how about a swim? The pond's a mite chilly this time of year, but it sure beats the hell out of taking a bath."

Three hours later and halfway back to Sylvan Lake, Marv asked, "Do you guys smell smoke?"

They sniffed the air. Nothing.

Marv said with embarrassment, "I could of swore...?"

Cheater said, "I wish the C.O. would start up some fire fighting sessions."

"I'm praying for rain," Howie said, "and I'm not even a praying man."

"What we need," said Dolph, "is a rain dance."

"What we need," said Marv, "is a new C.O."

The rest of the way back to Sylvan Lake, Howie tried to picture the woods surrounding him exploding into flames and sending splinters of sapling every direction but down. It was a picture he couldn't quite paint clearly in his head. And for that he was thankful.

The first car that came along passed the four Cs by. Cheater raised his middle finger to the rear of the speeding vehicle. The next car pulled to the side of the road.

"Where you fellas heading?" the driver asked.

"Camp Iron Mountain," was Howie's reply.

"Well," the man said, "I'm heading as far as Custer City if you fellas want to come along."

The four looked at one another, shrugged, and got in, Howie in the front, Marv, Dolph, and Cheater in the back. After all, they knew it would be easier to get to camp from Custer than from way out here in the middle of nowhere.

"So, what's the likes of you fellas doing out thumbing rides?" the man asked.

"Just our constitutional," Howie said. "We're with the Corps, our day off."

"Been hiking Harney Peak," Marv said.

"Ah, I see. Harney. I hiked it once myself. A religious experience, that, isn't it? Was for me."

Howie noticed the man's collar, the thin white choker around the neck with the black rim. A priest. He looked back at Marv, Dolph, and Cheater and grinned that special grin of his, but his friends paid him no mind.

The man continued, "At this camp of yours, Camp Iron Mountain, is it? You fellas have services you attend there or what?"

Cheater started to answer, but Howie cut him off. "There's a preacher comes by every Sunday morning," he said.

"Yeah," said Cheater far too loud and with too much personal pride, "but none of us has got any use for that sort of thing."

The priest caught Cheater's eye in the rear view mirror. "That right? No use what so ever? That's what you're telling me?"

Cheater laughed as he said, "All that religious stuff's just a crock of shit, right guys?"

Dolph started to answer, but he saw the look on Howie's face. Howie was either in pain or constipated, he didn't know which. So, Dolph just shrugged and looked out the car window at the passing trees.

"Tell you fellas what," the man said. "I'll give you a ride all the way to Camp Iron Mountain—"

"Hey," said Cheater, "that'd be great."

"—IF—if you'll tag along with me for a couple of hours this afternoon."

Cheater laughed again. "Hell, man, you ain't some sort of weird one are you?"

"Well, I suppose that's for you to find out, sonny." The man looked at Howie and smiled. "What say, young man, you go to mass with me, I'll truck you fellas wherever you want to go."

"Mass?" hissed Cheater. Then he caught a glimpse of the black and white collar. He sat back in the seat and groaned.

"Sure," Howie said. "That'd be just fine."

No one said anything for a good minute or so. It was Cheater who broke the silence when he said, "I'm a God-fearing Catholic, Father, and I ask your forgiveness for the language I used in your presence just now."

With that, Father Leary, as he introduced himself, lectured the four Cs on the necessity of religion in their lives and made a point of praying for them, especially Cheater, with growing passion three times before they arrived in the city of Custer.

The Catholic church was small, built from stone and logs, the sanctuary dimly lit by candles and a few hurricane lamps. Every seat in the building was taken by the time they arrived, every seat except for half a pew in the very front. The four were ushered to this conspicuous bench as Father Leary excused himself and went into the church by another door.

Howie glared at his buddies as they slipped into the front pew, Cheater stopping long enough to kneel and cross himself before finding his seat. "I ain't never been in a Catholic church before," Howie whispered to Cheater.

"Well, take it from a pro, Cracker, this one ain't much."

"Marv?" Howie whispered. "You ever been in a Catholic church before?"

Marv whispered back, "'Course not. I'm Jewish."

"Ah, come on!" Howie said aloud.

"Shhhh!" Cheater hissed at him.

Howie looked at Marv with renewed interest, as if he was seeing the hulking teenager for the first time. "You're serious? You're a Jew?"

"Anything wrong with that?"

"No! Nothing's wrong with that. I think it's fantastic. I just never would have guessed, that's all."

"Does it make a difference, my being a Jew?"

"You better believe it does, Marv. You're a Jew, Dolph's a Mormon, I'm a Baptist. How're we gonna know what to do in a Catholic Church?"

"Blind leading the blind, Crack," Dolph whispered.

"Don't sweat it," said Cheater. "Just follow me and do what I do."

They stood up, they sat down, they sang songs and heard the Gospel read in what Howie figured had to be Greek. Then Father Leary came forward, everybody stood again, and he kissed the Bible, crossed himself, and read again in the same foreign tongue. They sat again and Father Leary began his sermon and all four of them knew, sitting in the front pew as they were, they would not escape the lashing that was surely headed their way. The priest stared at and through the Cs as he began his lecture once again, the same he had shared with them on the drive into town, his lecture on the need of religion as a cornerstone in a person's life.

Howie listened with curiosity. The words were the same Poppa used; only they were shaped differently. The passion was lessened, the urgency almost non-existent. In the place of passion and energy was the priest's logic and sincerity.

Yes, Howie found himself agreeing with what the priest said: one does need religion in his life—as long as he was willing to accept the presence of a Supreme Being. He had experienced trouble with the last part from the time his Poppa started forcing him to go to church. He had problems with it even still. And Father Leary had nothing new to say on the subject, and that was that.

He got along fine with the service and was actually enjoying himself until the priest had finished his sermon and blessed everybody within the sound of his voice. Then the strange part started. All the worshipers around him, except for Marv and Dolph, who were just as confused as Howie, bent their knees to kneel. The two of them were left standing like stop signs at an intersection. Cheater hissed at them to join him on his knees.

Marv and Dolph did.

Howie sat down instead.

"Kneel, damn it," Cheater whispered.

And Howie whispered back, "I can't."

Up, then back down. Howie was getting confused. Then the parade started. Back home, they passed the communion wafer and the grape juice down the pews so nobody had to leave his seat. Here, everybody got up, walked down to the priest, and had the wafer placed on tips of their tongues.

Being in the front row, the four Cs were the first down the aisle. Howie didn't know what to do; neither did Marv or Dolph. They moved with the flow, down the aisle and to the priest. Howie faced the man eye-to-eye, not knowing what else to do. Father Leary crossed him and spoke some words in the foreign tongue, but he didn't give him the host, nor did he offer him the cup. Instead, he whispered loud enough for those in the rear of the church to hear, "Move on." So, Howie moved on, up the aisle, and out the main entrance.

Dolph, Marv and Cheater followed and joined him on the running board of Father Leary's automobile. They sat in silence as the rest of the congregation left the building and went on their ways. Howie stood rapt in his own thoughts.

After a time, Cheater said, "That was fun."

"Yeah," Marv said and chuckled. He had been given the host and it had tasted good.

"Why didn't you kneel, Howie? I mean, Marv knelt. Dolph knelt. When you go to Mass, you kneel."

"I don't," Howie said.

"Why not?" Cheater insisted.

Howie sighed. He knew why, but he wasn't sure he could explain it, so he said instead, "If I had bent my knee in that church, my Poppa would have killed me."

"That's dumb. He'd never know," said Dolph.

Howie nodded his head. "Oh, yes he would. My Poppa would know." He thought for a second before adding, "Besides, with a Baptist it's a matter of pride. No self-respecting Baptist bends his knee before no man, not of his own choosing. Not if he can help it."

"What about before God?"

Howie shook his head. "Before no god neither. Don't mean to belittle you or your faith, Cheater, but that's just the way of it."

True to his word, Father Leary gave the four a ride to Camp Iron Mountain, dropping them off at the main entrance and continuing on his way to his next parish. All across the mountains, Cheater and the priest talked Catholic talk while Marv, Dolph, and Howie sat in the back seat in silence.

Howie was quiet only on the outside. Within him was a raging debate. Why couldn't he bend his knee in the Catholic church? After all, he wasn't a confirmed Baptist. His Poppa might be a preacher and everyone else in his family a born again Christian, but that didn't mean he himself had been born again. Sure, he had come close that time Preacher Williams had come to Liberty Baptist for the annual Fall Revival when Howie was ten. He had gotten all involved and emotional in the Invocation, while the evangelist made his call to salvation, his plea for redemption, and he had gone up front to receive the right hand of Christian Fellowship, only he knew even then, even as the congregation passed him with joyful hand-shaking and the other converts stood at his side crying and as his Momma May Lou threw herself on him with tears of joy, he knew it wasn't for real, that he was faking it, hoping to get Momma and Poppa off his back. And then that afternoon, that hot August Sunday afternoon, when he and the rest of the saved had traipsed down to the edge of the Dog River and Preacher Williams had waded up to his waist in the cold mountain stream. The line began moving out to the preacher, there where he prayed over them, bringing God's attention to what was happening, and then placing the white handkerchief over people's noses and mouths and dipping them down into the water with words of salvation issuing like candy from his throat. Howie, knew it was all a sham, that he still was only faking it. That's why he had waded right on by the preacher, stopping only long enough to shake his hand before pushing past him and on to the other bank of the Dog where he pulled himself out of the water and into the mountain laurel that tangled the woods into a brambles. He knew even then, even at the age of ten, that baptism was a serious thing and he simply was not ready for such seriousness, not then, not now. And it confused him. Why, then, could he not bend his knee in a Catholic mass? Marv could, and he was a Jew. Dolph did, and he was a Mormon. But he couldn't when he was a nothing, a nobody. He simply could not do it and that was that. No need to ask why. There was no answer.

No more than a week later, the C.O. clanged a couple of pots together at supper mess.

The buzz of chatter that was constant during most meals at Iron Mountain petered away as everybody turned their attention to their captain.

He cleared his throat a couple of times before he said, "Reveille's at five in the morning, gentlemen. We have us some big doings starting tomorrow, so we'll get an early start. Lights out an hour early tonight. All you guys pack a light duffel. We'll be gone three, maybe five days. Consider yourselves on your first extended fly camp." He clanged the pots together again, noting the end of his message. But the buzz of conversation didn't return.

Instead, one of the Cs who'd been in camp the longest asked, "What's up, Captain?"

And Old Clyde called out, "Finish your supper. Reveille at five. Get a good night's rest, gentlemen,"

At five the next morning the bugle sang out and the whole camp gathered in the early morning chill to answer roll call. Instead of the usual morning drill of O'Kelley's calisthenics, the boys were hustled into the mess where they ate a quick breakfast of oatmeal with brown sugar and milk. No eggs. No meat. "Didn't have time for meat," Meatloaf said when asked.

When they came out of the mess fifteen minutes later, the bird cages were parked, bumper to bumper up the drive, all pointed out of camp.

"Okay, fellas," O'Kelley called from the running board of the lead truck, "everybody get aboard. We're taking us a hell of a ride."

"Where we going?" somebody asked.

"Ask me no questions, I'll tell you no lies!" he shouted with a grin on his face. But anybody could see, the grin was made of wheat paste. It wouldn't be long before it was gone.

"Where're the tools?" somebody else wanted to know.

"Just get on the trucks, boys, tools are waiting for us where we're going."

"Where's that?"

But there was no answer.

The Cs climbed aboard the bird cages until there was room for nobody else.

This was a first: the first time all of them had left camp in one bunch to do one job. Usually they went in different directions to manage different tasks. For some reason, the apparent magnitude of the job ahead of them turned the Cs to silence. So the trip began, as they pulled away from Iron Mountain, with a strange sense of quiet.

Howie settled next to Dolph. They didn't talk. There was nothing to talk about.

The night before, they had hardly slept as they stayed awake, sharing their greatest fears, their most sincere dreams and hopes and desires. They didn't understand it themselves, but Old Clyde's announcement at supper the night before had sobered them far more than anything before, and they didn't know why.

Dolph told Howie about his girl Loreen back in Utah, a tall, willowy seventeen-year-old with green eyes and wavy auburn hair. She was waiting for him, he said, because he had asked her to. She had agreed to wait, not only for his time in the Cs but for his subsequent two years of mission with the church.

Since Howie knew little of the Mormon religion, the two talked at length about what it meant to serve the church, the need of the mission years and becoming an elder, in that part of the world where Dolph hoped to carry out his service. He had his mind set on a south sea island, but those assignments were hard to come by.

He intended to marry Loreen as soon as he could. They wanted to have five kids, three boys and two girls, and build a home on land Dolph's father had given him outside his home town of Logan—land that Dolph said was the prettiest he'd ever seen. His house, he said, was going to sit on a little ridge overlooking the most beautiful valley in the world. Behind him would be the Uintas and under him would be the ranch he knew he could build. Horses, quarter horses and maybe an Arabian stallion for stud service. A few cows. Sheep, of course. No hogs. He hated hogs. It was perfect in his dreams, and he hoped he lived to realize them.

Howie hadn't really thought much about his future until their late night whispering. Dolph's plans sounded so definite and possible. They made Howie feel at loose ends. He didn't have Dolph's devotion to religion, certainly nothing like being willing to devote two years to a mission, and even though he had promised Indella that he'd return home and marry her, he hadn't thought much beyond that single act. Marry her and then what?He asked himself and Dolph as they whispered back and forth. Marriage was such a big step, he said, and an important one, but then what? Work in the mill, he guessed, like his Poppa and his poppa before him.

Everybody he knew in Douglasville worked in the damn mill. It was their birthright, their obligation, their reason for being born... That was one of the reasons he'd been so eager to join the Cs in the first place, he admitted, the damn mill. Company owned his Poppa's body and God owned his soul. Alexander Stevens, since he was a teen, had worked at the loom and read his Bible, preached down at Liberty Baptist when they asked him to, held prayer meetings in his own sitting room, and not much else. Howie looked at his Poppa and knew there had to be more. He had tried to talk to his Poppa about it before he stepped on the bus, but Alexander Stevens didn't understand. The mill simply was; nothing really to talk about. You were born, you went to work for the cotton mill, and you died. Selah. He had no mission to look forward to and his daddy didn't have any land to give him, and he had only mentioned to Indella in passing the prospect of having kids, kids that, if matters held true to form, would spend their lives behind the looms as well. What in God's name was he going to do? He and the future seemed to have so little in common.

They rode in silence through the Hills, to Custer, and then west. It wasn't long before they left the Black Hills behind and entered the vast desolate landscape of Wyoming.

"Never been to Wyoming before," Howie said. "Don't look like much so far."

"It's a big state," Dolph said. "Give it time."

Their talk of the night before had filled Howie with questions. Dolph's conviction to his religion fascinated him and would not leave him alone. So he asked, "To be Mormon, you got to be baptized?"

"Sure."

"Oh." And Howie sat silent.

"You got a thing against baptism?" Dolph asked.

"Not me personally," Howie said. "but Momma puts a whole lotta stock in it. Something like, you gotta be baptized before you can enter heaven."

"Well, it's not a bad idea."

"Maybe for some," he said and slipped back to silence.

May Lou had insisted on it, this baptism thing. Not gonna let you leave this house until you've been baptized, she had announced two days before his bus left Buddy's One Stop. As he rode across Wyoming, he could almost hear his Momma's voice chastising him, "No son of mine's gonna leave the nest without the grace of the Lord bestowed on his head." And she meant it. But he resisted. You gotta be saved first, he argued, and she had said, "You mean you ain't been saved yet?" And he had said, not that he had noticed.

"How's a body come to join up with the Mormons?" he asked.

"You interested?" Dolph said.

"Could be."

"You just accept the Lord Jesus as your savior and you're in," Dolph answered.

And Howie shook his head. "I've heard that one before."

His Momma had insisted. "You die out there in that Corps thing you've joined and you ain't in the fold, I'll never see you again, son. Won't you let the preacher baptize you before it's too late?" And he'd declined the offer. "Nothing's gonna happen," he said. From where he was sitting, half-way across the empty state of Wyoming, he wasn't so sure of that any more. Was it too late? How could a body get itself baptized in the middle of Wyoming? There wasn't any water to be found anywhere, and it made him just a little bit scared.

They stopped for dinner in Gillette. The sandwiches were dry like Meatloaf had fixed them in a hurry the night before, and the water they had to wash them down with tasted of mineral salts. "Wyoming backwash," somebody called it.

During dinner, the C.O. took one fellow from each bird cage and briefed him about where they were going and what they were to do when they got there. After they were back on the road, the fellow could inform the rest.

From Howie's cage, the guy selected was Roosevelt Tucker, tall studious, a college student who had dropped out after his first year, a fellow who didn't have much to say. Rosie was a nervous sort with a jerky kind of speech that seemed to be popular in these parts.

Back from the briefing, Rosie got everybody's attention and said, "Well, boys, we're heading to the Bighorns."

A buzz of excitement swept thought the truck.

A thrill passed through Howie as he mentally transformed the Bighorns into the Rocky Mountains. Be Jesus, wait till Pierson hears about this!

"All I know is this," Rosie continued. "there's a big fire going out there somewhere and we've been ticketed to take it on. We'll learn more when we reach fire headquarters, some-time tonight. That's all I know, except we stop for supper somewhere around Sheridan. Enjoy your ride.''

They were taking on a forest fire? The idea didn't sit well with Howie. He wanted to see the Rockies but not from inside a burning inferno. If only he knew more about how to handle himself, he'd feel better. But this, going in unprepared, filled him with the kind of fear he hadn't felt before. He didn't feel ready to face a fire, especially one in a land that was as foreign to him as Hell itself.

He sulked and picked at the frayed edge of his shirt sleeve. His memory of Reliance Panott and the story he told was too vivid to let him settle into this great adventure across the state of Wyoming and into the face of the unknown.

"Just relax,'' Dolph said, "It's not going to be so bad.''

"None of us have any idea how to deal with a fire.''

"Has to be a big one, too,'' Dolph said, not offering anyone who heard him any comfort. "Pulling us out of the Black Hills like this, they've got to be desperate for help. Must be one big dragon-breathing fire.''

"Just wish I knew what to do,'' Howie said. "I hate being stupid about things.'' He was approaching hero territory, and he was scared.

He and Dolph rode the rest of the way through Wyoming in silence.

The landscape remained the same for hours. No trees anywhere that Howie could see. Occasionally, they passed through a small town of four or five buildings or saw a tiny ranch house off on the horizon. He didn't understand how anybody could live in a place where even grass refused to grow. It almost struck him as funny. Here they were, on their way to fight a forest fire and there wasn't a tree to be seen anywhere.

This dark a night Howie couldn't remember. The mass of smoke that hung over the small valley the rangers called fire post was thick and billowing, almost alive. If there was a moon, nobody around their bivouac knew it.

Howie, Dolph, Marv, Cheater Evans and six others from Iron Mountain pitched their peaked tent in one of the clearings made by huge earth-moving machines. They had passed through Sheridan as the sun disappeared through a dense haze, giving Howie his first though distorted view of the majestic Rockies he had heard so much about. He wasn't impressed. After all, he grew up not far from the Great Smokeys. Now there were some mountains, he said to anybody willing to listen.

He crawled into the tent and held the rear pole in place while the others tied it down.

The mountains might not be as grand as he expected, but they were sure cold enough. Here it was only the end of August and already he was shivering. What they needed was a good warm campfire.

He smiled at the irony of the thought: in order to fight a fire, he had to build one to get warm. He held the front pole while it was tied down and the tent was pitched. Now, time for that fire.

His teeth were chattering, and he couldn't make them stop. Never been so cold in his entire life.

But the campfire would have to wait.

A sergeant in the regular Army passed through the camp and ordered the Cs to report as soon as they could to the command tent just down the path. "Make it snappy," he said and moved up the row of tents with the same less-than-friendly suggestion.

"Old Clyde's not enough. Now we're really in the Army," Marv said.

"If I ever go into the service," Howie announced, "it'll be into the Navy. None of this marching foolishness for me."

"You can swim?" Marv asked.

"Sure. Can't you?"

"Never found enough water to learn."

"Well, we get back to Iron Mountain, I'll take you down to Center Lake..."

"Like hell you will."

They found the command tent. It was a massive piece of canvas, big enough to hold five hundred men, and by the time the Cs showed up it was already three-fourths full.

Men from all over were there; regular Army, Rangers, volunteers from Sheridan, Cody, Buffalo, even from as far away as Cheyenne, Helena, Idaho Falls and Rapid City. The place was alive with young, eager men.

Word spread. The Blackwater Burn, as it was being called, was raging out of control deep in the Bighorns and was laying waste some valuable land, thousands of acres of timber every half hour. Something had to be done, and that was what all these men were about.

A little shrimp of a fellow dressed in a Ranger's uniform got up on a raised area near one end of the tent and had two other men hold up a large map of green and brown and blue. The Ranger spoke with a big voice, much bigger than his body: "Let's have some quiet around here."

The throng of men shushed themselves and turned full attention to what was being said.

The Ranger slapped the huge map with a stick. "We're here." He slapped it a second time. "The fire's here." The two slaps seemed awfully close together, Howie thought. A third slap. "Fire's already ate most of this area. Wind's taking it here." Another slap. "Our job is to attack the beast face front and keep it from going here." Another slap. Howie wondered what was underneath that last slap. "We already have over five hundred men and heavy equipment spread through here" slap "and here" slap. "They should have things pretty well under control by morning, that is if the conditions remain constant.

But it looks like she's heading"— another slap —"here. I tell you, brothers, if she makes these trees, she's gonna be hell to hold. These mountains are about as tough as any you'll find in the world. Down in this area there's nothing but trouble. So, we keep her pinned in here"— slap—"and here"—slap— "we'll be fine. Any questions?"

Silence. Nobody knew enough to ask questions.

From the looks of things, Howie determined, they were to fight the Blackwater Burn by slapping at it with pointed sticks. Until the slaps turned to hot spots and defined objectives, they'd be lost.

"Okay," the man said, "your squad leaders have been briefed. Every last one of you is important to this battle, and it's not a battle I expect to lose. The guys on the lines have been there better than forty-eight hours without rest. At o-three hundred, that's five hours from now, most of you fellas will head in and they'll head out. You'll stay in the trenches until you're relieved. It could be days before we see you again. But that's the way these things work. Now, I know we've got a lot of greenhorns around here. Don't worry. An hour facing off at the front and you'll be baptized veterans. Now, get some sleep. You'll need it."

As they strolled back to their tent, Dolph said with a smile on his face, "Think of it, Howie. This time tomorrow night, you'll be baptized into the Church of the Veterans, and you only seventeen years old."

Howie answered back, "I'd just as soon not, thank you very much."

Later, Old Clyde stuck his head into the tent. He had worry etched across his brow. He looked his charges in the eye and tried to smile. "You boys're gonna do just fine," he said. "Any questions?"

There was a moment of silence before Dolph asked, "Yes, sir, I got one."

"Let's hear it, soldier."

"You got any idea what a firebrand is, Captain?"

The C.O. stared at him, looking for some sort of answer in Dolph's eyes. "Can't say that I do, son. What's your point?"

"Don't know what a firebrand is and you volunteered us. You're one damn good soldier, Captain Munk."

"You've got a problem, Mr. DeSmet? You got a problem, I want to hear it." The iron jaw was set for attack. His eyes were as hot as any firebrands Howie had ever wished to see.

Dolph breathed out, slow and easy. "Got no problems here, Captain. No problems at all."

Old Clyde disappeared. His bark could be heard as he moved from tent to tent. Dolph was quiet after that. He had nothing more to say.

Before turning in, Howie wrote Indella his longest letter yet. He didn't mention where he was or what he was about to do. Instead, he shared with her his thoughts regarding their future and what they might plan on and how they might go about realizing those plans. He even suggested they have five kids, three boys and two girls, and that she should let him know what she thought about all this. He mentioned his growing interest in the Mormon Church and if she would look into it with him. He liked the idea, he said, of going on a mission and then coming back to Wyoming and maybe buying a little piece of land in the Bighorns. The country, he wrote, is among the toughest in the world. Finally, he closed by saying, "You'll be pleased to know come tomorrow, I'll be baptized, but don't tell my Momma. She'll only misunderstand. All my love, Howell."

O-three hundred came too early. Howie was stiff from the long ride across Wyoming, plus he wasn't used to sleeping on the ground, especially when it was newly cleared by machine and still contained large tangles of roots and stones.

His tent was part of Squad 14. He was told not to forget

that number. Squad 14 was made up of twenty-four men, the ten from his tent, Iron Mountain men, and fourteen from a C.C.C. camp over in Idaho. They had come a long way, too, to help put the brakes on the Blackwater Burn.

Squad leader, Norton Farr, a lad from the National Park Service, Yellowstone Office, led Squad 14 off into the still morning dark, and they walked the Fire Post and into the mountains.

As the sun came up, Howie could see the craggy range in front of them. The smoke was thick as ever, but thanks to a wind at their backs, it hovered high over their heads. There were no other signs of the fire.

Around ten in the morning, after walking what felt like half a week, Squad 14 came over a rise and stumbled onto the group they had been sent to relieve. They were greeted with cheers, hugs, and back slaps. Howie was surprised at how easy it was to be hugged by total strangers when they are so pleased to see you. He liked the feeling of being important to somebody else and he looked forward to the sight of his replacement coming over the same rise and greeting them just as freely with hugs and cheers and back slaps.

The original group wasted no time. They shouldered their personal belongings and headed off the way Squad 14 had come, leaving their tools, tents, bedrolls, and meager food supplies behind. They didn't care to set awhile and chat a spell.

"When did you sleep last?" Howie asked one of the boys in the group.

The fellow shrugged and said, "Damned if I remember."

"Where's the fire?" Dolph asked another.

The fellow pointed in three directions.

"What you been doing here, building a firebreak?" Howie asked.

The fellow shrugged again, "Damned if I know."

Then they were gone. It was then that Howie felt most alone and deserted. It was just him, Dolph, Marv, Cheater,

Norton Farr and eighteen other youths against an enemy they could not see, hear, or feel. But Howie knew it was out there somewhere, and his job was to keep it from getting past him. Only trouble was, he had no idea how to go about accomplishing his task.

The crew worked through the afternoon, digging and clearing a twenty-five foot wide firebreak. As Norton Farr explained it, the first squad had prepared one firebreak in closer to the nose of the fire. This second was a safety valve in case the first didn't hold. In the dirt he drew a rude map of the terrain and pointed out where they were, where he thought the blaze was, and how they could contain it if they put their backs to it. He sent the fourteen Idaho Cs off to the right seven or eight miles. They were to start a stretch in a hollow that was particularly vulnerable and work their way back to their present position. Then when the break was connected, they could move back a mile or two and prepare the third break. The beast was going to be tamed, no question of it. Norton Farr was a true believer and he made converts of all the rest.

Norton was in radio contact with headquarters as well as the other wing of his squad. He was told by the folks back behind the lines that he and his men were to make their way forward, that the fire had been sitting quiet for long enough to assume the first break was holding.

So forward they went, toting their shovels, spades, knapsacks, bundles, canteens and other valuables. From all reports, the Blackwater Burn was on its way to extinction a whole lot easier than anyone ever thought possible. The modern firefighting techniques were working, Norton bragged.

The day was hot. Howie removed his shirt and tied it around his waist. His back was tired, but right then he was feeling fine, as fine as he had ever felt in his life. He had been on the fireline half a day; he was a veteran. This was truly living. Couldn't have times like this back home in Douglasville. If his brothers could see him now, shirtless, sweating, spade over his shoulder, a canteen slung around his neck, they would know: Howie Cobb had the makings. He was a damn man, for God's sake. Just look at him.

A strong wind came up. It was sudden and blistering, a scorching blast of wind from their backs.

Norton Farr stopped and pushed the boys aside. "My God," he said aloud without realizing it. He took in the wind with his nose and skin. This wasn't good, no, not good at all.

"What's wrong?" Dolph asked him.

Norton didn't answer. Instead, he hailed the home base over the short-wave radio. "This is Squad 14, Nose Point 8. The wind's shifted," he yelled into the instrument. "What's happening back there?"

"No wind shift here. No problems. Proceed as planned," the friendly voice said back.

"Have you guys started any backfires around here?" he yelled again.

"Sure, north of you. No problems."

"This wind's hitting us from due north. What's going on!"

"Stop worrying and do your job, man. The closest hot spot's five miles from you," the voice said.

Norton switched off the radio without signing off.

The wind was growing hotter and stronger by the second. He climbed a large boulder and looked off to the north and west. Smoke was billowing from beyond the ridge and blowing in their direction. If headquarters was right, the smoke should be going the other way. Now this wind. He knew as did the rest of the squad, it was a breeze with demon designs.

He hailed the other half of his squad, the group of Idaho Cs. Nothing. He hailed again and again. Nothing. "My God," he whispered again, more a prayer than an attempt to communicate with his men or a supreme being.

"Let's head back," Cheater suggested.

"Damn good idea," Marv said.

"Can't," Norton said. He pointed in the direction they had come and saw it at the same time as the rest of his squad. "Jesus Lord, it's switching back on us. It's switching back."

"What's that mean, switching back?" Cheater yelled.

"Shut up!" Norton Farr yelled back. He quickly surveyed the lay of the land. There was no place to hide, and the fire was in its own personalized jet stream, racing with wild disregard for any and all vegetation and life in its path, headed directly toward them.

"Do you know these hills?" Howie asked.

"Not that good. Come on." He rushed off the boulder down the hillside.

"What're we gonna do?" Cheater yelled, the panic in his voice louder than his words.

"Stay close. Come on!"

They splashed through a small stream. Norton stopped and rolled in the water, getting everything on him wet. The rest followed his example. The water was mostly ash and smelled of alkaline and lye soap. Howie soaked his shirt and put it back on. He rolled in the small stream like he'd seen musk rats do back home. It felt good until the scorching heat of the wind that kept growing stronger and stronger hit his wet skin and threatened to raise blisters.

"Wet your tarps and bedrolls," Norton yelled, struggling to be heard over the fire's roar that was increasing by the second.

Then he raced up the stream bed away from the fire, keeping the wind to his back. Ahead was a huge pile of granite, the sides almost shear, rising a hundred feet or more above the low-growing brush. Norton began to climb.

He didn't need to order his squad to climb with him. It was obvious, this was the only way. Hell was on their heels, and it was climb like mountain goats or lay your burden down.

Even in his constitutionals, noted for their difficulty,

Howie had never attempted this kind of rock before. It was rough and tore away skin when the foothold was lost. The stone was blisteringly hot and slick from ash. And it was as steep as anything he had ever seen.

"Find a chink and bury yourself," Norton screamed. He pushed his squad on, shoving the slow ones with the end of his spade. "Don't look back, bury yourself!"

Howie climbed with all his might. He could feel the tongues of fire flickering out for his boots. He reached a plateau of stone that sported a scrub juniper or two. As he rushed past one of the bushes, it burst into flame and disintegrated before his eyes. God was in the vicinity. He had to be. Howie almost wanted to laugh out loud at the thought: so this is how Moses felt when God Almighty was after him!

Cheater was in front of him, standing still and tall. Howie tried pushing him forward, but Cheater wouldn't move. He was mesmerized by the raging fire that rushed about him now on all sides.

Then, the canteen slung around Cheater's neck burst open, spewing steam and water out and down. The string holding the canteen about his neck flared like a lit match. Cheater screamed and threw the beast away from him.

Howie reached for his friend's arm, but missed. Cheater raced not up the rock, but back down. He was yelling something into the fire, maybe a challenge, Howie didn't know what. There was a horror in Cheater than nobody could have contained. He ran with all his might into the fiery air and disappeared over the edge of the rock.

Howie emptied his canteen over his head and rushed on. The rock burned his feet through the leather soles. It felt as if the eyelets of his boots were going to brand his feet with molten lead. He threw his belt off to get away from the burn of the metal clasp. Then he found a crevice in the stone, not deep, but as deep as any he was apt to find. Two other Cs were already huddled there. He fell on top of them and spread his soaked tarp over himself and the others. He lay as still as he possibly could as the sound of a hundred steam engines roared around him.

The C beside him screamed as loud as he could, yet his voice was a mere whisper. The heat forged over, around and through them, and the rock itself felt as if at any moment it, too, would burst into flames. Howie prayed aloud, "If this be the time, Lord, so be it, if this be the time."

Then, as suddenly as the firestorm had come, it was gone, raging with incredible speed and insatiable hunger over the ridge and away. At first, Howie was afraid to move. His muscles weren't ready to be engaged right then. Give him a minute to find himself. That's all he needed, a minute or two. He needed longer. He couldn't force himself out of the chink in the rock. He slept instead and dreamed of the annual pig roast given by the mill in Douglasville for folks who lived and worked, worshiped and died in that God-awful place.

They found what was left of Cheater Evans at the base of the rock. Howie hoped Cheater had been dead before he hit the ground. That would have been merciful.

The fire had eaten away most of Cheater's skin, leaving the flesh exposed and charred and smelling of burnt earth. Howie could not imagine a more painful way to die. His own seared back, legs and skull were hateful to the touch, yet his wounds were as nothing compared to those on Cheater's destroyed body. He felt like a liar, caught in his lie. He should be dead, too. All of them. They should all be dead. But only Cheater could lay claim to that state of being.

Howie felt the need to cry. Not from the pain of his back and head but from such a loss. He'd never looked into the face of death and beheld somebody who only a few moments before had been a man with a name and feelings, a man just like himself, from a certain very special place with loved ones, family, friends, hopes, and a future. Dolph knelt beside Cheater and rammed his fists into the charred dirt as tears streamed down his face. Let Dolph cry, Howie said to himself, he can cry for us all.

They rolled Cheater's body into one of the few remaining tarps and began the long, long walk down the mountainside, back to headquarters, that as far as they knew still thought the Blackwater Burn was five miles away and under control.

Howie, Dolph, Marv, Norton Farr, and the others spent a week in the Sheridan hospital. They were treated like heroes, and none of them knew why. They had gotten trapped by a fire. There was no glory in that. The fire had no brain and they did. Yet, the fire had won, won decisively. Stupid things aren't worth bragging about. Yet, there they were, heroes of a sort in everybody's eyes. They even got their names in the Cheyenne paper as gallant men worthy of Pulaski medals.

Howie remembered Reliance Panott's words: "There ain't a fire around that man can extinguish that nature herself can't take care of you just give her time. Fighting fires is downright foolishness, an act for those who feel the need to be challenged. If you'd just leave the damn fires alone they'd burn themselves out."

That's what the Blackwater Burn did. A day or two after the squad was caught unprepared by a sudden shift of wind, the skies dumped tons of rain and snow over the area and turned the burn into a heap of ashes, and the Bighorns returned to their natural state in spite of man, laughing, Howie could imagine, at man's incredible capacity for foolishness.

Then word came. The bodies of the other fourteen members of Squad 14, the fourteen from the Idaho camp, had been found. All fourteen of them were huddled together in an open meadow. It looked as if they had tried to encircle themselves with a quickly managed firebreak. But it hadn't helped. None had survived.

When Howie heard about them, he finally wept. He didn't know them, could hardly remember what they looked like, though they had been part of his squad. They were nameless, faceless, embodiments of himself and his Iron Mountain friends. He washed himself with weeping. His eyes rained tears like none he had ever allowed himself before. But it didn't help. The more he cried the more he wanted to. He could cry for a week and it would not make him feel one bit better.

The Corps arranged for Cheater Evan's body to get back to Fort Meade where he was given a hero's memorial service before his remains were shipped to his home in Aberdeen, South Dakota.

It was another week before the Cs from Iron Mountain climbed into their bird cages and headed back across Wyoming, back to the safety and comfort of the Black Hills.

Five minutes after leaving Sheridan, there wasn't a tree in sight. Howie looked over the vast open desert and secretly longed for the deep woods. Even with things like fire, the woods were still the best place to be.

"I've been thinking," Howie said to Dolph. Dolph's bandages were already coming off, though Howie's had to stay on a little longer, to keep infections from setting in.

"Yeah?" Dolph said. "Should we give a cheer or what?"

"I'm serious, Dolph. When I get home—" Howie shook his head as the thought sunk in. "If I get back home—I'm going to buy me a grocery store."

"Where in the world did that idea come from?"

"I don't know. I like to eat. I like to sell things. It just seems a natural thing, doesn't it? Running a grocery store." He let the idea sit there for a bit before adding, "At least nobody in my family will ever go hungry with me running a grocery store."

"Sounds interesting. Where you going to get the money?"

"I figured I'd hire myself out as a fire fighter, seeing as how I've got so much first-hand experience." He was quiet for a time and then said, softly almost as if he didn't care if Dolph heard him or not, "Someday, I'm coming back out here, me, Indella, and the kids and put a little marble cross atop our rock. I think the Lord will appreciate that. Cheater, too." He was going to put his cross, not where Cheater Evans had died, but where he, Howie Cobb, had been baptized into the fold.

Poet Laureate

Marisa Louise Clackson was five-feet-two in her stocking feet. Howie hadn't seen her in her stocking feet, so he was supposing. She had the blondest hair in the world, plus a full figure that turned heads when she passed. Howie liked his women with full-figures, as did most all the enrollees at Camp Iron Mountain. In short, Marisa Louise Clackson was a looker, and all the young men looked, as best they could, the short time she was in camp twice a week.

Where Professor Watkins, Iron Mountain's education director, found a writing teacher like Marisa Louise, nobody knew, but the enrollees were proud of him for his foresightedness.

Anything was better than the arithmetic class with G.I. Klanner or shorthand with Miss Logg, the biggest damn female this side of the Bighorns, or basic biology with the limp-wristed Claus Farquhar, better known in camp as Claus the Faggot Hare. Oh, yes, Professor Watkins knew his business when he hired Marisa Louise to teach penmanship.

Hers was the only class that had full enrollment and near perfect attendance both times it met each week. To Professor Watkins' way of thinking, attendance went hand-in-hand with significant learning.

Howie fell in love with Marisa Louise, in spite of his best intentions. So what if he had given his word to Indella Shealy?

158

She was two thousand miles away, probably messing around with some other guy now she was growing up. Most likely she had forgotten all about Howie Cobb now that he had been gone four months, even though her letters arrived every day, filled with affection and vows of life-long devotion.

Besides, Marisa Louise was present tense. Here and now, not part of the Georgia history he wanted to keep in its place.

Besides, he liked the Black Hills, now that his hair was growing back and his seared skin was recovering without leaving scars. Cool nights, pine scent in the air, scenery like none he had ever thought possible, mountain lakes perfect for skinny dips on nights of full moons, land of natural blonds. The food was good, the pay was skimpy, but he could live with that, and the work wasn't nearly as hard as he had first feared. His new friendship with Bert van Dorst and his waning one with Dolph DeSmet filled his spare time with poker and things like that. So, he just might decide to re-up, maybe after that even settle down in the Hills. And if he did, he might be in the market for a Dakota gal if she were anything like Marisa Louise.

Custer wouldn't be a half bad place to call home, either. There was always work for young men willing to get dirty. Now, book learning was even fun. "Dear Indy," he wrote in his head. "Remember what I told you that time outside the house? About coming home? Getting married? And all? Well, it seems I might have been lying to you a little."

When he had signed up for the Cs, Howie had no intention of taking part in an educational program. After all, he had a third grade education. He could read with the best of them, thanks mainly to Poppa's Bible. He knew his addition and subtraction well enough to figure out when he was being gypped. He could write letters that Indella called brilliant. What he already knew was good enough for him.

Then *she* drove into camp in her black, shiny, thirty-four Ford coupe. It was so new-looking it seemed to shimmer as it pulled up outside the commissary in a cloud of mica dust.

Howie was coming from the rec hall when she stepped from her coupe across the road. All he could see were the lower half of her legs. Oh, what calves. Such perfectly shaped, perfectly manicured, perfectly stockinged calves. Then, up the steps, to the door. Her rear end. So delicate. He had never thought of a woman's derriere as being delicate before, but hers was. Perfect delicacy. What must the soft snow-white skin beneath her flowered figure-forming dress be like? Who was she? What was she doing here? How long was she going to stay?

Please, Lord, let me meet her.

...Dear Indella.

The first day of writing class, one he had been forced to take by the Professor, who claimed his penmanship was horrible, Howie had wanted to cut. But, like Bert told him, you don't cut the first day! That's a slap in the face of the teacher, no matter how lousy a person he might be. So, Howie showed up for class, complaining all the way, bitching about his grade school teachers, berating all with education greater than his own, and generally making everybody's first day inside the Iron Mountain classroom holy hell.

Then, suddenly, it was "her" up there at the portable chalk board with her back to all of them, scribbling her name in an unintelligible scrawl.

Beneath her straight-seamed plaid skirt, her cheeks were rigid, flattened and tight. Her calves, which led to feet stuffed into spiked shoes too small for the meat pressed into them, were halved up the center by the black line of her silk hose. A vision of forgotten possibilities, all the men sat in their chairs with hands clasping midsections with varying tightness. Howie was stuck in a chair near the rear of the room. Next time, he promised himself, he would come to class early, get a front row seat, and have an unobstructed gander at whatever the woman selected to highlight next.

She turned from the board. She was twenty-two if she was a day. If she was over twenty-two, Howie silently vowed to eat

JoJo's footlocker, dirty socks and all. Those eyes. Blue as a Dakota sky after a mid-summer cloud burst, and as moist. Like she had something in them, like a speck maybe or bits of chalk dust. Full lips. Kissable lips. Lips made to drive a man to passion. The sight of her lips made him lick his own. Oh, yes, a front seat next time for sure.

She stood before the silent gawkers with all the pride of position that her youth and training would allow. She pointed to the board. "That's my name," she announced. "Can anyone read it?"

No takers.

"Just as I thought." She had a haughty superior look in her eye. "That's because most likely, my name is written in the same way many of you write your own. Sloppily. Illegibly. Stupidly. What's the good of writing—writing anything, your name, your girlfriend, your banker—what's the use of writing if nobody can decipher the message?"

She turned back to the board, erased her scratchings with full swipes of the chamois cloth, and with a sure, positive, elegant attack of the chalk, she graced the board with "Marisa Louise Clackson."

The relaxed flow of her butt mesmerized everyone, especially Howie. No longer tight, no longer flat, her rear end was as lose and squeezable as any he had ever admired. Oh, this is the one, this woman is —

"Now," she turned. "What's my name?" Everyone in the class belted the words. Marisa Louise Clackson. It was music. It was sweetness. It was her.

"Dear Howie," the letter began. "I hope you are well..."

It was difficult conjuring up an image of Indella Shealy. After all, she was still a child. Years from being a woman—like Marisa Louise. Oh, Indella, how wrong can a man be in making promises...

He dreamed of Marisa Louise and woke in a small pool of wetness.

He entered the Ponderosa pines of the Hills, axe and hoe in hand, with an eagerness for Tuesday and Thursday late afternoons and Miss Clackson's writing class. Was it "Miss?" No one knew. Everyone used the "Miss" out of respect and hopeful anticipation.

In the evening as taps neared, he wondered about her. Was she home now? Home? Where was home? Was she alone? A boyfriend maybe? A husband? Squelch that thought. Then, what kind of home? Where would she live? Custer? Deadwood? Rapid City? Make it Custer. It was easier to get to Custer than any of the other small towns.

He knew so little about her. Nothing, in fact. Except she was an artist with a piece of chalk and a makeshift blackboard. And a woman. And probably older than him by a few years. But who cared about such things as a few measly years? When a man and woman were made for one another, what did a few years matter?

"I miss you so much, especially these past three weeks." Indella. She must have taken a writing class too. Her letters were always so easy to read, her lettering perfect, just like Marisa Louise's. Except that Indella didn't put big fat zeros on top of her "i"s. Maybe he should tell Indella about the "i"s. Soon.

Indella. Black hair. Black as midnight down in Wind Cave. Marisa Louise's hair was Black Hills gold. Indella's skin was soft, yes, but with the olive tone of her Spanish ancestry.

Soft, sure. What do you expect when you're not yet sixteen? But Marisa Louise. Her skin was fragile, like if you touched it too tightly it might wither and die, soft and fragile like the underside of a yucca blossom, and as fresh. And she was already past twenty! Skin as delicate as a baby's buns.

"Since your letters have stopped coming. Is everything all right? Won't you let me hear from you?"

Dear Indella, he wanted to write. Dear Indy, I've discovered that I love someone else.

He couldn't write such a thing. He had hardly met Marisa Louise. She didn't even know his name, except "Mr. Cobb." She insisted on calling everyone by last names. No one dared call her anything but "Miss Clackson." Besides, every enrollee in class was madly in love with her, which she seemed to know and enjoy.

She ignored their affections in every way. Except for sandy-haired Roosevelt Tucker, Rosie as everyone called him, everyone except Miss Clackson who insisted on calling him "Mr. President," was Teacher's Pet. And everyone hated him for it. It wasn't Rosie's fault. Miss Clackson selected him and the honor stuck. Rosie, the whimp, couldn't swing an axe if he had to. Which he didn't. A college drop out—a year at South Dakota School of Mines before enrolling in the Cs—made him "special." Should keep such college kids out of the Corps, Howie decided. They upset the balance. Rosie was so inept that the C.O. put him in the commissary to type official reports and told the Civie who had been hired by the government for such work to stay the hell out of camp. All Rosie Tucker did, day in, day out, was type reports and lure away Miss Clackson's attentions. What does he need a writing course for? someone wanted to know. He can goddamn type his letters, for Christ's sake. But there he sat, every Tuesday and Thursday, center front. "Maybe Rosie'll catch pneumonia and die," Marv Drexler said after Rosie Tucker scored the highest grade in class for the fourth time.

Dear Indella, I've met someone I'd like to get to know better. I'm sure you'll understand...

But Howie couldn't write it. Not yet. He was still too ashamed of his sloppy handwriting to send any sort of letter to Indella. He stopped writing his Momma. When Hev sent him a scorching rebuke for dropping out of touch, he still couldn't force himself to write. He had to make a perfect score on penmanship first. Then he could write home again.

They should have closed the camp in November and sent everyone home. But the bridges had to be secured. There were deadlines set by folks in Washington. The politicians out East didn't know about the winter storms of western South Dakota and the Black Hills. Keep the camp open, keep the guys at the pigtails, keep the metal strapping and the drills hot and the dynamite popping. Get the ditches dug and the undergrowth cleared. No matter what.

Mid-month with a foot of snow on the ground, Marv Drexler taunted Howie. "Don't worry, Cracker," he said. "It'll get cold soon."

Two below zero with wind adding on to it; Howie had never dreamed of such cold. He didn't know that cold could burn as badly as fire sometimes. Let it drop off the gauges, and cold will hurt.

Marv was from Minot, North Dakota. "You want to see cold," he was fond of saying, "spend Hanukkah in Minot. You need thick blood to make it in this country," he said. "Hang around the Hills long enough, your blood'll thicken. Your skin will insulate. Then you'll never like hot climates again."

It got so if Howie stepped outside, the hairs inside his nose froze, instantly forming stick-like bristles. The deep freeze invaded his lungs and left them throbbing with a cold that felt like brimstone. Nothing had prepared him for such a life, coming from Georgia as he did, and it was still early in the season, not even mid-month, nowhere near Thanksgiving yet. Hell. Back home, the trees'd still be dropping leaves.

"Give it time," Marv said. "It'll turn nippy 'fore you know it."

Howie's gloves froze to the handle of the pick he had used the day before. On returning to work detail the next day, he slipped his hands inside them, hoping his hands would warm them quickly so they in turn would keep his fingers warm and semi-nimble. No such luck. Soon his fingers were numb and he had to nearly stick them in the flames of the work site fire to feel anything in them again. Cold is a wickedness, he discovered, just as much as a raging firestorm. He was growing more and more convinced that such wickedness wasn't for him.

The Dirty Ditch was the tackle for the day. Get down and dig. Wham the pick home.

But the ground was like concrete. It resisted the edge of the pick, like wet oak resists the blade of the splitting axe. Try to punch your way through the newly cut stump of a tree with the axe edge and the off bounce might land the thing between the eyes. The same with the pick. Wham it home and it glanced off like the dirt had been poured with rubber and let set twenty years.

"No go here," he told his foreman. "Can't penetrate."

The foreman cackled. "I've heard that about you Southern fuckers. All tongue and no thrust." And the laugh spread up the Dirty Ditch and spilled into the vaulted ranks of the Rockers. Howie laughed, too. It was a good joke. Crude but good.

"Need a blow torch in here, Schuster," someone called. "Be the only way we'll get any head today."

The discussion made the diggers even colder. Whamming fists against torsos didn't do doodly-squat for the cold. It just created a breeze, and there was already enough of that without making more. Hug your arms about you as tight as you can, keep the feet moving, and make sure the bandanna around your lower face is tied tight and kept in place.

Howie's eyes hurt most. The air caught the edges of the eyes and gave them the runs, and the moisture globbed on the eyelids and froze them shut. Howie listened to all the advice about surviving the frigid Dakota weather and still shivered deep inside his marrow.

"This is God awful," Howie called out to nobody in particular.

"Just be thankful we ain't higher up the mountain," someone said.

"Give it a while, Cracker. It's only November. It'll get cold soon."

The workers plugged away at the digging.

The tenth week into class, Marisa Louise was as mysterious as the first day. Who are you, everyone wanted to know. Tell us about yourself, Miss Clackson, if indeed you are "Miss" Clackson. Help us with our drooling.

But no. Nothing doing. She would not digress from her lesson plans, no matter how persistent the attempts to divert her.

Howie tried all he knew to do. It was another attempt to survive the intense cold. Keep thoughts on the teacher and you'll be just fine, he said to himself. So in class he tried to engage her in conversation. He asked what he considered intelligent questions, like is it permissible to dot an "i" instead of drawing a little curlicue over it? She ignored him. It was as if she expected foolishness and refused to endorse it by answering such questions. He finally stooped to asking what he considered to be stupid things, like do you always have to sign a love letter with the words "Love, Howie"? At least he made certain she had heard his first name. She responded to irrelevant questions with a studied terseness and forged on through the syllabus, not to be derailed.

Once, a question caught her off guard. It came from Rosie Tucker, of all people. "If I were to write you a letter, Miss Clackson, would it be permissible to address you as Dear Marisa?"

There was a moment of silence before she responded: "It would be permissible to address any letter with the salutation of 'Dear'."

"No," Rosie persisted, "I mean a letter to you." Even a fool could see the desire oozing out of Rosie's jaundiced skin.

She stammered a response no one understood, glanced kill-ingly in Rosie's direction, and continued, flustered, through the remainder of the day's lesson.

Howie learned the sound snow makes under heavy boots. It squeaks, like stepping on a set of little girl dolls that squeal when squeezed. After melting a little during the day, only to re-freeze over night, snow crunches, like eating peanut brittle.

A heavy snow loaded the spindly Ponderosa pines, and the cook went outside with his mixing bowl, filled it half a dozen times or more with snow, and stirred in a concoction of milk, raw eggs, vanilla extract, and powdered sugar. Nothing tastier in the world than snow ice cream on a cold November night.

"Never eat yellow snow," the cook told them.

"Why not?" Howie wanted to know, and everyone laughed.

"If I ever get out of here," Howie whispered one night to Marv after lights out, "I swear I'll never step foot north of the Mason-Dixon Line again."

"Getting to you, huh, Cracker?"

"I can't get warm."

"You ain't the only one."

In the barracks, one pot-bellied stove was located at each end; one was in the center of the room. The guys nearest the stoves looked like baked snapping turtle after a night's rest, while those farthest away shook like they had ice cubes hang-ing from their ear lobes. All the trees in the camp had been cleared so the only thing left to stop the wind, since the postcard-thin walls couldn't do it, were the bodies of the men wrapped inside their eight layers of homemade quilts.

"Dear Momma," Howie wrote home out of desperation, "you're gonna have to put more ticking in your quilts, cause what you've got now just ain't giving service."

He got a letter back with a new and thicker quilt. "Good to hear from you again, son," May Lou wrote. "You seen your brother Pierson out that way?"

That damn Pierson, Howie fussed to himself. He's off tramping again. But he'd never make it this far. Howie was convinced of that and would write his mother as much if he was able to pen a proper letter again. There was no way Pierson could make it to the Hills, especially with the kind of weather they'd been having. Pierson would be home soon. Just let him get hungry for May Lou's cooking.

Howie discovered the pleasures of Chinooks. The warm breeze came over the Hills and released the camp from the claws of the deep early winter freeze. Off came the over coats and the long underwear and out came hiking boots.

Howie held a passion for long walks, his "constitutionals" he called them. Point him in the right direction, he was fond of saying in the mess hall, and he could walk to the Pacific coast and back again.

"Why don't you take a hike home, then?" somebody asked. And Howie laughed. "Too damn far for that," he said. He had ridden the bus and knew. "But to the Pacific? Piece of cake. Hell, Lewis and Clark did it, right?"

"Sure, in a canoe," Marv paid. "and they had an Indian squaw to show them the way."

Bull said from his side of the poker table, "Who gives a shit about Lewis and Clark anyway?"

As long as weather permitted, Howie took his after-dinner walk. Then, the November cold snap took his late afternoon hikes away. Now with the Chinook hovering over the Hills, he was tempted again into the deep woods, walking stick in hand and well-worn boots on his feet.

His favorite hike was to the lake, around the edge, over the dam and the spillway, up the hill, down to the creek, and home again. Or over to Iron Mountain and up and over the rocks for a good long distance view of Mount Rushmore. That was the real constitutional, over to Iron Mountain and back, getting up there with the mountain goats—he had never seen one—and pulling the crisp, dry air into his lungs. Refreshing. Damned if it wasn't.

Sometimes Dolph took a constitutional with him, but recently, Dolph had been out of things, somber, almost like the Blackwater Burn, and now the deep freeze, had taken away his sense of humor.

Nobody joined Howie on this day. Even with the Chinook, it was only thirty degrees outside, too cold for most folks' blood.

But Howie could stand it. The air, finally fit to breathe, made him feel alive. Made him feel not quite so lonely to make contact with Marisa Louise. When he was off by himself with the pine trees for company and the clean air for solace, he was almost satisfied. So, after dinner on a Saturday afternoon, off he went and out of sight, up the road toward Iron Mountain.

Half an hour out of camp it started drizzling. Less rain than ice. It was a fine, glazing mist that left a slippery coating on the earth. But that didn't bother Howie. He was a lusty fellow. He had seen ice storms back home in Georgia like none other in the world. This little glaze was nothing.

He kept on, up the mountain side and over the rocks to his favorite spot, a flat granite outcropping that offered a spectacular view of Mount Rushmore miles and miles away and the faces that were emerging from solid rock.

He filled his lungs with the chilly air. He pulled his coat around his throat.

Colder than he had thought.

He didn't understand enough about Chinooks to know they were as fickle as a teenage lover. The deep dark green of the pines was growing dulled as layer upon layer of ice formed. Then the bottom of the cloud turned loose, dropping a mist over Mount Rushmore, hiding the figures, and over the forest below, and over him there at Norbeck's Point. "Be goddamned," he said to nobody, "this don't look so good."

He started back toward camp. The compass in his head told him this way, always this way. Down the rock, now more like glass from the freezing mist. Nothing funny about this, he thought, must be careful as a dog on a slat bridge. Go easy, go slow. And don't slip, not this far from home base.

The slant wasn't all that bad. He had walked up it, standing tall. But now, going down, he lay on his belly, searching for holds, hoping the holds he found were true.

One hold wasn't.

It crumbled under his weight. He slid like a kid on a sliding board, down the face of the rock. His fingers grasped at anything—a sapling, a cactus, a sprig of grass. Nothing. His feet flailed for a spike of rock strong enough to stop his fall. None. Faster down the rock face, like being on a roller-coaster without a safety bar.

His sins paraded past his eyes. The rotten egg in Hev's baseball cap, his peeking through the washroom keyhole at his sister Annie as she took a sponge bath, his telling Poppa a bald-faced lie about not smoking a cigarette outside the tool shed when he had rolled and smoked at least half a dozen. He was sorry for that, Lord, sorry for everything, even the things he couldn't remember or things he wasn't sure were sins. Indella's face popped into his head. Oh, God, he wanted to scream, what about our children! Here I am about to die and I ain't even planted my first kid! But it wasn't Indella's name he called out, it was Marisa Louise's and he shouted it over and over to the clouds hanging low in the sky as he slid ever further, ever faster down the icy face of the granite outcropping.

Suddenly, and not knowing why, his skid stopped. He lay prone on the slippery rock and turned his head so he could see what lay before him. His boot had caught on a small ledge that was protected from the sleet by a three foot juniper not six inches from his nose. He grabbed the stubby trunk of the bush with both hands and held on for fear his free-fall would begin anew.

He breathed like air had been denied him for years. His heart pummeled the inside of his chest with the wham of a pick axe on frozen ground.

When his eyes cleared of fright and he could focus again, his stomach rose into his throat and his grasp of the juniper trunk became a hug. Below him was the abyss. His foot had found the ledge of a precipice, a bottomless drop that disappeared in the mist. A fall of six more inches would surely have sent him home inside the promised Black Hills pine box. Or worse. The fall might have left him a pitiful cripple for the remainder of his days. Or even worse than that, it could have dumped him somewhere at the bottom of an Iron Mountain cliff, only half dead. He would have been food for coyotes and buzzards and worms, never to be heard from again. Lucky. That was how he explained the ledge and juniper bush. Sheer, inexplicable luck. Or Providence. Or a mixture of both.

As he clung to the tree, he shared with his Momma the tale of his near catastrophic fall over the side of Iron Mountain.

Inside his head he heard her tell him it had to be Providence, that tree, that ledge, no question of it, and the sooner he admitted Jesus into his life, the safer he'd be, especially if he insisted on making this God-forsaken place called South Dakota his home after his year in the Cs. He smiled and shook his head at his Momma's railings. It was luck, Momma, he tried to convince her. Simple luck, that was all. "Call it what you want," he could hear her saying, "cause I know the truth."

The wind came up fierce as he clung to the side of the mountain. It was trying to lift him free of the rock face and fly him upward to safer ground. It urged him to turn loose and trust it to see him safely home. But he knew better. This wind, this evil and tempting wind, was trying to loose his grasp of the small juniper tree and hurl him like so much empty trash into the abyss below. It tore at his clothes, and his hair, and his nose and eyes and ears. It frosted his fingers with an icy glaze that made him feel a little bit warmer. Almost as warm as the time in the Bighorns when the fire swarmed over him. This, the wind, the freezing rain, was doing the job, too, that was traditionally reserved for water. It seemed he could hardly make a move these days without some element of nature trying its hand at chastising him for his failure to believe and he was growing down right disgruntled with the efforts. "Oh, Momma, Momma, Momma, if only that trick of yours had worked," he moaned into the wind as he clung with ever decreasing strength to the fragile juniper tree, whose roots, thank Jesus, remained true to their charge.

His Momma had come at him that last night he spent in Georgia before getting aboard the bus to head west; she was armed with a bucket of water from the rain barrel. Him sound asleep on the small cot on the screened-in back porch, she had raised her free hand to the heavens and whispered, "Oh Lord, I hereby baptize this sinner in the name of the Father, the Son, and the Holy Spirit. Praise Lord Jesus." And she had doused him with two gallons of cold water, catching him full on the head with the main stream, urging him awake, sputtering, gasping for a breath free of baptismal fluids. "What in God's name're you doing, Momma!" he had yelled. And she had simply smiled in that way of hers and said, "You done been baptized, son, and now I can rest easy." "But this don't count," he had hollered as she marched off back inside the house. "All you done is wet my bed, Momma, for Pete's sake." But to her way of thinking, her boy had received the grace of the Lord before leaving her roost, and for that she was most almightily thankful.

He knew he had to crawl up, out of the danger. Tenuously, he lifted his leg up off the ledge, pulling himself up with his arms at the same time. He continued the slow struggle until finally he found firm footing.

When he finally reached the cliff's edge, he eased himself into the forest away from the rock face. In the closure of the woods he found a rest from the howling wind that had come so close to taking away from him that thing he treasured most: his life.

"Some day," he whispered to the Ponderosa pine that he hugged like a long lost friend, "I'm coming back to this place and put up a cross." He looked around him, alone in the wilderness, not another human being within miles and he yelled into the darkening storm, "How many times, oh Lord? How many times?"

He got no answer. For that he was thankful.

Nine o'clock, and he dragged into camp, an exhausted lump. "If you weren't back in four days," Marv Drexler told him, "we were going to send out a search party."

"I was close to being a goner," he said, telling the story of his slide down Iron Mountain's bald side, keeping the guys in Old K.P. up well past lights out with the drama of his adventure.

"That's it for me hiking alone," he announced. And he stuck to his pledge—at least until the next Chinook found the Hills.

"We're gonna have to get you into the church before you kill yourself," Dolph told him as they lay waiting for sleep to find them that night.

"Might not be such a bad idea," Howie whispered. "The wind out here's indeed something else, ain't it, Dolph."

"Yes, indeed, something else," he said and then lay quiet. And Howie said, more to himself than to Dolph, "Back there in the Bighorns, you know, I never doubted I'd come through just fine. Never doubted. Even as I lay under that tarp and prayed for salvation. But today, Dolph, I don't know. Today. If it wasn't God out there taking care of me, I wonder who it was?"

"Your Momma," Dolph said and went to sleep.

Eleventh week. Only one more, then Marisa Louise would be gone—at least, until after Christmas.

Gone. Howie hated the thought. He hated knowing only her name, not knowing what her life away from camp was like, if she was married or not, if she cared at all for men, and if so what kind. He couldn't let her leave camp a final time without learning something about her, without making contact somehow or other. He was nearing desperation.

Tuesday, he cut class. The first cut in penmanship class by anyone during the entire fall class period. Miss Clackson called his name from the role; no one answered. Bert van Dorst and Marv Drexler both almost answered for him, but decided against it. Let Howie stew in his own broth. Let him suffer the wrath of a justified educator like Professor Watkins on his own. It was no skin off their behinds.

As the other enrollees lavished Miss Clackson with attention that Tuesday afternoon, Howie raced up the camp road to the intersection of the Needle's Highway to the bridge across Squaw Creek he had helped build the summer before.

Neatly piled rocks formed the foundation for the wooden bridge and underneath there was room for a man to sit and contemplate the meaning of bridges. He had done so several times during the summer, in this his place for contemplation.

He slipped down the creek bank and out of sight under the bridge. He waited there, beneath the bridge, sitting on the frozen surface of the creek bed. He shivered, but the cold was worth suffering if he could only succeed in his plan.

While he waited the hour for class to end, he took out his pocket knife and etched a heart in one of the log cross pieces. It was there to stay, that log. And if he carved his heart deep enough into the coarse wood, it would be there to stay as well. Inside the heart, he carved "HMC + MLC." Marisa Louise. There was music in the name. Marisa Louise. Slapping his arms against his torso and stomping his feet on the frozen creek bed, he sang her song.

The sound of a car. Right on time. He heard it change gears as it left the camp entrance. He waited for the auto to make its way up the gravel road toward the intersection.

He caught a glimpse of it through the trees. It was black. Yes, it had to be her thirty-four Ford Coupe, black and shiny. He ripped open the canvas bag of tomato juice he had stolen from the kitchen that day during lunch. It was half frozen and sent shockwaves of fire through his whole body as he allowed the red juice to ooze over his hands. And he splashed his face with the sticky stuff and almost shouted with pain. This had to work, by-God, or else all this hurting was for nothing.

The car drew nearer. The Ford Coupe. It was time. He staggered from his hiding place beneath the bridge, red bandanna in hand, waving, red tomato goo, frozen in globules, dropping from his hands, and the tip of his nose. He stumbled with legs stiff with cold into the path of the car, collapsed to his knees with eyes filled with pleading, eyes that focused momentarily on a vehicle that held questionable qualities— was that a Chevrolet insignia on the front grill?—and wobbling, fell face first into the dry powdered snow of the gravel road.

He lay there. Moaning. The vehicle ground to a halt. The brakes squeaked as if they needed new pads. He could fix those for her if she would only give him the chance.

The driver's door opened.

Two heavily booted feet touched the gravel.

They approached his prone body.

The space between steps seemed longer than what he would expect from Marisa Louise and her dainty tread. And his nose told him the smell wasn't right. There should be the aroma of her perfume, the scent he had identified with passion, the odor of honeysuckle and peach blossoms. Instead, there was the smell of sweat. Male sweat. Mean male sweat from a hot Chevrolet.

"What the goddamn hell's going on around here!" The

C.O. stood over him, hat off, fingers scratching his head where hair had once been.

His wife's voice came from the car. "Is he hurt, Clyde?" Howie raised his face from the dirt. Specks of powdered snow clung to the glob of tomato juice still frozen to his nose. He smeared it with his red and frozen drenched hand. He attempted a smile, but the C.O. wouldn't tolerate such a thing.

"I asked you question, mister. If you've got a tongue, I'd advise you to use it."

Howie cleared his throat as he got to his feet and brushed himself off as best he could. "I—uh—I tripped," he said.

"He looks hurt, Clyde," the C.O.'s wife called.

"Cobb?"

"Yes, sir."

"If you ain't the craziest son of a bitch. You hurt, son?"

"I don't think so," was all Howie could say.

"Then, what the hell's all that red stuff on you?"

Howie couldn't think fast enough. He could see the Ford Coupe approaching from camp and the object of his dreams at the steering column. Quickly, quickly. It's now or not at all.

"Nose bleed, sir. Nothing serious. I get them all the time."

He put out his thumb. But the Coupe with its blond wonder behind the wheel eased past them to the intersection, and turned left—left toward Custer? The Lodge? Hermosa? Hot Springs?

Howie's spirits sank. His shoulders slumped forward, his whole body drooped.

"He is hurt Clyde," the C.O.'s wife said. "I told you he was hurt."

Howie watched as the Ford Coupe disappeared.

"Cobb," the C.O.'s iron jaw set. "If it ain't one thing it's another. What is it with you anyway?"

"Sir," he said, fingers crossed behind his back so the C.O. wouldn't shoot him for impertinence. "If you're heading to town, could I oblige you for a lift?"

There was only one telephone book in camp. It was kept in the commissary. Very few of the enrollees had access to the building since it held all records, money, and governmental stuff. One of the few who did have access was Rosie Tucker.

"I just want to see the book," Howie said. "Is it a federal crime to look at a telephone directory? For God's sake, Rosie—"

"Look, I'm not getting in trouble for you." Rosie had a whine in his voice that made him sound like a fifteen-year-old when actually he was older than most of the enrollees in camp. Howie hated the whine, but for once he was willing to put up with it, if putting up with it meant getting his hands on the valuable telephone book.

"This is important," he said, deciding to lie if he had to. "I've been having stomach pangs and I need to find a doctor in Hot Springs who can help me." Lord help me, he thought, if Momma finds out about this.

"It's just gas."

"Well, how the hell would you know?"

"Cause I'm having the same stomach pangs, and Doc says it's just gas. Meatloaf's cooking. It's just gas, Cracker."

"Okay." He pulled out his billfold but didn't open it. "A dollar, Rosie. Just bring the directory to K.P. tonight, give me twenty minutes with it, and a dollar is yours."

"You serious?"

"Not really. All I've got is two bits. The two bits are yours though—"

Rosie showed his teeth in a sneering grin. "She's not in the directory. I've already looked."

"I don't know what you're talking about."

"I've checked every goddamn town in the Hills, Cracker. No Marisa Clackson is listed. No Louise. No M. L. Nothing. It's like she doesn't live anywhere. That or she doesn't have a phone. She just comes here, gives us benefit of her perfume, and disappears. I tell you, Cracker, there aren't any Clacksons listed in the Black Hills area."

"You serious?"

"You bet. Serious enough to tell you that there's no way you're going to get in that woman's stocking drawer. No way in a blue moon."

Forget it, Howie decided. Too much trouble. Last time he had been in Rapid City, he had called all three Clacksons listed in the phone book. None of them knew a Marisa Louise. Now, if he was to believe Rosie Tucker, there was no Marisa Louise Clackson to be found.

He drooped back to Kensington Place, crawled into his bunk and pulled the wool blanket over his head. It was a cold night in the Hills.

It had been five weeks since he had written Indella. She probably figures I've gone to China. Should write her. Really should.

Forget it. He wasn't interested.

The last day of class. The final exam, so to speak.

"Like being in college again," Rosie Tucker said, rubbing it in.

Give us a break, for God's sake, Howie wanted to say. Hate college guys, he decided, if they were all like Roosevelt Tucker.

Howie took the test.

Marisa Louise had a new hair style that made her look just like the pin-up photos of those movie stars whose names he couldn't remember. She stayed behind the desk and watched the men as they struggled with the exam.

Howie decided to fail. It was his last chance to get her attention. Just flunk the beJesus out of it. Let her know that she didn't teach him a damn thing.

So, he left each section of his exam paper blank, except for an occasional doodle as he tried to capture her profile.

As others began returning their completed tests, he flipped his over and wrote on the back as clearly as he could and, as beautifully as he knew how, "i"'s crowned with perfect curlicues, the following message to his true love:

> How do I love thee, let me count the ways—If I knew the rest of this poem, I would write for days, For I love thee, far more than you will ever know, And how I hate that today from me you must go.
> Love,
> Howie

Three days later, class grades were posted on the bulletin board in the rec hall. Top of the list for the writing class was the name, Roosevelt Tucker. Just as everyone had expected, damn teacher's pet. But the second name down shocked them all. There, in Marisa Louise's impeccable hand, was the name, Howell M. Cobb.

Posted near the list was one of the tests. Across the top of the paper, written unmistakably in Marisa Louise's script, was the note: "An example of perfect penmanship." And beneath it in Howie's careful hand: "How do I love thee."

From that day on, Howie was no longer just plain Cracker. He was the Poet Laureate of Iron Mountain.

Poker Face

Classes over, Marisa Louise no longer in camp, Howie's thoughts turned to home. If he wanted it, he could arrange a ten-day Christmas leave. The C.O. had promised any of the Cs as much.

May Lou in her letters urged him to come home. So did Indella. Their letters were full of longing and need to see him. May Lou wasn't ready to spend her first Christmas without all her kids around the kitchen table, though she still had no word from Pierson and Hank was threatening to head off on his own, too, soon as he got his chance.

Indella was lonesome and longed to see his face, or that was what her letters said.

He lay on his bunk, remembering that first time he had kissed the woman he was fairly certain he would someday call wife.

Rudy Shealy, Indella's impossible little brother, had seen to it. He traipsed the whole town looking for Howie Cobb, and when he found him, he said, "My sister's gonna marry you."

The rumor spread: the second of the Cobb boys was getting married to that poor little Shealy girl. At first, Howie had laughed off the snide remarks about him and his forthcoming marriage to Indella Shealy. It was a little funny, even to him, and a whole lot embarrassing. After all, he was a seventeen-year-old man. Free, thank you Jesus. And she was just barely

179

turned a teenager. What would folks in Douglasville think about him if they ever took the rumors, which were spreading faster than the mumps, to be true?

After two weeks of questioning from friends, relatives, neighbors and even strangers he met on the streets about his forthcoming nuptials, Howie determined the time had come to put an end to the entire shebang once and for all. No matter how often he said: "There's nothing to it, folks," nobody seemed to listen and went about their business of giving him a difficult time.

The only way he knew to put something like this behind him was to find the girl, confront her, and deny the rumors to her face if necessary and witnessed, too, by God, and get this marriage business behind him once and for all. He wasn't in the market for marriage, especially those days when he was more interested in discovering how things worked. Besides, there was Carol Bauman, two years his senior, who was paying him a lot of attention at church these days, sitting with him when she could, even holding his hand under cover of the hymnal and giving him a kiss now and then in the church parking lot after Sunday night services. And he could court either of the Statum twins with no trouble whatsoever. Hev's fiance, Merle, had a sister, Lacy, cute as could be who was an old woman compared to this Shealy girl—Lacy was all of fifteen and "ready for Freddie," according to Hev. At any rate, it was time, past time to be exact, to put this marriage mess behind him.

One afternoon after he got off the cotton-thread shift at the mill, a job he had held for going on three years, Howie followed Rudy home. He took Pierson along for witness since Hev, being too infatuated with Merle to have anything to do with his younger brother's marital problems, refused, especially now that he and Merle were talking along those lines themselves.

Howie and Pierson stood outside the fence as Rudy rushed up to the white-washed house and disappeared inside. The two brothers fidgeted. Howie plucked a straw from the sage brush growing around one of the posts and used it to pick his teeth. The field across the way had sprouted cotton and was etched a deep green against the far row of trees and the redness of the road bed. And honeysuckle. Somehow or other, it seemed honeysuckle followed him whenever he came close to the Shealy place. Its warm moist aroma was so thick he felt he could reach out and touch it.

Rudy returned. "She ain't coming out," he called to the brothers at the fence.

"Why not," Howie wanted to know. He felt his face go red with heat and disgust. His ears burned his mouth turned dry.

"She just ain't," said Rudy as he sauntered to the fence and hung against it by standing on the lower board. "She's a girl. Who ever heard of a girl acting right?"

And Pierson nodded. He was thinking of Martha and Annie and Brenda and the half a dozen or so girls around his house that he found particularly obnoxious. "Girls are pains in the boom booms," he said.

"You want to see my place?" Rudy asked Pierson.

"What place?"

"The Wildcat Den. It's back in the woods behind the house." The two younger boys scooted out of sight before Howie could stop them.

He paced for a bit in front of the house. He should leave. He had made the effort, but she wasn't gracious enough to honor it. Forget her. Her and all girls like her. Her and her honeysuckle. She wanted to marry him? Well, hell could freeze over as far as he was concerned. Hell freeze and the heavens melt, and he'd still be his own man, his and nobody else's. Not even Carol Bauman, who had kissed him at least a dozen times the past month in the darkened parking lot of Liberty Baptist Church, could deny him that. He figured she'd heard the rumors of his marriage to the Shealy girl and was taking the opportunity to place her claim on him before it was too late.

The stone he threw at the row of mail boxes clattered against the first and put a small dent in the metal. He was startled. He had not considered it possible that he might hit something and felt as if he should apologize to somebody for putting a dinger in their box.

"Do you want something?" Indella was standing on the front porch, dressed in a pink print dress, a white bow in her black hair and new saddle oxfords on her feet. Howie's heart rate increased two-fold. This girl is fourteen? My God, he thought, she looks older than Carol Bauman.

"You get back in this house, young lady," he heard her momma call from inside. But Indella ignored Glory Bea and sat on the top step, clasping her legs together at the knees and hugging them as if to keep them from knocking against one another.

Sitting there, like that, he remembered her from before. When was it? Weeks ago. She was just a kid then. Now, she looked like what she was: an "almost" woman.

"Hi," Howie said across the fence.

"Rudy said you wanted to talk to me."

"Well."

Glory Bea came onto the porch. She had a leather strap wrapped around her right hand, ready for whatever might be the young man's intent. "You're too old for my girl, you hear me?" she bellowed. "She's just a baby. Just be on your way and everybody'll be happy."

"Go inside, Momma," the girl whispered.

"Indella, I'm not about to let you—"

"Go inside. I'll take care of this."

If a mother's looks could kill, Howie was dead ten times over. But Glory Bea turned on her heel and slammed the door behind her, muttering, "I don't know where they get their ideas these days."

"Care to sit with me on the porch?" Indella called.

"I ain't done nothing to your momma," he said.

"I know. Come on over, set a spell."

"I don't take to women with straps in their hands," he remarked as he edged through the gate and down the path lined with tulips and red bricks. The tulips weren't blooming yet, but they would be soon. "My name's Howie Cobb—" he started.

"I know who you are."

"So I hear."

"You're sixteen? "

"Seventeen."

"Seventeen, sorry. Work in the cotton mill, have four brothers and three sisters, your daddy's a preacher down at Liberty Baptist, but he works in the cotton mill, too, and so does your momma and older brother. His name is Heviathan, or Hev for short, and he's in love with a girl name of Merle Addams. You've been seeing a girl named Carol Bauman—"

"Now wait a minute—"

"But that's okay by me. You'll get over her. You live in the mill village in Douglasville. You love baseball and are pretty good at shortstop, whatever that means. You dropped out of school after the third grade to help support your family, and you're about the best looking boy I ever set eyes on."

"How do you know all that?"

"I know."

"You've been talking about me to other folks?"

"I have the right. After all, I've decided I'm going to marry you."

"Now, damn it—."

"Don't you swear in my front yard, young man!" Glory Bea yelled from inside the house.

"You want to go for a walk?" Indella asked, touching his arm with her soft hand.

He paused. Did he? He didn't know this girl and she didn't know him, though she seemed to have some pretty impressive facts about him, and there he was looking at her and liking what he saw, listening to her threats of marriage and not taking flight like something inside him said he should. She smelled good. She had eyes that sliced through his defenses and left him dangling like so much ham in the smokehouse. And her touch was soft as a bee wing on an azalea bloom. It sent sparklers through him and made his blood rush about without reason.

"Sure," he said. Stupid fool idiot, something inside his head said, you better get out of this while you can.

"If you leave the yard, I'm calling the police," Glory Bea yelled from the house.

"We don't have a telephone," Indella whispered as they stepped through the gate and into the road. "Closest phone's a quarter mile away. She knows we're getting married. She'll get used to the idea."

Howie stopped and turned to her. He had come to face her about all this marriage stuff and by God he wasn't going to be railroaded into something, especially by a fourteen-year-old wisp of a girl. "Listen, Miss Shealy—"

"Indella."

"—I do not know you, I don't know if I want to know you. And all this talk you're spreading around about— things, well, it's got to stop. Okay? Will you stop it?"

"Don't you think I'm pretty?"

"Well, you're pretty enough."

"I put on some toilet water. Don't you like the way I smell?"

"That's not what I'm talking about, damn it."

"Then what are you talking about?" And she added under her breath a quiet "Damn it" to match his.

"This marriage business."

"I'd love to."

"That's not what I'm talking about either!"

"You just said it was."

"Cripes. Just don't talk for a minute, okay?"

"Okay."

They walked down the road, he kicking at the dirt and gravel with the toe of his right shoe, she being very careful not to disturb any dust for fear it might soil the luster of the new oxfords which pinched her toes. Their knuckles brushed against each other and he stuffed his hand in his pocket and she crossed her arm.

"You don't know anything about me," he said soft enough not to be heard if Pierson or Rudy should be lurking in the bushes beside the road.

"I know lots."

"Facts, maybe, but you don't know a thing about me— about who I am. Besides, well, I don't know anything about you."

"What would you like to know?"

"What's your favorite color?"

"Pink."

"Favorite ice cream?"

"Strawberry"

"How about church?"

"What about church?"

"I don't believe in it much."

"I do."

"Yeah. You see? There you are." He walked a little faster, but she kept up.

"I could learn not to believe in it much," she said.

"Well, now, that's dumb. Would you want our kids to grow up without Sunday School and prayer meeting?"

She hung her head slightly and repeated his words, "Our kids."

"Now, look, I didn't mean that."

This was getting out of hand. He loved her aroma. He wanted to grab a handful of her hair and caress it. He wanted to put his mouth over hers and feel her body press against his.

At the same time he wanted to get as far from her as he could. If he didn't, he wasn't sure what might happen.

"I've got things to do, you know? Things I want to do more than anything, and getting married isn't one of them."

"Not ever?" she whispered.

"Well, I don't know about ever. I mean, ever's a long time. Besides," he added, "I've joined the C.C.C.s."

"You have?"

"Signed and delivered."

"What's the C.C.C.s?"

"Civilian Conservation Corps. We plant trees."

"Why?"

"Cause trees need planting."

"I mean, why did you join it?"

"My folks need the money. It's good money. Twenty-five dollars a month and I get to keep five of it for myself. The rest is sent home. Besides, if you join the Cs and ask for it, you can travel to other parts of the country and learn a lot. I've already been assigned to a camp somewhere out west."

"West of what?"

"Here. Out west. Indians and cattle drives. You know."

"You don't like it here?"

"Douglasville? Well, sure, it's okay. Don't care all that much for the mill. And that's all I've got to look forward to if I hang around here. Same as my Poppa and his before him. A life in the mill. I want more than that. Know what I mean? I want to travel and learn things and be part of something bigger than this little town and its cotton looms. You can't understand that sort of thing. You're a girl."

Tears swelled out of her. They weren't fake, he could see that much. She was weeping, unashamedly, profusely, and he didn't know what to do about it. He didn't have a handkerchief. His shirt tail was dirty and so was his sleeve. So he pulled her to him, whispering, "Don't cry, no need to cry." He held her as tightly as he felt proper.

Her sobs came from deep inside her as she buried her head in Howie's shirt front.

"I'm sorry," he said over and over. "I'm sorry, I'm sorry."

"I'll wait for you," she said. "I know you're not asking me to, but I will."

Her mouth was too young and fragile and alluring to resist. It could have been his first kiss from the surge that swept through him. He was, after all, experienced in such things as kissing, thanks to Carol Bauman.

It was without a doubt her first, though. He could tell. He recognized the symptoms. Through kissing him, she was learning, she was giving all control to him and allowing him to do with her as he wanted. He ran his tongue into her mouth, and she almost fainted. So did he. Instead he exploded. Oh Christ, he almost yelled out. What is all this? And there it was daylight, too. Was the wet spot going to show?

"I'll be back in a year," he said.

"Okay."

"I'll marry you then—if you'll have me," he said.

"Okay."

"I'd like to see you again, before I leave," he said.

"Okay."

He slipped an arm about her waist as he ushered her back to the house where her momma sat waiting just inside the front door, waiting to prevent the very thing that had taken place, waiting to prove beyond a shadow of a doubt how powerless a parent can truly be when facing young love.

So Howie figured it: four days there, four days back, and he had two days to spend with family and friends. Was it worth it? Something inside him said it was.

He checked. Fifteen dollars round trip on the bus. He didn't have fifteen dollars. He was lucky to have five. He needed ten more just for the ticket and probably three more to feed himself en route. Thirteen dollars. Where can a guy go to get thirteen dollars?

He had nothing to sell, no collateral to use in borrowing. What he had was the nightly poker games in the rec hall. But they were high stake and cut throat. He had gotten into them a couple of times and was lucky to break even. Now, he was thinking of them as a means of coming out ahead, enough ahead to get him home and back.

The first night of playing serious poker he came away sixty-five cents to the good. At that rate he would need more than four weeks of winning poker to manage the thirteen dollars he needed. He had to do better than that, no question of it.

By the third night, he discovered something: if you don't have it, don't bet it. Chances were you wouldn't get it in the draw. So, his tendency was to fold early unless he had a potential winner in hand; when that happened, he stayed in the round and raised the pot at every opportunity. To his surprise, using his new strategy, he came out three dollars and forty cents to the good by the end of the night.

The fourth night the other players were wise to his game. When Howie raised a pot, all others folded so that the best he did that night was break even.

Time was slipping away. After four nights of dedicated poker playing, he only had nine dollars, half of what was necessary if he was to take advantage of the ten day leave which was coming his way in less than a week.

The fifth night, Howie changed his tactics: he stayed in more hands, raised a few losers, and actually found himself winning with lousy hands more often than with real winners. He discovered the bluff. That night he counted his winnings: six dollars and fifty cents. One more night and he had all he needed.

Actually, he had enough in hand to purchase the bus ticket with fifty cents to spare. And it wasn't any too soon.

He considered taking his winnings and staying clear of the poker table, but he knew fifty cents wasn't enough to stay fed during the four-day trip home. He needed one more night of moderate winnings to insure that he didn't lose weight while on the road. He returned to the poker table the sixth night.

The very first hand of seven card stud, he received a pair of aces in the hole and a third one dealt face up. He raised the ante each time he got a chance until finally it was just him and Bull left. Bert sat across from him with a couple of low spades showing after all cards were dealt. Howie had nothing to back up his three aces, but with what he saw in front of Bull, he didn't need anything else. He raised a full dollar when it came his time.

Bull looked at his show, grimaced over his hole cards then matched the dollar and raised another two. It was bluff. Howie had used the bluff enough the past few days to recognize it. Besides he had over four dollars in the pot already. Two more was all he needed to ante in order to assure his passage home.

He studied his cards; he studied Bull's.

After a bit, he said, "Call," and placed two more dollar bills on the sizable pot. Bull grinned and turned over three more spades.

Howie gasped. God. Only the first hand and he had lost six of the dollars he needed to buy passage home. He hated the goddamned grin Bert the Bull had on his face. But there was nothing he could do.

Before the night was over, Howie was back where he had started at the beginning of the week—five dollars. Bull had the rest.

He didn't know how it had happened, but he was stripped of five day's earnings, of his plans to go home, and of his pride in poker playing. His Poppa had told him to stay clear of such sinnings as gambling, but he hadn't listened. If there was a God somewhere out there, Howie was sure He had taken pleasure in his demise that evening.

"So, you're heading home for Christmas?" Bert said next morning at breakfast.

"Not anymore," Howie said, still too upset to be nice to his poker nemesis.

"How come?"

"You know goddamn well how come."

"Hey," Bert said, "it ain't my fault you don't know how to keep from tipping your hand."

Howie was suddenly interested. "How you mean, tip my hand."

"I mean this." Bert scratched his nose with his right middle finger. It was a small gesture, hardly noticeable. Howie wouldn't have recognized it as a gesture of his if Bert hadn't drawn attention to it.

"I don't understand."

"Any time you hold a halfway decent hand, you scratch your nose, Cracker. Notice I say 'a halfway decent hand,' not a good one or a bad one. When you got a sure winner, you fold your arms in front of you on the table. Any time you scratch your nose, I know: stay the mile and force your hand. You make it easy, Poker Face."

Howie felt disgust rising inside him. He was his own worst enemy. And Bert was the smart one after all. He had found Howie's poker flaw just as Howie had discovered Bert's in boxing.

Or was Bert the smarter? Might there be a way for Howie to use Bull's mastery against him just as he had done to Howie in the boxing ring? It was worth a full measure of thought.

That night, Howie returned to the poker table. It was his last night. His bus, if he was to be on it, left from Custer the next morning at nine a.m., and he intended to be on it or be damned trying.

He took his place at the table and won just enough to be a little ahead when his time to deal came around.

He took the cards and shuffled them four or five times

before Bull demanded, "What's the game, Cracker?"

"High card draw," he said, and placed five dollars in the middle of the table. "Five dollar ante. No betting. Ante up."

"What are you talking about?" JoJo said. "I've never heard of any poker game called High Card Draw."

"It's my deal and that's what I'm calling," Howie said. "If you're in, ante five dollars. I deal everybody one card, face up. Person with high card wins the pot. Two cards of equal face value regardless of suit get one more card. The high second card takes the pot. Anybody in?" And he tapped his five dollar bill in the center of the table.

It took some soul searching among the players. Five dollars was a lot of money to any C, but finally five of the seven players placed five dollars apiece in the pot. JoJo said he'd just watch.

Rosie Tucker said, "I don't have five dollars."

"Guess you're out, then."

"Got a Black Hills gold ring, though," he said and pulled it out of his pocket and placed it with the pile of money.

Bert fingered it and handed it around. "I don't know jewelry from gall stones. Anybody know how much that thing's worth?"

Rosie knew. "I spent eight dollars on it three months ago in Rapid City. I gave it to my girl but she gave it back. I don't want it any more. What about it, Howie. Am I in?"

Howie didn't care. There was already twenty-five dollars in the pot. A Black Hills gold ring made no difference. "Okay by me. Pot right?"

"Pot's right," JoJo said. Twenty-five dollars looked like Fort Knox to the suddenly quiet and serious poker players.

As Howie shuffled the cards, Bert said, "What're you trying to do, Cracker, bust our bank?"

"If it's any of your business," he said, "I'm trying to get home for Christmas."

He dealt the first card, a ten of spades to Roosevelt Tucker. Rosie sat back. He had a chance, though a slim one.

Next card was a five of diamonds to Marv who almost spat in contempt. "This ain't poker," he said and left the rec room in disgust.

Next card was a king of spades to Bert The Bull. He sat back with a shitty grin on his face. Rosie threatened to rip his ten of spades in half but laughed instead. "Good riddance to a bad investment," he said to his Black Hills gold ring.

Next was a three of hearts to PeeWee Phillips, who let loose a loud lingering fart that nearly cleared the room. Then a queen of clubs to Manny Lakso who shrugged his shoulders and said, "We gotta do this again."

Finally Howie came to himself. He dealt his card face down.

"I haven't looked at it Bull," Howie said, hands folded in his lap.

"I can see that."

"Ever since breakfast this morning, I've been wondering what kind of poker player you really are. What kind are you, Bull, do you know?"

"What are you getting at. Turn your card over."

"In a bit." Howie didn't take his eyes off the burly C sitting across the table from him. "There's twenty-five dollars and a ring in the pot just in case you have difficulty with things like counting. I don't turn my card over, you me split the pot right down the middle—fifteen dollars apiece. Ten to you and the ring if you want it. Or I turn my card over and take the pot. I walk away with loot, you walk away with nothing. It's your call."

"You're gonna need an ace to do all this walking."

"That's what I'm betting I've got."

"And I'm next to certain you ain't."

"How much you bet?"

Bert sat still. He stared as hard as he could at Howie's face. But there was nothing there to read. "Go ahead, take a look at what you've got," Bert said. "Then we'll bet."

"No, sir," Howie said. "This bet is on you, not me. You want full pot, half, or nothing."

"Some game you've concocted, Cracker. What do you call it?"

"Screw You."

"Fitting name." He thought a bit longer, then said, "Tell you what, Howie. You call it."

Howie took no time at all. "I want to go home," he said.

"Fifteen dollars is all I need to do it. I say forget my card and split the pot."

"I say you're full of chicken shit," Bert said. "All or nothing, winner take all."

"Are you sure?"

"Roll your damn card."

Howie flipped his card over.

Ace of clubs.

He was going home. Glory hallelujah and praise the Lord, Howell Madison Cobb was going home.

Christmas.

Indella.

Oh, how she had changed. Six months and she had found a beauty like none other. She had breasts, beautifully high-riding breasts that seemed to float in front of her. Her waist had turned inward. She was at least three inches taller. When Howie asked her what happened, she smiled at him in her way.

Her face was different now, too. She seemed five years older. Her lips had developed a pout. She had been studying movie star pictures printed in *Harper's Magazine*. She even wore a little eye make-up to show off her long lashes and her jet black eyes. She had become a woman in a bare six months, and Howie was confused. She bragged about her blossoming, too. She had become the perfect woman, she said, for Howell Madison Cobb.

It mattered little what changes had occurred in Indella as Howie tried his best not to notice. He was preoccupied when with her. All the time, his mind was somewhere else.

Oh, sure, he spent as much time as he could at the Shealy place, paying as much attention as he could to Indella and Glory Bea and even Rudy—six months gone, and Rudy had gotten younger, bigger sure, but still a kid. Maybe it was the time he was spending with Hank over in Douglasville. Or maybe it was just Rudy's nature to refuse to grow up. Howie didn't put much thought into it. He didn't put much thought into anything except the two days he had to wait before he boarded the bus one more time and headed west again.

On Saturday night while Howie was at the Shealy place, Sylvester came home, drunk, and busted up the place. He staggered all about the house, knocking over Glory Bea's little porcelain dancers that Indella had given her the Christmas before and spilling whiskey on the living room rug. Rudy hid in the hall closet. Glory Bea locked herself in the bedroom and refused to come out. Howie sat in the living room with his arm around Indella. They didn't speak.

Sylvester smashed a few things in the kitchen trying to find the apple butter he claimed he brought home the week before. Indella went into the kitchen to find it for him.

Howie was used to drunks. He had helped drag JoJo and Fleance Schmidt and even Marv Drexler back to barracks after a number of roisters in Custer. But they were easy drinkers and made no demands on anybody.

Not like Sylvester Shealy, who was by Jesus going to have his apple butter on some toast if he had to kill everybody in the goddamn house to get it.

When Sylvester took a swipe at Indella's head with a soup ladle, Howie figured enough was enough. He pulled the old man aside and whispered in his not-too-drunk-to-comprehend ear that if he, Sylvester, ever laid a finger on either Indella or Glory Bea again, or Rudy for that matter, he, Howie Cobb, would take it as a personal insult and knock his, Sylvester's, nose to the other side of his head, and he, Howie Cobb, could do it, too, he promised, because that was what he had been taught in the Cs.

"Do what you like away from the house," he said, "but leave Glory Bea and Indella and Rudy alone."

"Who do you think you are, boy?" Sylvester said.

Howie grabbed a fistful of ear, hair, and skin, and twisted it until Sylvester whimpered.

"You don't know who I am, Mr. Shealy?"

"I know you, I know you."

Howie turned him loose. "Then know I keep my promises." Sylvester left after that and didn't come back until long after Howie had returned to Iron Mountain.

For Indella, if not before, after that night, Howie became her knight in shining armor, her personal Launcelot, Sir Galahad, and Arthur all rolled into one.

But even though Indella and Howie spent as much time together as they could during his brief time home, and even though he walked with her and held her hand and even kissed her as much as he liked, Indella could tell, his soul just wasn't in it anymore.

When Indella asked what was wrong, Howie got defensive and blustery, something like Sylvester had been, and almost shouted at her, "Nothing. Nothing's wrong."

He told Indella about the sights he had seen. She listened with rapt attention as he described Mount Rushmore. "The faces don't do anything," he said. "They just sit there and draw thousands of people. It's really something, though," he said, "how they could carve such massive look-alikes of important people out of a mountain side."

But what she wanted to know about were the things he didn't want to share. Things like what life in camp was like, who his friends were, what he had to eat for supper, where he went on his days off, what it felt like living so far away from other people. She had wanted to say "women" instead of "people," but refrained.

Instead, he told her about the Needles and how on a full moon you can go up there and sit and conspire with the Great Spirit. He hadn't done it yet, but he was going to. He told her how the Lakota considered the Black Hills to be sacred ground. He told her about Paha Sapa and the time the Indian on his pack mule came through camp begging for a handout.

He didn't tell her about Tilda Eaglewing.

He told her about the work, about the pigtail bridges on the Iron Mountain Highway that he had worked on for a while, and the cold and how the hairs inside his nose froze each time he stepped outside during the November cold snap. He even told her about Chinooks, but not about his slide down the face of Iron Mountain.

What he didn't tell her about was how he had improved his handwriting. He didn't tell her about a blond named Marisa Louise.

He did tell her, after her vow to absolute silence regarding the matter, about the Blackwater Burn, about how his half of Squad 14 had scampered up a cliff to safety while the other half hadn't made it. He told her about Cheater Evans and his dash off the cliff into the inferno and about how God awful it felt after the fire storm had past to find the cooked remains of his friend and fellow C. He showed her the news clipping that had appeared in the Sheridan, Wyoming newspaper. She was weeping as he pointed out his name. He told her how some day he wanted to return to the Bighorns, find the rock that had saved his life, and erect a cross with Cheater Evans' name carved on it. And he told her about his idea of buying a grocery store when he got out of the Cs, about maybe becoming a Mormon, and possibly going on a two-year mission to earn elder status. She wept through all he said and he felt confused.

"Why are you crying?" he asked her.

And she said, "Because you could have been killed, and then what would I have done."

"Found somebody else. You know." He thought such words would give her comfort. Instead, she wailed as if her heart were breaking, and she buried her face in his jacket and held him so tightly it hurt.

"If anything should happen to you," she whispered, "I don't know what I'd do."

The guilt he carried inside him was enough to fill four bird cages, and he had no idea about how to get rid of it. She clung to him as if he held real value. Yet he knew better. He had been through fire and ice, and he knew there was very little value to be found in his guilt-ridden soul. Still she held him with a terror of losing him, and his guilt increased ten-fold. The best thing for him was to leave. No, the best thing would have been not to come home in the first place. Then his guilt might have been something to be borne.

He caressed her silky black hair and said, "You know, sweetheart, get you a white sweater with beads on it and put a ribbon in your hair, and you'd be the spitting image of a Lakota princess I danced with one night."

She looked up at him, tears still clinging to her fleshy cheek, "You danced with a princess?"

"Just a joke, sweetheart," he said, quickly realizing the dangerous territory he was near. "Go on back to your crying."

As it was, two days home in Georgia around a weeping Indella was more than enough for him. He was ready to board the bus and get back to the Dakotas and the Hills and Camp Iron Mountain. When the day came for him to leave, he hugged his Momma's neck, shook Alexander Steven's hand, chucked Hev on the shoulder and slapped Hank on the back. Pierson hadn't been heard from in four months. He kissed Indella Shealy long and deep on the mouth and told her he'd be back. He promised. He would come back home; he would see her again. He bound the promise by slipping a Black Hills gold ring on her finger.

"What's this," she asked, blushing deeply at the idea of a ring.

"A souvenir," he said.

"Oh my God," she said and began to cry once again.

"What?" he almost shouted. "What's the matter now?"

"Does this mean we're engaged?"

"Shit no," he said, immediately regretting his word choice.

She allowed her tears to stream down her cheeks. She said, "Yes it does."

"Now, Indella—"

"You go on and do what you've got to do," she said.

"We're not engaged, honey," he said.

"Go on now. I know what I know."

He got on the bus and sat on the opposite side of the vehicle so he wouldn't have to look out the window and see his girl standing there, adoring the finger he had decorated. My sweet Jesus, he thought, what have I done?

A brand new year, another four-day bus ride, and January in the Hills was what he had to look forward to. And a fiance waiting for him back home. Life was certainly a strange kind of thing.

Halfway across the frozen tundra of Iowa, he was home-sick again, this time for Georgia. Just no pleasing him. He was becoming an old codger in his advancing years. It was too damn cold. Besides, he was turning eighteen away from home. It was going to be his first birthday away from his Momma's cooking. He was growing old and there was nobody on the bus who knew any thing about it or cared one way or another.

Dear Indella, he wrote in his head, how I miss you. But he didn't write it on paper. He couldn't. Not yet. First, there was something back in the Hills he had to do.

Teacher's Pet

"You can't take writing again," Professor Watkins told Howie as he tried to sign up for Marisa Louise's class in January.

"Why not?"

"Well, look, Cracker, last session you were second from the top of the class. If I let you take the course over, it would piss a lot of guys off. I mean, it wouldn't be fair, their having to compete with a top-notch student like you."

"But there's so much more to learn," Howie said.

"I just can't do it." The professor made it sound so final. "Why don't you take English instead."

"What for? I can already talk English. For God's sake, I want to learn more about curlicues."

"I really think you'll like this English class."

"Nothing's stupider than studying English, Professor," Howie said.

Professor Watkins nodded and said, "Miss Clackson's teaching it."

"That right?"

"That's right. She did such a bang-up job for us last session, we're giving her a second course this time around."

"You're joking, right?"

"Cracker, would I joke about such a thing, especially to Iron Mountain's own poet laureate? Miss Clackson's the finest teacher we have. I'd be foolish not to take advantage of all her abilities."

"You call her 'Miss' Clackson. She's not married?"

"Son, I'm afraid you'll have to find that out for yourself."

"I've been trying," he said.

"So, try harder."

Howie signed up for English.

First day of English class, there she was, radiant as ever.

There were so many enrollees and regular Army signed up that the class had to be moved to the mess hall over Meatloaf's protest. The tables were pushed aside to make room for a blackboard and chairs. All of which were full. In fact, five extra had to be added.

Professor Watkins beamed. His education program was actually working.

She called roll. The Cs answered names with a loud "here" except for an occasional "yo."

Then she came to his name. "Howell Madison Cobb."

"Present," he said.

A few sneers came at him.

A half whispered, "The Poet Laureate's present," was heard.

When he answered, Marisa Louise looked up from the lengthy roster. She found him in the mass of male faces. She formed brief eye contact with him. And smiled. Then back to roll.

His blood was made of chili pepper and all of it seemed to gather in the most awkward place.

It was good being back in the Hills.

Like everyone predicted, it finally got "cold." The heat of Hell couldn't be much worse than the Black Hills in the middle of a January blast. Let the preacher change his tune about hellfire and brimstone: make it four weeks of twenty below with a forty-five mile an hour northwest knee knocker wind, and he'd scare Jesus into all the poor suckers who insisted on remaining in the Devil's grasp.

Howie had heard tales of it getting so cold dogs stuck to sidewalks. In the Hills, there were no sidewalks, so dogs were sticking to the front porch of the mess hall and biting off parts of toes to get themselves free. Meatloaf whipped up dog mittens for their feet, and Howie was amazed to see the animals leave the lightly tied pieces of cloth alone, as if they knew the cook's silly concoction was for their well being.

Howie would not have believed it if he hadn't seen it. The windows in Old K.P. froze up solid. The moisture from the stoves and the men's breathing condensed on the glass and formed large upside down icebergs that kept growing until they were five inches thick and covered most of the window and hung over the sill. The extra insulation the ice gave must have helped, as the barrack held warmth much better after the windows were encased.

Work on the Iron Mountain Highway, Old Clyde complained, was too slow. The pigtail repairs had to be finished despite the weather turning bad.

Howie couldn't remember ever working so hard.

Strapping around the giant timbers was tedious and dangerous. The job had to be managed just right or the metal would slip and slash out at the nearest C. It was bad enough doing such work when the air was warm, but now with frozen metal straps, it was doubly difficult. Two men had already been rushed to the hospital in Rapid City, one with a cut so severe his hand clung to his wrist by only a sliver of flesh. Thank God for the cold. It froze the man's wound and probably kept him from bleeding to death. The other man received a deep gash in his upper arm and required forty stitches to close the wound.

Since the post-Hallowe'en freeze of November, folks had promised him: "Just wait. This ain't nothing, Cracker." Now, in January, with new snow nearly every morning and frigid Canadian cold spells coming through weekly, he considered himself dead and gone the other way.

He tried writing his Momma about the biting chill, but he couldn't find the words. January would have to remain as something he experienced without sharing with folks back home.

At first, the Cs had been set to clearing the roadway of underbrush from the asphalt fifty feet in. Then, the C.O. got it in his head that the pigtail bridges had to be finished before tourist season. Maybe somebody was on his tail about it, but that didn't matter.

The Cs were on edge. After all, cold like this January can be dangerous. It was time, maybe, for a new C.O. "Run him out of this place," Howie said to Dolph over mess, "else he's gonna run me out."

"You mean that?" Dolph asked.

"Maybe."

"You'd really go AWOL?"

"Don't tempt me," Howie said.

The C.O. in his surge to get the pigtails finished changed everything from amount of liberty on weekends to the kind of mess the Cs received.

"The man thinks we're regular Army," Dolph said when word came that lights out would be at nine instead of nine-thirty and reveille at the ungodly hour of five in the morning. The new order of the day was: the cold be hanged. They were going to fix the bridges, no matter what.

"I joined the Cs to plant tress," Howie said to Dolph after lights out. It was mid-January and his breath froze two inches from his face. "Not to do this kind of shit for Old Clyde." His palm throbbed from the creosote splinter that had pierced his glove and refused to work its way out of his flesh.

"Come with me," Dolph said. He lay on his back, arms under his head.

Howie hung over the edge of his top bunk. "Come with you where?"

Dolph had had his fill of C.C.C. life. With his refusal to play the championship baseball game, he had earned the scorn of nearly everyone in camp. Only Howie remained his friend. Few people spoke to the two of them when they were together, which was a good bit of the time. When Dolph tried out for the basketball team, no one let him touch the ball. When he stretched for a rebound, he was fouled time and again. The bruises on his legs and arms told him he had no future playing for the basketball version of the Cougars. It was time to bid farewell to Iron Mountain. He recognized it, but Howie didn't.

"I'm going home," Dolph whispered. "I'm going AWOL. Come with me."

"I can't do that," Howie said.

"You ever been to Salt Lake City?"

"Of course not."

"You'd like it. We could make a God-fearing Mormon of you, if you'd let us."

"My Momma tried making me a God-fearing Baptist, but that didn't stick. So I don't think so."

"My folks say it's time for my mission. I could wait, I guess. I intended to wait. But Old Clyde's such a bastard these days, I figure now is as good a time as any. Did I tell you where my mission's going to be?"

"No."

"Fairbanks."

"Where's that?"

"Alaska."

"Alaska? You're crazy, Dolph. Winters are bad enough here. But Alaska?"

"They say it's pretty nice up there."

"Who's this 'they'?"

"I don't know. Them."

The two lay on their bunks, quiet and thoughtful. Howie closed his eyes and envisioned Indella waiting for him. She was dressed in a white frilly dress that hung over her knees near the top of her white socks and saddle oxfords. Her hair was curled and pulled back from her face with a pink ribbon. She was smiling the biggest smile in the world. He turned over, thinking Dolph had gone to sleep.

"Wish you'd come with me, Cracker," Dolph said. "We make a pretty good team, you know."

"I've still got four months left to my hitch," Howie said. Going AWOL was something he couldn't manage. It was against everything he held dear. He wasn't a quitter, and neither was Dolph. He told his friend as much, too.

"I won't be here in the morning," Dolph said.

"You're joking, right?"

Dolph didn't answer. Pretty soon, he was snoring, or pretending to.

Howie slept fitfully that night. He dreamed of going AWOL and being chased by Military Police and having to sleep in a pig sty to keep from getting caught. What woke him in the morning was the dream of May Lou and Indella chastising him for being a quitter. "Cobbs don't quit," they yelled at him. The dream left him in a cold sweat. It wasn't light out, but he could see: Dolph was still around. He breathed easier.

"You wanted to see me?" Howie said as he stood before Marisa Louise, the mess hall emptying as the guys headed for the warmer barracks or rec room or fire-fighting class.

Her perfume was almost too sweet. It was disconcerting smelling honeysuckle in a frozen world of brown snow. Regardless, the aroma aroused his pepper blood. If her smell could make him horny, then what would her touch do? His fingers itched to grab hold of her sleeve and caress it. "The final exam you took last semester—"

"Sorry about that," he said, afraid to look her in the eyes.

"Oh, don't apologize. I thought your parody of Browning's poem was delightful."

"My what?"

"Mr. Cobb, you are obviously much more widely read than the other young men in camp."

"Well, I read some." He had read a book by Walter Scott once on Indella's recommendation and hated it.

"Your take-off on Elizabeth Barrett Browning, not too terribly clever nor original. Still, it reveals a knowledge of literature that I find refreshing in this cultural desert."

"You do, huh." He had no idea who Elizabeth Barrett Browning was or what a cultural desert looked like, but he was willing to go along with whatever kept him near Marissa Louise.

"Is Browning your favorite poet?"

"Oh, no," he said. "Not at all."

"Who is your favorite then?"

He was stumped. The only poems he knew were nursery rhymes. He didn't think "Mary Had a Little Lamb" was going to impress Marisa Louise. So he took his Poppa's advice: when in doubt, answer a question with a question. So he asked, "Which one's your favorite, ma'm?"

"Oh, gee golly. I don't know. I like so many. Keats, Shelley, Wordsworth. Almost all the British Romantics. I have a fondness for the American poets, as well. Like Whitman." She was glowing. It was obvious: talking poetry with this woman was a sure way to keep her interested.

So he said with total recognition in his voice, "Ah, Whitman."

"What do you think of Whitman?"

206

"I never chew," he said. And she laughed out loud. It was the first time he had heard her laugh. He had decided she didn't know how.

"I love your sense of humor, Mr. Cobb."

He felt himself ready to limp into a sodden sack of meal. She had used the word "love" to him. Did she mean it? Did he really have a chance?

"Anyway," she continued, "I am thinking that my planned syllabus for our English class could easily bore you. Perhaps I might arrange more serious readings for you? I mean, the others in class will be stuck with silly little things like *Silas Marner* and *The Scarlet Letter*, things I'm certain you've already explored. Would you like a more challenging reading list?"

"Challenging?"

"You know, Benet, Melville, perhaps a little Dreiser. There's this new writer, John Steinbeck, that I find exciting. Of if you prefer the classics, I have a few works by Hardy in my personal library. Longfellow, Poe, maybe some Twain. Or Jane Austin. I adore Jane Austin."

"I read a Hardy Boys once."

She laughed again, this time with less interest. "You are so clever, Mr. Cobb."

"Howie."

"I suppose you've already gone through all of Dickens?"

"You bet," he said. He didn't know what the dickens she was talking about.

"Do you prefer poetry?"

"Well..."

"Good. I don't usually let my students read him, but I think you're ready for Whitman. He's my very favorite. Whitman is worth 'chewing on' as you say. He'll give us a starting point for discussions. Private discussions. Do you have Whitman in your personal library?"

"No," he said, feeling like he was disappointing her.

"Well, we'll take care of that. I have his complete works. See you Thursday."

The cold weather had its good points. In addition to becoming "teacher's pet," a label that left him feeling foolish, Howie learned to bob sled, ice skate a little, and ski. They didn't have a real bob sled in camp—they used a piece of ribbed tin roofing. Skating was nothing more than getting out on Center Lake and sliding around with boots on. And for skis they used pieces of warped one-by-three, smoothed and carved and stained—almost as good as the real thing. Drilling rods worked nicely for poles—a bit heavy, maybe, but who cared. The road from the top of the camp down to Center Lake made a pretty good bunny slope for the inexperienced. The grade was scant and you had to work hard to raise any speed, but it would do for guys like Howie Cobb who had seen precious little snow before, much less been asked to manage snow skis.

This is great—CRASH—Up again and down the slope. Not bad—CRASH.

Meatloaf stormed out onto the porch to see which fucker was banging into his north wall. Hey, suck on it, Meatloaf.

Off again. Make sure you hit the bridge—miss the bridge and—CRASH.

Maybe somebody else should try this thing. You should stick to vehicles on wheels, Cracker. Safer. God knows this ain't the place to find a broken arm or leg or busted skull or all three.

Howie stuck with it. Soon, he and Marv and four or five others made the run to the Lake like pros. The bunny slope was conquered.

That sent the guys looking for hills with a bit more challenge. Like some of the grades on Iron Mountain Highway they were working on. Sure. But getting there in two feet of snow? It was worth a shot.

Howie stood on the brink. During digging and blasting and hacking at trees and dragging logs to creek beds, nobody paid attention to the steepness of the grade. But now, here, perched like a bird fresh out of the nest on two home-made skis, with poles that must weigh twenty pounds each, Howie wasn't at all convinced the Iron Mountain adventure was that good an idea. What if he missed the bend? It was a good twenty feet to the bottom of the embankment, and at the bottom of that was the forest. If he missed and crashed over, over, over and down, there was nothing to stop him but the goddamn trees. And if he and a Ponderosa pine should make acquaintance in such a fashion, it was obvious which would be the worse for wear.

Are you sure abut this, Howie Cobb? Do you really want to be sent home to Momma and Poppa, Indella, Hev, Pierson, and Hank in a box made out of Black Hills pine, your skull smashed, your arms ripped away, your legs snapped like twigs? He pondered this as he perched on the brink. Sure, why not.

"Hey, Teacher's Pet's gone limp-kneed. He's sweating rabbit piss. Would you look at him? He's gonna pee all over himself."

The taunts were all he needed. It was shut up or put up time. It was like poker. You play the hand you're dealt; take what you get, or fold and wait for a different game. It was like baseball. If you have a problem with the base runner coming in with cleets crotch high, then you don't play the game. It wasn't in Howie's constitution to fold without good cause. He glared down the snow-covered grade. The bend glared back. Time to put the bastard in his place.

He pushed off. He crouched. He poled for more speed. The trees to his right and the embankment to his left zipped past. Not bad, not bad at all. This Georgia boy's flying. He's got buffalo broth in his veins. He's—CRASH. Nowhere near the bend.

He tumbled a few yards and then stopped in a pile of skis and poles and snow and laughing flesh. Good God Almighty, he could learn to love winter. The bastard won this hand, but time was on his side.

Marv Drexler jeered. "This is how you do it," he yelled as he pushed off.

Howie and the others rah-rah-rahed him on.

Marv poled for speed, which he found. The dry powder was perfect for skis, home-made or not. Marv whooped. He had done this since he was a boy. He was the master, the one who knew what skiing was all about.

He soared, and Howie raised his arms as Marv zoomed by. He laughed. They all laughed.

Then the bend.

Marv, out of control, disappeared over the edge.

That finished downhill skiing at Iron Mountain. The C.O. put a stop to it, then and there.

It was Marv Drexler who got the free trip home, not in a pine box, but in a plaster cast from ankle to hip. The doc in camp set the shattered leg as best he could and shook his head over how ineffective the appendage would be in future jogs down mountain slopes.

"Gonna miss you, buddy," Howie said as Marv got in the front seat of the bird cage. "Won't be the same around here, you know."

"So come visit me in Minot," Marv said. "You think it's cold down here? Come see what cold's really like."

Howie wanted to give his friend a hug, but couldn't. Instead, he stepped back and gave him one last little wave of the hand before turning his back and going inside Old K.P. where it was a little warmer, but not much.

Leaves of Grass. What in God's name is all this about, he wanted to know. What was the guy doing, writing about grass and never mentioning the stuff? Where does he come off, writing poetry that doesn't rhyme?

"Why don't you come to my house sometime and we can discuss it." Marisa Louise had changed her scent. Today, it was orange blossoms. So strong it hurt his sinuses.

"Huh?" Howie didn't trust his ears. Go to her house? Discuss poetry? But more important, *go to her house?*

"Why not?" she said.

He was so close to her he could feel the sleeve of her coat brushing his arm. Was she telling him something?

"You have Sundays off, don't you?" she asked. "I mean, I live so nearby. I bet you could walk. Or ski?" And they laughed. "Will you?"

"Just point me in the right direction," he said, feeling ready to crow.

And she did. The Game Lodge. Go through the woods, down Squaw Creek, and her house was less than three miles away. He couldn't believe it. Three miles away all this time. He felt as if he had been cheated.

"Do you mind walking?" she asked.

A piece of cake for a man like Howie Cobb who loved to walk almost as much as he loved to eat. If she only knew.

Her stepfather, she told him, was an assistant manager at the game lodge, and she was living with him for a year or so while she, as she put it, got her life back in order. "Can you come on Sunday?" she wanted to know.

"You bet your bottom dollar," he said with a surge of joy that he had difficulty hiding.

"Sunday?" She smiled.

"You bet." A mere three miles away. All this time, she had been within hollering distance of camp and he hadn't known.

"Can you stay for lunch? I think it would be fun discussing Whitman over a chicken leg, don't you?"

He didn't care. A leg of lamb, a leg of jackalope, he could not care less.

Howie suffered through Friday's firefighting class. Everything pointed toward Sunday. Sunday, the best day of his life.

"Cobb," the instructor of class yelled at him. "When's the best time to ripple a wild fire?"

"Best time to ripple a wild fire?" Howie said.

"That's right. Ripple a wild fire!"

"On Sundays," he said.

He loved the sound men made when they laughed so hard it hurt.

Saturday may have been the longest day of his life, made even longer by Dolph's growing depression, Bert van Dorst's release from camp life due to his mother's sudden illness, and the two letters he received from Indella, both pointing out to him that he was the man of her future, the father of her children (she couldn't be pregnant, could she, they hadn't done anything—had they?), and the white knight of her dreams.

Dear Indella, he almost wrote but didn't. A dear John letter could wait. Sunday would tell all.

The walk down Squaw Creek was made easy by the logging road skirting the banks. The snow was packed and slick, but he was used to walking on such stuff.

He arrived on her front porch on time. But hesitated. Was he really up to a poetry discussion with a woman who was light-years ahead of him in her comprehension of such stuff? He brought the copy of *Leaves of Grass* with him, but he hadn't been able to read much of it.

What if an opportunity came along to, uh, make his move? What would he do? What would his Momma who lived in his head allow him to do? Well, hell, wasn't he a grown man.

Couldn't he do what he liked? He tapped on Marisa Louise's door.

Her stepfather was at work, she told him, and wouldn't be home until after nine that night. "We have the whole afternoon all to ourselves," she whispered as they settled on the sofa in an overly warm room.

"Can we open a window?" he asked.

"What for?"

"Excuse me, but I'm awful hot."

She smiled. "I'm pleased to hear that."

They had a picnic in the middle of the living room rug. The chicken leg was over cooked; the baked potato was almost raw. It was cold on the inside like Walt Whitman's rhyme. But the wine was pretty good. He supposed it was good. After all, he had drunk wine only once or twice before, so he had little room for comparison. It must have been okay since he felt lightheaded from having drunk it. He felt a little ashamed of himself, being lightheaded after only two glasses of the stuff. Usually, he could put away a pitcher of beer and not feel a thing. But wine was more potent than beer. May Lou had told him once: "Look out or you'll become a wino before you can say Millard Fillmore. It only takes one time, you know. So stay away from Catholic services."

He told Marisa Louise all that and she laughed. "You have such a marvelous use of the English language," she said.

"What do you mean?" he wanted to know.

"Your accent."

"I ain't got an accent. What are you talking about?" And she laughed again. He was rather pleased with himself, being such a comic and not even trying.

The copy of *Leaves of Grass* lay between them on the rug like a barrier. She picked it up and thumbed through it. "So, what do you think of Whitman?" she asked.

"Well... He's sure a poet."

She led the way back to the sofa, leaving the picnic in the

middle of the floor. She sat with her feet tucked beneath her. He sat at the opposite end, hands in his lap.

She shifted toward him, holding in the middle of the sofa with her arm resting on the back. He wanted to take her hand in his and feel the texture of her skin but didn't dare.

"Beautiful stuff, isn't it," she said.

"What, your hand?"

"No, silly," she flipped at his shoulder with her finger tips. "Walt Whitman. I love his work. I mean, really, there's no greater poet than Walt Whitman."

"I don't know about that." He was thinking that greeting card companies hire better poets every day.

"Here. Here's my favorite part." She moved again, this time coming to rest beside him, her shoulder resting comfortably against his. Her perfume was too strong at this range. Oranges were okay in their place, but here, so close, in an over-warm room and after the wine, he wasn't sure he could keep his chicken in his stomach where it was supposed to be. He felt a sudden need for fresh air.

She showed him the section of the volume and read aloud: "The smoke of my own breath,/ Echoes, nipples, buzz'd whispers—"

Howie pointed at the page. "Ripples," he said.

"What?"

"Here. The word is ripples."

"Oh." She smiled a faint, self-conscious smile and continued: "Echoes, ripples, buzz'd whispers, love-root, silk-thread,/ crotch and vine. / My respiration and inspiration, the beating of my heart,/ the passing of blood and air through my lungs.."

She breathed heavily. She sighed. She looked through her eyelashes at Howie. He was reading ahead.

"...belched words?"

She read: "The sound of the belched words/ of my voice loos'd to the eddies of the wind, / A few light kisses, a few embraces, / a reaching around of arms..."

She stopped. Howie pulled air from his belly and let it slip out of his mouth in a deep-throated, frog-like burp. He grinned and said, "Bet I could belch words with the best of them."

She didn't smile. She didn't seem to care what he burped. She sat quietly, very close. What the hell? The poet seemed to have the right idea. Howie slipped his arm behind her, letting it rest on the back of the couch.

She tapped him on the chest. "Doesn't it get you right here?" And she laid her head on his shoulder.

His hand slipped to her back. She didn't move.

She placed her free hand on his thigh, dangerously close to his crotch, which was already taking on a life of its own. She whispered, "Whitman reminds me of... my ex-husband."

"Beg pardon?" He looked around as if expecting a tall, bearded older man much like the portrait of Walt Whitman on the jacket of the book to step out of a crevice in the room, point a finger at him and say "What the hell do you think you're doing with my wife!!"

"Oh, don't worry, Jack's long gone."

"Jack?"

"We were married for almost two years."

"Were?"

"The divorce was finalized just after Christmas."

"And this Jack, he was a poet, too?"

"Oh, no. But he was just like Whitman in another way. He was a homosexual."

Howie's mind whirred. What was she trying to tell him? So close.

Too close. He couldn't breathe.

"You have no idea how distressing it was to discover that Jack's mistress, my competition so to speak, was another man. I was afraid for a while there that it might have turned me against men. It hasn't." Her fingers caressed Howie's leg, moving closer to his crotch.

Couldn't be any more distressing than to hear you tell about it, ma'm, Howie wanted to say. He needed to get the hell out of there and the sooner the better.

"Can you imagine how it felt?"

Her mouth was moving toward his. He could feel her full breast pushing against his arm. He gulped.

She kissed him.

Never had he had that much tongue in his mouth. Sure, he had put his tongue ever so slightly in Indella's, and, of course, the time before that, Carol Bauman. But this. Her tongue explored every centimeter of his oral cavity. His teeth. His nose, for God's sake.

He gagged.

She ran her hand inside his shirt and played with his nipples and his chest hair. Her other hand was inching closer and closer to his red hot organ. And then it was there.

She touched him.

He erupted with volcanic heat. His semen, hot as melted rock, spilled uselessly into his baggy underwear where it turned icy cold. This time, he knew, the wet spot would surely show. There was no way to prevent it. He jerked away from her lest he be further embarrassed by letting her know what he had just done.

She looked shocked, momentarily stunned. Obviously the wine was affecting her as well.

He stood up, putting a distance between them, not knowing what to say or even if he should say anything.

"Don't you like me?" she asked as if she weren't already vulnerable enough.

"Of course, I like you."

"In the poem you wrote me you said you loved me. Do you still?"

"I like you a lot," he said. But he knew he loved Indella. He saw her clear as day in the center of his memory. Dear Indella, he wrote in his head, I've been such a fool...

"Then come on back over here, sweetie." She offered a tempting hand.

"I can't."

"Sure you can." She adjusted her position on the sofa, assuming the same posture Mary Pickford had used so many times.

"No, really, I can't."

"Why not?"

"I just can't." He wanted to say that he was engaged, if a Black Hills ring could mean that much whether he meant it to or not. That he was true to his one and only love. That he had mistaken his feelings for his teacher. That he had to get back to camp as soon as possible and write a letter home. An important letter, one he had postponed writing far too long.

Instead, he looked at her. It was as if he was seeing Marisa Louise Clackson for the first time. What he saw amazed him. She was overly plump with lumps of flesh in places they shouldn't have been. She had a squint about her eyes and a twitch in her upper lip that made her seem like a rabbit sniffing a carrot. No, this woman couldn't hold a candle to his Indella. The only thing she had over Indella was present tense—she was here and now. And that was no reason to do things that might ruin his life.

"You're not another Jack, are you?" she asked.

"How do you mean?"

"You know." She almost whispered the word, "Queer."

"Jesus Christ!" He laughed. She laughed, too.

"Then come back over here, sweetie."

He kept his hands folded in front of his crotch. Was there a wet spot forming down there? This whole thing had been one gigantic mistake. "I've got to go," he said. Dear Indella, how I miss you . . .

"I'm sorry, Howell," she whispered, sober now. Completely sober. Too sober.

"I am too, Miss Clackson."

"Do you have to go just now?"

"Yes, I do."

She tried to hide her hurt, but it slipped out her eyes. Oh, sure, be a bastard, she seemed to say, like all men, just a bunch of goddamn bastards...

Instead, she said, "Then go. Nobody's holding you." And she tossed the volume of *Leaves of Grass* to him. He caught it. "Present," she said.

Howie didn't learn a thing in English class. Marisa Louise selected another enrollee to receive her time and energies. His name was Claude Edison. He was from Sioux Falls, a high school graduate who quoted Shakespeare all the time, or at least quoted something that sounded like it should be Shakespeare. Howie migrated to the rear of the room, refused to read any assignment, doodled in his notebook, and wrote letters to Indella without using a single curlicue.

He watched Claude Edison leave camp every Sunday morning, headed down the logging road toward the Lodge. Nobody understood why Howie called Claude Edison "Chicken Leg" all the time, and he didn't make any effort to explain. But the nickname stuck until Chicken Leg went AWOL and was last heard from in Pocatello, Idaho, working as a plumber's mate.

"Chicken Leg was chicken shit," Dolph said one night.

"Why do you say that?" Howie asked.

"Going AWOL that way. It takes chicken shit to go AWOL." Then Dolph was silent. Howie could only watch his friend slip deeper and deeper into his depression.

Dear Indella...He shared everything with her now, everything he dared. He wrote:

"Dear Indella, How do I love thee?
Let me count the ways..."

Chicken Leg

As soon as the first thaw began, work on the pigtailling started up again. The snow was piled up deep and Iron Mountain Highway was closed until the tourist season. But the horrible conditions didn't stop Captain Clyde Munk.

He kept the bird cages crossing the Hills until on a down grade, Howie, who had become an excellent driver since joining the Cs, lost control of one of the trucks on the icy road and it plunged down the side of the mountain.

Howie was the first to bail out. He saw no reason to play captain and "go down with his ship," so he leaped free. Next came the Cs out the back of the cage. The snow was deep, slowing the truck's descent enough to allow everyone to clear and providing a cushion of sorts for the landings. The rickety old truck meandered a hundred yards more until it slammed into a large Ponderosa pine, bounced backwards and rammed it again, sputtering to a halt.

"This probably means the end of pigtailling, wouldn't you think? At least until the snow is good and gone," Howie said to Dolph.

But Dolph shook his head. "I wouldn't count on it if I was you."

The C.O. surveyed the accident site. "Who was the driver of the vehicle?" he asked.

All heads turned to Howie.

"You. My Lord in Heaven, it's you. Mister, you've been nothing but a pain in my rear end since you came to the Corps. Now this," he said, pointing to the truck's engine, which was now resting in the driver's seat.

Howie nodded. It was a good thing he had jumped when he did, otherwise he'd have been wearing a six-cylinder engine as a navel stone when they sent him home.

"The next time you decide to vacate your post while on duty, soldier," the C.O. said, "I want to know about it ahead of time—in writing. Do I make myself clear?"

"I'm not a soldier," Howie said.

"Did you say something?"

Howie could almost hear the bristles on the C.O.'s back popping to attention.

"I'm not a soldier ... sir," he said.

"In my camp," the C.O. said, "there are two kinds of people. There are soldiers, whom I love, and there are civilians, whom I hate." He was nose-to-nose with Howie by now. "You're telling me I'm not to love you, son?"

"I'm telling you, sir, that I already got me one daddy. His name's Alexander Stevens Cobb. He lives in Douglasville, Georgia, and he works a loom in the cotton mill and preaches on Sundays at Liberty Baptist Church, when they let him."

The C.O. bellowed: "Put this man on latrine duty, O'Kelley!" The Old Man stormed off, slipping up the snowy mountain side, struggling hard for some military presence in the face of the snow.

O'Kelley grinned. "Maybe we should just move your bunk into the latrine, Cracker. Save you some steps each day."

Everybody within hearing laughed, everybody except Howie. He was sick of cleaning up other guys' shit. He would prefer it if somebody else cleaned his once in awhile.

The bird cage was pulled by winches back to the road bed, and then hauled to Fort Meade where it was repaired and returned to active duty.

Once it was back in camp, Howie greeted it like an old friend. But he wasn't allowed to drive again. That pleasure went to somebody the Old Man loved.

Captain Clyde made his decision: if the roads were too slippery to drive across to the pigtail bridges, then they would relocate camp. It was warm enough. After all, the bridge work had to be finished before the next tourist season, and it was his assignment to see that it was ready. If he failed in his charge, all those touristy folks would be denied their chance to see the faces at Mount Rushmore, and we couldn't have that, now could we? The answer is No, Sir, We Can't Have That Sir! Dedication, that was what the C.O. wanted from his soldiers: dedication to a project completed and well done. None of this stuff like Howie Cobb bailing out when the going gets tough.

Nobody dared look at Howie when Old Clyde said all this. Instead, they inspected the ground for earth worms.

The Captain wanted men in his camp who would go the distance and suffer pain in order to enjoy the pleasure of surveying a job well done.

A fly camp was set up just off the Iron Mountain Highway near one of the pigtail bridges. The men, with grumbles and complaints reserved for when the C.O. wasn't around, cleared the trees, dug the latrines, and pitched the tents. Over three-fourths of the camp was moved to the new site, Howie and his latrine duty with them.

It was his task to dig the hole, build the three-seater bench, locate it over the hole, and pitch the tent so there might be a bit of privacy when anybody took a piss. It was his daily chore, morning and night, to keep the rolls of paper handy, the wood seats clean, and the droppings coated with a sprinkling of lime. Shit work if he ever saw it. This was in addition to whatever else his crew supervisor found worthy of his time.

Then, just when Howie's blood was beginning to thin a bit, it turned cold again—January weather in early March.

What Howie had complained about before was almost equalled by the Arctic blast that swept south from the Canadian Rockies. Howie wore all the clothing he owned, but it wasn't enough. He shivered like an aspen leaf, and everybody knew aspen leaves had no business hanging around in weather like this. He couldn't get warm—no matter what he did.

The strapping on the pigtail bridges slowed to a snail's pace. Three men in one tent suffered severe frost bite and were rushed into Rapid City. They didn't return. Rumor had it one of the three lost four toes on his right foot. But work on the pigtails went right on.

Everyone had a head cold. If a C coughed, he just had to live with it. If blood came up, he reported to the doc back in the base camp and let him have a look. Usually, the doc sent the guy back to the bridges with a fistful of little pills and a directive to take one every four hours for three days. If blood was still involved, the rule was: don't bother the doc, just pull a Chicken Leg and go AWOL. That was the only way. Many made the decision to do just that. Others didn't.

Rosie Tucker, who had been reassigned from his clerk duties to road crews—Old Clyde claimed he was too short-handed to let a well-bodied man like Rosie Tucker devote his talents to paper pushing—nearly coughed his guts out one night. Rosie didn't have the strength to go back to the camp infirmary by himself, so Howie and Dolph and a few others escorted Rosie across the mountain.

The doc listened to Rosie's chest, tapped Rosie's knee with a wood hammer, said it was a bad cold, nothing more, and sent Rosie back to the pigtailling.

Rosie refused to take the little white pills doc gave him. "Nothing but placebos, anyway," he said.

The number of Cs in the fly camp dwindled and no new recruits arrived. Each morning at roll call, another handful of men were no longer in camp to answer the sergeant's call. They slipped away in the night like the spirits the Indians claimed occupied the Hills.

No one ever knew where they went. No one cared. Going Chicken Leg was on everyone's minds these days.

Howie watched the fellow next to him, a farmer from up around Lemmon, pack his duffel bag after lights out. Secretly, Howie wished he could join him and the dozens of others who simply walked into the woods. But Alexander Stevens sat inside his head and scolded him over and over, "No son of mine is a quitter. Quitting ain't the Cobb way."

Then one morning, Rosie Tucker didn't show up for roll call. He lay in his bed, head turned toward the tent wall. He was having an unusual amount of difficulty breathing. His every attempt was a struggle, tapping the meager reserve of strength he had left.

The Seargeant sent for doc, but he had been called to Camp Narrows to consult about an influenza outbreak there. It was a three-hour trip both ways in this weather.

By the time doc made it to the fly camp, Rosie was through breathing. The effort got too much for him, and he simply quit. A different kind of Chicken Leg.

Howie had been sitting by Rosie's bunk when the rasping stopped.

He felt helpless sitting there. So fragile. So eager to go home. Get as far away from this as he could. He pulled an Army blanket over Rosie's body and waited for orders to start building the special Black Hills pine box.

An enrollee from Scottsbluff had served a time back home as an undertaker's apprentice. He laid Rosie out nice and neat. Rosie looked better than he had in weeks by the time the box was ready for him.

Howie had been around death enough to know what it was like. But his experience didn't help him fend off the growing feelings of personal loss. After all, he and Rosie had shared a tent there in the fly camp. Dolph had been there, too. They had listened to Rosie's cough for nights on end. They had complained to O'Kelley that Rosie needed some real help, and needed it quickly. They had nursed Rosie as best they could. The coughing went on. The sound had sent shivers up and down both their backbones. There but by the grace of God...

First, Cheater Evans out in Wyoming. Now, Rosie. Dead. Howie was far too awe struck to let his feelings show.

The doc said it was Rosie's basic unhealthy constitution, but all in the camp knew it was pneumonia. Just showed what the doc knew. If anything like that happened to himself, Howie vowed in the secrecy of his head, he'd find a way into Rapid and a real doctor. But that was a contingency, not reality. Rosie, lying cold and still, was real.

Howie felt like crying, but he didn't have any tears, not after that time in Sheridan. Besides, he was getting too old for that sort of thing. Too old to cry.

Instead he grew angry. He wanted to lash out at the hated C.O., the incompetent doc, the United States government, anybody or anything that kept them in this God-forsaken place of ice and cold. He wanted to yell "This is wrong!" but he didn't know which direction to aim the shout. The C.O. needed to see, damn it, that there were two kinds of people in the fly camp: live ones and dead ones. And right then, Howie didn't much care which group he belonged to.

The C.O. didn't see. As the lid on Rosie's box was nailed in place, he ordered everybody back to the pigtailling. There was nothing anybody could do for Rosie Tucker now and there was still work to be done.

Old Clyde and his direct order back to work were ignored. It hadn't been planned. Nobody had talked about it. None of the Cs had discussed such a possibility. It just happened. Nobody moved. They all simply stood there silently looking at the pine box.

It was a curiosity, this sudden failure to obey an order from the commandant. There was no leader in the protest, no agreed upon boycott of work. It wasn't mutiny, only a simple realization that Rosie deserved this much: a day of mourning, a day of calm and thoughtful rest.

That was what he got.

Nobody worked. Once he saw what was going on, the C.O. decided he needed a day off as well. Old Clyde returned to Camp Iron Mountain and spent the day, according to one of the Civies back in camp, chopping wood for his fireplace and playing horsey with his baby girl.

After an hour or so of doing nothing, Dolph, wandered into the woods. It was too damn cold for a walk, Howie tried to tell him, but nothing would stop him. Dolph walked deeper and deeper into the trees until Howie could no longer see him. Howie called to him, wondering where he was going but got no answer. Howie returned to his tent where he remained the rest of the day, alone, waiting.

Dolph didn't return that night. Or the next day. Or the next. Damn it all, Howie thought. Dolph's gone Chicken Leg.

After threatening to do it for such a long time, he'd gone and done it. Goddamn him. Howie was left alone. To do what?

Nothing left to do but stay. Cobbs after all do not quit.

Into the second week of sub-zero weather and three days after Rosie Tucker's death, Old Clyde finally called the extension camp in. A weak cheer rose from the shivering Cs when word spread: the pigtailling would be postponed until the aspens grew buds.

The barracks at Camp Iron Mountain weren't much warmer than the make-shift tents, but they looked inviting to the enrollees as they unloaded in front of the rec hall. The heat produced by the pot-bellied stoves was swallowed up by the cold four feet away, but that didn't bother the guys who sat on regular bunks and removed four layers of socks from half-frozen toes. At least there was an attempt at heat and for that they were thankful.

By mid-March, the severe cold was replaced by a more moderate chill. By the twentieth of the month, the ground was beginning to peep through the snow in places. When March passed, so did the rest of the snow, and in its place was a deep, gooey sludge of black mud. Camp strength was reduced to its minimum. Cs just walked away during the night.

"Any more birds in this camp," Old Clyde said to whomever would listen, "and we'll be merged with Legion Lake. Where's the pride of Iron Mountain, fellas?"

And to his wife he said, "Need some more recruits."

Big Brother

The first really warm day of the new year at Iron Mountain, Howie had a visitor. Pierson Cobb walked into camp.

"Who're you looking for?" Meatloaf asked when the tall dirty boy stood in the doorway to the mess hall.

"Howell Madison Cobb," Pierson said.

Meatloaf must have smirked a little at the vagabond standing in front of him. Pierson smelled of months without a bath. His shoes were laceless, tongueless, and probably soleless. His pants were worn through at the knees, and his shirt was missing all its buttons. Rag-tag was the term Meatloaf used later.

"Try Kensington Place," he said and pointed out the side door. "And don't come back in here, kid. I don't need your cooties in my mashed potatoes."

Pierson wandered through camp. Howie was on work detail, clearing the roadway for the Iron Mountain Highway.

Pierson had no idea what to expect from the Civilian Conservation Corps. Howie's letter had been sketchy at best, the one he'd read. The camp was in a valley with heavily treed hills rising all around. Squaw Creek flowed through and on. Ice still covered its edges. At the foot of the camp was the garage where the bird cages, earth movers, and generators were kept in service. He liked the smell of that place and hung around, watching the civilian mechanics work on an ageless truck.

The grease pit was deep enough for him to slip into

227

without bending under the chassis. Pierson watched the men tug away at bolts and overheard them curse the machines, and smelled the tangy odor of oil spilling into waiting drums.

"Get out of here," one of the guys snarled when he noticed Pierson standing at his elbow. "Hey, Marvin, where do these kids come from?"

The hospital was nearly empty. There was one case of influenza, not severe, another of mumps. Both patients were cordoned off from each other. The rest of the beds were waiting for the next casualty, illness, or other emergency. Pierson wandered through the building with the ease of ownership. No one was around to tell him to get lost. Doc was probably across the road playing cribbage with the C.O.'s wife.

Pierson visited with the fellow who had mumps and talked about the Cs and Pierson's trip across country while riding the rails. It wasn't until the sick man grew tired of Pierson's stink that he was shooed on his way.

Up the hill from the hospital was the latrine/bath house. Pierson found a half-used bar of store-bought soap beside the lavatory. He tossed it in the waste basket. Who had need of soap? He relieved himself at the urinal and grinned at the luxury of it all.

Next, he explored the rec hall, the commissary, the various "hotels." He gazed with untrained eyes on the words above each barrack. It didn't bother him that he couldn't make out the letters. All he need do was ask: "Which is Kensington Place?" and folks would point him in the right direction.

One thing about Pierson, he wasn't afraid to ask anybody about anything. It was a trait that was bound to take him far.

When the bird cages dumped their loads in front of the mess hall, Meatloaf drew Howie aside. "There's a kid in camp looking for you, Cracker."

"Sure there is Meatloaf."

"No joke. I mean it. Last I seen him, he was stringing up a tarp-looking thing the other side of the baseball field."

"You're serious."

"He can't be more than thirteen-fourteen years old. When you see him, tell him to take a bath will you?"

"What are you doing here?" Howie nearly shouted when he saw Pierson.

"Come for a visit," Pierson said with that big winning grin of his. He sat on a rug the same color as the earth it was spread on. He had a small fire going in a stone-rimmed pit. A pot was suspended from a make-shift tripod made of pieces of junk metal Pierson had found around camp. The vessel collected as much of the heat as it could and turned it to good use, boiling water.

Pierson dropped a half-peeled potato in the pot as he got up to greet his older brother.

"Ain't you glad to see me?" he asked.

"No," Howie said. "Where'd you get the spud, Pierson?"

Pierson grinned. "You wouldn't believe the pile of potatoes they got over there in that building." And he pointed to the mess hall.

Howie didn't say anything. Let Pierson discover Meatloaf's wrath on his own. Teach him a lesson he won't forget. "How'd you get here?" he asked.

"Train mostly. I walked some of it." Pierson showed Howie his feet, lumpy and callused as an old man's, and then squatted at the fire. "Good warmth in a pit fire. Got an extra spud if you want it."

Howie squatted beside him. Yes, the fire felt good. "It gets cold out here at night, Pierson. Come into the barracks with me."

"Can't do that."

"Why not?"

"I don't belong there."

"Well, Pierson, you're my brother. You belong any place I belong. It's cold out here."

"Cold? I'll have to tell you sometimes about cold. Who's that?" and he pointed across the creek.

The C.O. stood on the hill on the other side of the creek, watching the two from a distance. He didn't like bums coming into his camp, teaching his boys all the wrong things. And this bum looked particularly loathsome.

Howie shrugged. "Don't let him bother you. He's got this idea we're in the regular Army or something. He'll probably prance down here and kick you off federal property. If he does, don't take it personal. It's just his way."

"I'm joining the Army one of these days," Pierson said.

"What for?"

"See the world. Lot of world to see you know." He grinned. "I done seen a lot of it getting out here. Do you know how many towns there are between here and Douglasville?"

"No."

"Me neither."

"Does Momma know you're here?"

"Guess I should of told her. I didn't know where I was heading when I started out. All of a sudden, I looked up, and what do you know. Here I am."

"You stink, Pierson."

"Well? I've been on the road near half a year now."

"And you ain't told Momma?"

"Don't 'spect she cares too awful much what happens to me."

"That ain't what she told me at Christmas time."

"You were home for Christmas?"

"Everybody was there but you."

"What'd she tell you?"

"That you're to get your ass home!"

"I 'spect I'll make it back to Douglasville one of these days." He stirred his potato with a stick he found on the ground.

"Come on, let's get you cleaned up."

"I'm fine just as I am."

"Fine for burying and drawing flies. Come on."

"Leave me alone, Howie."

"I said come on!"

It took two times in the shower for Pierson to come moderately clean. First time out, Howie took one whiff and sent him back. Second time out, Old Clyde was waiting for them.

"We're not turning this into a shantytown," he said to Howie.

"This is my brother Pierson, all the way from Georgia."

"He could be Charles Lindberg's kidnapped kid for all I care, but it makes no difference. I'm not having him turning Iron Mountain into a hobo haven."

"I'm just staying a couple nights," Pierson said.

"Not while I'm in charge around here you're not. You want to pitch your camp outside what's mine, that's okay by me. But you want to use my facilities, take up my boy's time, you have to be in the Corps. Do I make myself clear?"

"So," said Pierson, grinning that grin of his. "Where do I join up?"

"You don't want him in the Corps, Captain." Howie found the idea almost worth a laugh.

Old Clyde persisted. "How old are you?"

"Old aplenty," Pierson answered and grinned.

The C.O. scratched his balding head. He didn't like this. But the rate of desertion had left his camp depleted almost to the point of shutting down—or worse, being merged with Legion Lake. Any recruit was better than merger.

"You seventeen?" he asked.

"Sure," Pierson said without blinking an eye.

"You swear to me?"

"On my mother's Bible."

"Pierson, for God's sake—" Howie was stopped by his brother's toothy grin.

"You wouldn't lie to me, would you, son?"

"Hell no."

"Come with me."

Pierson followed the C.O. at a respectful distance. Howie trailed behind. He pulled at his brother's sleeve. "You're not seventeen," he whispered.

"Will be—some day."

"Pierson," Howie said, hoping his brother would show a little more sense "you're gonna burn in hell one of these days, I swear."

His admonition did no good. Pierson signed on the dotted line and took an oath that he was old enough to do as he pleased. He was assigned a bunk in Old K.P. alongside Howie. It was Dolph's old bunk. It felt strange to Howie having his brother sleeping in his AWOL friend's place, but he didn't say anything about it.

"You've run away from home?" Howie asked when his brother was settled in with regular-issue clothes.

"No!" Pierson showed his toothy grin. "I walked. I'd been spending most of my time out of the house anyway. You know me, Howbo, I got happy feet. I came to dinner one night to home, and Poppa said: 'Nice, ain't it, May Lou, having Pierson's shoes under our table again.' You know me. Never one for sarcasm, be it from Poppa or no. If you've got something to say to me, say it. I got out of my chair, right there, we was having fried chicken, too, walked out of the house, and just kept walking. I heard the toot toot of the freight, headed for it, and here I am."

"That was when?"

"Hell, I got no need for watches and calendars."

Howie shook his head. "Have you written them?"

"Why should I?"

"They're worried. Momma's worried sick about you."

"How come? I can take care of myself."

"I want you to write Momma tonight."

"You write her for me. Ah, Howie, Momma and Poppa

don't care where I'm at. Shoot, me away from the table's just one less mouth to feed."

"I'll write her then."

"Do what you want." He punched the mattress with his fist.

"Kind of soft, ain't it?"

"You're the craziest booger I've ever met, Pierson."

"Ain't I though? Shit, Howie, I've seen some sights since I left home! You ever been to Canada?"

"No."

"Me, neither. Let's go."

"What's to see in Canada?"

"Things. I've been in more county jails than you can shake a stick at. I got me a goal, Howie. Before I turn twenty, I want to leave my mark in every jail cell this side of San Francisco."

"You want to get put in jail?"

"Free lodging, ain't it? Food's pretty good. Warm. Besides, they some kind of interesting folks in them jails. Good folks."

"What do you do to be put in jail for?"

"Nothing. It's called vagrancy."

"You're a damn hobo, Pierson."

"Got a nice ring to it, don't you think, Howbo? I come to Rapid City in a cattle car. Cows make the warmest travel mates. I remember you saying how Rapid City's the closest big town to where you were, so I figured I'd look you up. I asked a fellow which way to Iron Mountain, and he pointed into the Hills. Said: 'That a way, two days at best, if you're walking.' Said I was, thank you. He said: 'Then you best not be slowing your happy feet.' Said: 'You stop, the brown bears'll get you.' So, I walked it all. Got here in thirty-six hours. Two days, my foot. That man didn't know what he was talking about."

"There're no brown bears in the Hills."

"That's what you think."

Pierson, that first night, slept in Dolph's old barrack bunk. Next morning he complained about it being too soft.

Without to do he returned to his tattered lean-to and filthy rug and pit fire. "If I wanted a feather bed," he said, "I'd stayed at home."

Pierson sampled C.C.C. life. The food was good. He filled belly and pockets at every meal. The rec hall was entertaining. He especially enjoyed the nightly card games and occasional beer that someone shared with him. He liked lounging on the banks of Center Lake with a line in the water and a worm on a hook. But he didn't much care for work. At reveille, he received his work assignment for the day, then returned to his lean-to where he slept until lunch. It didn't seem to bother him that he was the only C not doing his share. In fact, he didn't really notice such things.

"You're gonna have to do some work," Howie told him.

"What for?" Pierson wanted to know.

"Cause it's part of being a C. We earn our keep and five dollars a month at that, spending money. Plus they send twenty-five more home to our folks."

"Wouldn't mind having five dollars a month," Pierson said.

"Well, you'll have to work to earn it."

"I don't mean any disrespect, Howie, but I'm getting along just fine as it is. If I need five dollars, I know where to get it."

"Come on, Pierson, don't play stupid. When you get an assignment in the morning, you're supposed to do it. That's how these things work."

"I'll think about it," Pierson said.

"What the hell is this!" Old Clyde stood over Pierson, who was asleep inside his lean-to. "I thought you were with the planting detail over near the Needles," the C.O. said.

Pierson, shaken awake, grinned his grin, but this time it didn't work.

"Get your butt in gear, Civie, else I'll have it and that silly grin of yours in a sling."

"I'm not so sure I want to do that, boss," said Pierson.

Old Clyde planted his feet and set his iron jaw. "What did you say?"

"Well, I don't mind work, you see," Pierson said. "It's fine to make an exertion when it profits somebody. Like what it takes to hop a train that's going some place you ain't been before, or corral a muskrat for supper if that's what you want for your supper. But this jump-starting you expect from these poor fellows around here—I don't take much to that."

"Who do you think you are?"

"Ah, I'm just a nobody, boss. I prefer it that way."

The C.O. turned on his heel, marched up the hillside to his cabin, rummaged around inside it for a bit, then came back down to where Pierson sat, taking in the warm spring sun.

Old Clyde held a piece of paper in his hand. "This," and he shook the paper, "is your registration into the Corps. I haven't got around to sending it in yet, thank God. You signed this thing, remember?"

"I have a faint recall of it, I guess."

"This document, which you signed, states that you are a duly sworn member of this noble country's fine amassment of youth called the Civilian Conservation Corps. In signing, you agreed to serve the corps and your country in whatever fashion your commanding officer directs. I am your commanding officer. I command you to get off your ass and report to work detail. Now. Not in a bit. Not if you feel like it. Now! Is that clear? or do I need to expand on it a little more?"

Pierson grinned. This fellow standing in front of him reminded him of his Poppa back home. "Oh, it's clear enough, I expect. I'll get around to it a little later on, General, thank you kindly."

The paper crunched in the C.O.'s fist. "You'll do what? What is it you just said you'd do?"

"You know, they got some real nice ear horns in the Sears Roebuck Catalog. I bet you could get one sent to you, you want. Help out on that hearing problem you got."

The C.O. ripped the document in half, wadded it into a ball, and threw it at Pierson's head. He kicked the lean-to into the creek and scattered the firestones in all directions. When he finished, he glared at Pierson and said, "I want this trash out of here, mister, and you with it. You ain't out of here by nightfall, I'll call the sheriff and have you run in for vagrancy."

"What jail that be they be putting me in?"

"Does it make a difference?"

"Well, I tell you. Be it a jail I ain't left my mark in, I just might hang around and meet this here sheriff friend of yours."

The C.O. marched up the hill past the commissary to his cabin. Meatloaf was outside peeling carrots for vegetable stew when he heard several loud crashes coming from inside the C.O.'s house. The crashes were mostly of glass meeting wood.

When Howie came in from work detail, he found Pierson perched on the rock wall entrance to the camp, a wall Howie had helped build the previous summer. Pierson had his belongings rolled in his rag rug and stuffed in his pockets. His cap was turned bill to his neck–his travel sign. Howie knew it well.

"Old Clyde's kicked me out."

"What for?" Howie asked. "What did you do?"

"Nothing. It apparently don't take much. Well, I'll be seeing you, Howie. If you get home before I do, tell the folks I said hello and will be home quick as I can."

"But you joined up, Pierson. You signed the papers. You leave, you're a Chicken Leg." This was serious stuff, and he could see that his brother was on the brink of the greatest sin of them all: quitting. "You're a Cobb, Pierson, and Cobbs never quit."

"The general tore those papers up, says I'm out of here. I ain't one for doing much arguing with a man as temperamental as your general."

"You wait here." Pierson settled back on the stone wall as Howie turned his rising ire toward the C.O.'s house.

Old Clyde was in his back yard, pacing. Howie could see something had the C.O. riled. He knew without being told it was Pierson. Maybe this wasn't the time to confront Old Clyde, but it was the only time he had.

"My brother goes," Howie announced, "so do I."

"You leave this post," the C.O. answered, "and I'll have your AWOL carcass on the flagpole, Cracker. You understand me?"

"If Pierson leaves, he'll be AWOL, won't he?"

"The paper that son of a bitch signed isn't worth the ink he wasted on it. The kid's no more than fourteen. He lied. We don't need his kind in this man's Army. The sooner we're rid of him, the better."

"This ain't the Army! And that bitch you're saying he's the son of happens to be my Momma!!" Howie was perspiring in spite of the forty-degree breeze coming over the mountain.

"He's what I choose to call him. Now you got a gripe with me, you take it through channels. Stop wasting my time on garbage like that brother of yours."

Howie's gut instinct was to leave the place and good riddance. He wanted something, he didn't know what. Maybe he wanted Old Clyde to say: don't do this, we need you. But there was no relenting in the C.O.'s gaze or body stance! Howie took off his hat and tried to sound sorry for his brother's doings. "You're forcing me to do something I don"t want to do, sir."

"I'm not forcing anything but discipline. Something that goddamned vagrant don't know doodlysquat about. Now get back to camp and do your duty."

"You don't understand. Pierson's family..."

"That no count lump of garbage is a waste of the good Lord's time and you know it."

The C.O. had nothing left to say. He just glared at Howie

238

as if he was made of chicken poop or something.

"Captain," Howie said, "you're nothing but a—"

"Just say it, Cracker, say the word. There ain't a cell at Fort Meade small enough for you. They'll have to build one special."

Howie left the cabin. He felt in his gut he was forfeiting everything, and it was all Pierson's fault. But what else could he do? Duty to family was the greatest duty of them all.

Pierson was where Howie had left him, perched on the stone wall. "Well?" he said as Howie hurled stones at the Ponderosa pines.

"I'm thinking." Is this it? Is this why he had traveled four and a half days from the woman he loved, just to chuck it all less than a month and a half before his time was up? His Poppa was speaking inside his head: "Cobb's don't quit. We're not the stuff of quitters." Then May Lou's voice was there, too, saying, "We're family, Howie, never forget that. Above all else is family."

Twelve rocks was all the thinking he needed. He turned to his brother with his Momma's adage firmly in his head. "Hike down Squaw Creek to the Game Lodge. Wait in the Lodge for me. I'll be along around midnight tonight. Can you remember all that?"

"Sure."

"I'm serious, Pierson. If you're not at the Lodge tonight, I'll skin you alive. Now get out of here before the C.O. puts you in front of a firing squad."

"You don't have to go with me Howie. I got here without you, I can get to Canada alone, too."

"I'm responsible for you, kid."

"Yeah? Who says?"

"Momma. Now, get out of here, damn it."

Howie watched his brother saunter down the road toward Center Lake. There was a spring to his step that Howie wished he had. Pierson's feet were the happiest Howie'd ever seen. He obviously loved the feel of earth pounding the bottoms of his soles. Howie envied that. Howie wanted the freedom that happy feet brought. But it wasn't his by nature. Happy feet belong to the irresponsible.

Still, the circumstances tugged at him. It wasn't his choice. It was the C.O.'s. Old Clyde left him no alternative but to pack his things, wait for night to come to the mountain, and put drudging steps in place for the midnight hike to the Game Lodge. An injustice done to one Cobb was done to them all. That was the unwritten law of the clan, supported by the rules set forth by Momma.

Howie packed his duffel bag. He had arrived in Iron Mountain with the bag three-quarters full. He left with it that way. What he didn't have when he stepped off the bird cage that first time—C.C.C. issue shirts, pants, socks, underwear, he left in his foot locker. He thought about scratching his initials from the underlid of the trunk, but that would have been too obvious to the guys around him.

He sat on the edge of his bed, waiting for taps and thought of Dolph. This is how Dolph must have felt. When Dolph slipped off into the woods, Howie hadn't taken the time to consider how his friend must have felt. His feelings were what mattered. After all, they had gone through a lot in this piece of the Black Hills. They had played, and laughed, shared their loves and hopes for the future, worked like banshees, even frolicked like mermaids in the icy waters of Center Lake. And now he was putting all this behind him. All for the honor of the family, and his brother, Pierson. The thing he regretted was not getting that valuable piece of paper known as his honorable discharge. Without it, all he had experienced in the C.C.C.'s was for nothing. And he hated waste.

He perched on the bunk and wondered if Pierson was worth it or not. What would Indella say if she learned? Would she be mad? Would she understand? One thing for certain, she would never know. No on would ever know. He would swear

Pierson to secrecy, on pain of death. And he would mean it. He would make sure Pierson understood that he meant it.

Taps. Lord, he thought, such a mournful sound. Almost like dying and being put six feet under. In a way, part of him was dying. Dead. Listen to taps one last time. You won't hear the melody again, not like this. It was then and there.

A little before midnight, Howie slipped from his bunk, shouldered his duffel, slipped out the back door of Old K.P., and found he had Chicken Legs after all.

Pierson waited outside the Lodge. It was two in the morning, but he didn't seem to care. He was drunk as twelve skunks in a liquor still. "Jesus Christ," Howie said when he found his brother in a pickled state. "Where do these folks come off, serving a minor like you!"

"Just thought I was twenty-one," Pierson said.

"And who was it told them that?"

There was no need for an answer. Pierson sat in the middle of the road, refusing to move. Something inside him said: this is as far as I go, brother. Howie tugged at him, but Pierson had a mind that was under the control of a stronger force. "Not going a step further," he announced.

"If Old Clyde finds me here," Howie said in all seriousness, "he'll have my insides on a string. Come on, Pierson. Let's put some distance behind us."

"Not a step further," Pierson said, and meant it. They parked their carcasses on the side porch and prayed no one came along. They didn't. Howie's body rebelled against the hardwood decking of the porch. Pierson had had just enough alcohol. His muscles caressed the planks with welcome. He slept like a newborn. He didn't know that his brother kept a vigil over them, waiting for the sun to give them direction for what lay ahead.

Howbo

"Keep an eye open for the bulls."

"Bulls? Black Angus or what?" Howie asked.

Pierson expelled a breath of air that seemed to say, My word, but you're stupid. "They are big tall mean-looking fellows with sticks two feet long and four inches thick. They're mean bastards. Just as soon crack your head open as ask you howdy-do."

"Why would they want to do that?"

Pierson merely shook his head and continued scanning the parked freight a hundred or so yards ahead of them. Howie was seeing parts of Rapid City he didn't know existed. "Shouldn't we get on now?"

Pierson let out another breath of air. "Don't you know nothing? We wait for the toot toot-toot and for the train to start moving. Then we get on."

"While it's moving?"

"You know a better way?"

"Sure. When it's standing still."

Pierson shook his head. He said, "Shouldn't be too long. The bulls always check the cars half an hour or so before the toot toot-toot. They're just now giving them a look-over."

"Where?"

Pierson pointed. The man was dressed like all other railroad men. What distinguished him was the stick, strapped to his right arm. "He's a mean son of a bitch. I ran into him on my way in and he almost took my head off with that damn stick of his."

"Why don't we just get on the highway and thumb our way home?" Howie asked.

Pierson laughed. He shook his head and settled down behind the crates. "Might as well relax, Howbo. It'll be at least twenty more minutes before we roll."

"How do we know where the train's going?"

"We don't." Pierson was in high spirits. He whistled snatches of tunes and flipped pieces of gravel at a hole in one of the crates. "There's nothing like jumping freights, brother," he said flashing that special grin of his. "It's—I don't know. Makes you feel alive. Gets the old heart apumping! Gets you to where you can see just about anything. Hear just about anything. Hell. Nothing like jumping freights, Howbo, that's a fact. Got to keep your eyes open, all the time. And you never trespass on another hobo's space. Not without asking leave. We're a selective bunch and that's a fact."

"What if you miss?"

Pierson tossed another stone at the crate and refused to deal with that kind of question. He said, "When you hop a train, you go where it takes you and like it. You can ride inside for comfort and take your lumps from the bulls, or you can ride atop where you've got a runner's chance. You can ride in between where you've got a leap if needed or you can ride like me: you can ride the rods. The bulls never check the rods, and if they did, they can't hurt you till the train's stopped. By then you're long gone. Riding the rods lets you know quick just how alive you are inside."

"What's the rods?" Howie asked.

"They're about as thick as your two thumbs, half a dozen or so, that run from one end of the car to the other, on the underside. You swing under from the ladder or from the cattle door. I've seen men start for the rods and lose their nerve. That ain't wise. Once you go for the rods, you gotta go for them. There's no backing out."

"What happened to them?"

"They be lucky if all they lose was their legs. Some ain't hobos any more."

"Think I'll stick to riding in between."

"Yeah, that's safe enough. I knew a fella once who rode in between. Didn't know the freight was headed into a blizzard. His hands froze to the ladder. They had to be cut him loose with a blow torch."

"Are you making this up?" Howie asked. Pierson grinned. "How about on top? Is that safe?"

"Sure, if you know what you're doing. On my way out here, I spent half my time doing top runs. It's wise, though, to know where you are. I heard of a fella who was top running through the Smokeys and forgot to take into account the tunnels they got there. You got to set up for a tunnel, else it just sucks all the oxygen out and you suffocate. Well, this fella was riding with his back to the wind and didn't see the tunnel coming. His friends yelled at him and waved. He was a friendly sort and waved back. The edge of the tunnel caught him back of the head just above the ears. Took his head off like a scythe. Like I said, you've got to know where you are, all the time."

"This is stupid, Pierson."

"Not so, big brother. It's living."

The train jerked and clanged. It reminded Howie of a giant fangless dragon, waking up after a night's rest. "We go?"

"Have you heard the toot toot-toot?"

"No."

"Then, we don't go."

Howie reviewed what he had done and didn't care for it at all. He was AWOL. He was hiding from men with baseball bats meant to bash in his head. He was edging toward hopping his first freight, becoming a hobo like his brother. He was in the hands of something he didn't quite understand, and he didn't know how to go about changing the grip. It was Pierson. Pierson had fallen into his life and was now in charge. That had to change. He recognized that without a doubt, he had to get back on top of things.

Toot toot-toot.

The train jerked and clanged and jerked again as car after car began its lazy roll out of the rail yard.

"Now?" Howie whispered.

"When I say go, run like the Devil's on your heels. Don't look back. Grab the first car you get to and jump. When you get to the top, wait for me. I'll be along. Got that?

"I guess."

"There's no guess work in this, Howbo. You do it or you don't. There's no half-way-in-between."

The train lurched and was rolling free now, gaining momentum the same as Howie's heartbeat. His adrenalin burst through his veins when Pierson yelled "Go!"

The two brothers threw themselves across the empty track toward the moving train. Howie thought he heard a whistle behind him, but he didn't look. Ahead of them he saw four more men making the same mad dash. But they didn't matter. Pierson didn't matter. The thing that counted was the piece of metal that formed the bottom rung of a cattle car ladder. It was a yard away and moving faster than he. He stretched his legs and ran like he'd never run before, reducing the distance until finally, he grasped the old iron with a sweaty palm. Grab and jump, Pierson said. The wheels, like giant saw blades, glinted at him and waited for him to slip. Grab and jump. Don't hesitate. If you hesitate—

He jumped. His right hand slipped as his other grabbed a metal bar a bit higher than his first. His feet dangled like a slaughtered pig from a singletree, and for a split second, he imagined his legs severed from his body by the persistent sawblade wheels. He pulled. His right boot found a ledge. He pulled again. His feet were firm on the bottom rung. If you hesitate—

He was a monkey on a jungle bar, up the side of the box car. He threw himself flat on the cattle car roof and tried to breathe again. It was as if he had forgotten how, and now his body ached for oxygen. His heart was too big, taking up too much room inside him. It wouldn't stop hammering away in his chest and give his lungs a chance to do their job. If I ever do this again, he thought, I'll know I've lost my mind.

"Nice job," Pierson said. He sat on the box car near Howie's head, his smile in place. "You want to join me on the rods?"

"Get the hell away from me," Howie said. He wished he was back at Iron Mountain, strapping pigtail bridges or cleaning latrines. It didn't matter. Anything had to be better than this.

It got easier. Cheyenne. Denver. Scottsbluff. Omaha. Topeka. Oklahoma City. Fort Worth. Amarillo. Galveston. Howie was seeing an America he hadn't known existed. And everywhere they went there were more men just like them. All ages. All colors. He met his first colored person on the way out of Topeka and his second a couple of miles down the track. Both nice folks. And they would have traveled on together until they found out he was heading home to Georgia. Damn state they hoped like hell never to see again.

A bull almost got the two of them in San Antonio. Near Corpus Christi two hobos sleeping next to Howie and Pierson had their heads busted while they dreamed. The two brothers slipped away in the dark and could hear the pounding grow faint behind them. In Waco, they spent the night in jail for vagrancy, Howie's first experience with that sort of thing, and he vowed it would be his last. Still, jail food was the one decent meal Howie had enroute home. In Beaumont, they could easily have had a second night in the clink, but the railroad detective just wanted to sit and talk. It was too pretty a night to waste running in the hobos. Besides, as the bull said, if it weren't for the missus, he'd be a hobo himself.

"Married, huh," Pierson said and shook his head.

"Biggest mistake of my life," the bull replied.

"My brother here's getting married as soon as he gets home," Pierson said and slapped Howie on the back.

"Then, I hope you make it, son. Listen," the bull said. "Whatever you do, stay off the 921 in the morning. It's headed east and there's a lot of you guys hanging around these days. Something's brewing, I don't know what, and if you're not careful, you could get caught up in something that won't be very pretty."

"What're you talking about?" Pierson asked.

"Just stay off the 921. That's all I can say."

The bull wandered off. Howie listened to his whistle as he meandered down the tracks, looking for other bums to pass the time with.

"The 921's the train we're gonna take, right?" Pierson said.

Howie nodded. "It's the only one heading east," he said. "Atlanta by way of New Orleans, Pensacola, and Columbus. Suppose he knows what he's talking about?"

"Hell," Pierson said. "Bulls're dumber than me and that's saying a hell of a lot. Sides, if something's up, I want to be in on it. Okay by you?"

"I don't know," Howie said. "I just don't know." There seemed to be so many of them these days. There was more hobo cargo on trains than freight. They had been lucky to have been arrested only once in their travels. The only rational explanation for their good fortune was that there were simply too many of them to deal with. Vagrants were over-crowding the jails. Maybe something was up, like the friendly bull said, something meant to discourage kids like themselves from taking to the rails. On the other hand, Howie wanted to get home, deliver his brother safely into the bosom of the family, and then go courting. The easiest and fastest way to do that was the 921.

"Why don't we take a look at it to see," Howie said.

They found it, parked and waiting. There wasn't anything noticeably different about the train. It was shorter than some and longer than others. There were two cabooses, but that wasn't anything special, either. Lots of trains have two cabooses these days, Pierson explained. "Looks good to me," Pierson said.

As the 921 pulled out of Beaumont the next morning, Howie and Pierson Cobb were aboard.

Howie had come to enjoy the warm showers the trains often passed through. It was a good chance to take a bath, get some of the grime off his body and clothes. But this morning was hardly a shower. It was a gale, driven by warm tropical air that could easily be classified a small hurricane. The rain slashed at the two brothers with fierce intensity. On a day like this it would be nice to crawl into the comfort of a car, but the doors were all locked, filled with cargo. The only place to find shelter was the underside and the rods. Howie had taken to the rods a couple times before. The first time, he lost all his dinner. The second, not quite so bad. The third, a piece of cake. This time he followed Pierson's lead without pause and swung underneath a box car. There they lay on their bellies, and, using their arms as pillows, slept as best they could.

The train jerking to a stop woke them. Howie opened his eyes. Beneath him stretched rails and black ties that seemed to be held in place by a cloud of mist. Where was the gravel of the road bed? Something was wrong. Adrenaline poured into his blood system. "Where are we?" he whispered to his brother.

248

Pierson's breath hissed. "We're on some sort of trestle, I think," he said.

"Let's get out of here," Howie asked more than said. The chill had him shivering to his core. All he wanted was a warm fire, a soft bed, and a comforter for his feet. Then he would be happy. "Let's hop off," he suggested.

"And go where? It's a goddamn trestle, Howbo, nothing beneath us but air. Shhhh," hissed Pierson as he strained to hear.

From both front and rear, box car doors opened and slammed shut. Heavy footsteps could be heard overhead on top of the cars. The boots were cleated. They didn't belong to other bums. "The bulls," Pierson whispered. "A goddamned army of bitching bulls."

"What're we gonna do?" Howie whispered.

"Be quiet." And they lay without breathing.

Howie could taste his sweat in his mouth. Down the track he heard the thud of a bull's stick against the soft skull of a kid like himself, then a hushed cry that seemed to fall forever down through the mist beneath the rails. Then another. Thud. A swish through the air. A third. He couldn't stop counting. What number would Pierson be? Ten. Eleven.

The thudding was directly overhead now. He could hear the coarse whispery voice: "You survive, tell all your friends we've had our fill of your kind. You got that?" Thud. Swoosh. The vagrant was hurled from the train.

Howie caught a glimpse of the body as it disappeared into the mist below the trestle. He strained to hear the thump of the body hitting something firm, but it didn't come. Fifteen. Sixteen. The thudding moved on. The train lay still in its tracks.

"What do you think?" Howie whispered.

"We've got to get to the top," Pierson said.

"What for? We're safe here."

"Like hell." Pierson eased himself over the rods to the

edge of the car. "Come on, Howie!" he whispered. Howie followed.

They swung free of the rods and climbed the ladder to the top. There they crouched low to the contour of the freight, but not low enough.

First the whistle, then the shout: "Here's two more! Come on guys."

Pierson ran one way; Howie the other. It made no difference. Howie stopped as the bull with the whistle grapped Pierson by his coat collar and landed the butt of the stick in his stomach.

Howie threw up his arms. He had seen the gesture in movies and considered it the universal sign of surrender. If he had possessed something white, he would have waved it.

The stick crashed down across his shoulders and back. He collapsed in a heap.

A heavy nailed boot found the soft underside of his belly and lifted him momentarily free of the train with a crushing blow.

With half-glazed eyes he watched his brother being thrown from the top of the train into God only knew what might be below. A mouth full of hot liquor-laced breath leaned into Howie's face and said, "Let me see you hop a freight again, kiddo, after the ride I'm gonna give you."

Arms stronger than his hoisted him into the air and held him there for an eternal second as a thick Texas voice said, "We baptize you in the name of the Hobo God!" And then he was hurled out and away from the train into the mist where he felt for a moment as if he would remain suspended forever surrounded by empty air.

He reached for something to grab, but there was nothing. He seemed to hang for a moment as he glanced back. The bulls, three of them, were watching his flight, their faces filled with a pleasure Howie was at a loss to understand.

And he flew, for the first time in his life, and he vowed,

if he ever put foot back on solid earth, he would never fly again.

Dear sweet Jesus, I'll do what ever you want. . .

Indella, I'll marry you if you'll have me. . .

Momma, I'm doing my best to get Pierson home. . . And I believe, I want you to know, I believe. . .

Captain Clyde, you're not such a bad sort, not really. . . Wish you were here. . .

Dolph, Dolph, where are you Dolph? What does one do to become a Mormon. . .

Is this how you felt, Cheater, on your dash into the fire. . .

Where's a juniper tree when you need one. . .

Down, down... rain stings when it hits you this hard. If I could breathe, I might learn to soar. . .

Yes, Indella, I'll be yours for ever and ever and ever. . .

He saw the river seconds before he entered it. Feet first, thank God, his boots took the blast of impact. His legs bent into his mid-section as he tumbled like so much dirty laundry in the deep dark current of the Mississippi. Hitting the water crushed out all air he had in him. And he sank. I baptize you in the name...

As a child, Alexander Stevens had taken him by the arms and hurled him into the Dog River, saying, "Okay, boy, it's up to you. Sink or swim."

"Okay, Howbo," a voice he'd never heard before said, "It's up to you—sink or. ."

Howie pulled himself to the surface as he gasped for air that was too full of rain and mist. Could he swim? Were his legs still attached? Was anything broken? Would his arms work if he asked them to? There was pain, in the middle of his chest and the bottom of his back, but yes, he could swim.

"Baptized a third time, dear Jesus," he said aloud. "Thank you, Lord, thank you."

Which way to shore? If he selected poorly, he could wind up in the middle of the Gulf of Mexico. He had a fifty-fifty chance. So he swam with what little strength he had left against the current toward what he soon hoped would be land.

By mid-day the storm had blown itself out. The sun returned and the air was filled with steam and liquid air. Howie lay in a heap on the river bank. He had gotten as far as he could, and there he would die, if necessary, but be-damned if he could go any further. He could see the trestle seventy-five yards or so up the river, which at this point was well over a mile wide. It was a joke, that's all, an awful joke he didn't find very funny. Both his legs hurt along with his stomach, chest, head, and back. His lungs ached from the water he had inhaled. What he needed was a cigarette and a shot of whiskey. He had neither. What he needed was a warm fire and dry clothes. What he needed was his brother. Doggone it, look what you've done to us, he'd say when he got his hands on Pierson. I told you something like this would happen, didn't I? If he could get his hands on Pierson... If he saw him again.

What he needed was rest. Sweet gentle sleep. He slept as soundly as the dead, there on the banks of the mighty Mississippi.

When he woke, he wandered up the river. If anybody else survived the free-fall, they'd be at the trestle. God only knew where Pierson might be. Washed into the Gulf by now.

"Hey, Howbo!"

The grin was there, bigger than ever.

Pierson sat at an open fire, heating a tin of beans. His grin was now partially damaged as one of his front teeth was gone. He had a massive abrasion across his forehead and an arm in a sling. But other than that, he was good old Pierson, happy as could be, with twelve or so other vagrants huddled around the fire at the base of a trestle tree.

Howie was welcomed by everybody there like a long lost cousin. After all, they had something in common. All of them had survived the soon to be fabled 921 from Beaumont, Texas.

"Hey, Howbo," Pierson said as he hugged his brother's neck with his one good arm. "This is the life, ain't it? Jesus Lord, Hev should be here cause I swear this is the life."

Howie's balled fist found the soft tissue of his brother's right eye. The blow threw Pierson backwards in a heap. He landed on his already hurting arm. The cry of pain that flew out of him took all of Howie's anger with it, leaving him so drained he had no energy to fight off the tears that insisted on release. He stood there, weeping, the only words he could form falling out of his mouth over and over, "Goddamn you, Pierson, goddamn you." He wept for Cheater and Marv, for Rosie Tucker, Dolph, and Cold Steam. He wept for his Momma May Lou wondering where her two precious boys must be, for the C.O. back at Iron Mountain who was probably losing his camp because too many of his trusted boys were going AWOL. But mostly he wept for himself, tears of fear and dread and joy of being alive, of finally coming so close to the core of himself that he could no longer avoid confronting it. He sat on the muddy river bank, a sodden rag of a man, but a man nonetheless.

Pierson crawled to him, holding his broken arm tightly against his side. "Hey, Howbo, you okay?"

Somewhere inside his core Howie found the will to fight one last time. He held Pierson's grin at bay with the strength of his eyes alone. "You know, Pierson, if it wasn't for Momma waiting at home for you, I'd leave you here to rot."

The two brothers sat side by side, Pierson's good arm draped over Howie's shoulder, but he didn't mind. Even when the low-hanging drizzle drifted in from the sea and changed to a cold penetrating rain, they didn't move. Neither wanted to lose what they both knew was slipping away.

Howell Madison Cobb

Howie and Pierson slid to the ground as the slowing freight neared the outskirts of the Atlanta rail yard. Pierson's broken arm had hindered them a little in making progress home, but after the adventure aboard 921, Howie wasn't in too great a hurry to get anywhere.

Now, so near Douglasville and home, he was even more hesitant to go any further. The two brothers reached the fence intended to keep hobos away from the tracks there in the Atlanta terminal, and Howie stopped.

This was it. He couldn't go on. It wouldn't be right.

"What's wrong?" Pierson asked.

"I can't do it," Howie answered, looking at the last hurdle, the fence, and knowing there was no reason to take it.

He had come so far. Yet he knew, he couldn't go any further.

Cobb's don't quit, and that was what he had done. Cross the fence and the next thing he had to do was face Alexander Stevens and explain to him what he had done and why. Then he would have to explain it to Hev, and he knew Hev wouldn't understand. May Lou wouldn't either. Would Indella? Oh, Lord, he would have to tell Indella of his failure, and he simply could not do it. The fence said all this to him as he stood there, fully knowing who he was and what he and only he had to do.

"You sick or something?"

"No." But Howie knew, if he crossed the fence, he would be sick, sicker than he'd ever been in his life.

254

"Well, let's go, Howbo. Just a twenty-mile hike and we'll be home. Got to tell you, I'm looking forward to one of Momma's home-cooked meals."

"Just can't do it," Howie said. He knew he spoke the truth.

"Twenty miles? Shoot, brother, that's nothing."

"That's not what I'm talking about, Pierson."

He rubbed his hand through his greasy, smelly hair. The backs of his hands were blackened with dirt and cinders, his clothing was reduced to rags, his shoes were shattered pieces of leather. This wasn't the way he had envisioned his home-coming. "I can't face Momma and them like this."

"So let's go get us a bath! I got nothing against a bath every now and then."

"That's not what I'm talking about, either." The rail yard was a den of activity, trains coming and going in every direc-tion. Maybe one of them would be heading west, maybe going as far even as South Dakota and Rapid City and the Black Hills. He didn't know. But after a week on the rails with Pierson, he knew how to find out. "I've got some unfinished business," he said. "Jesus has seen me this far. He'll see us both the rest of the way. Can you get home by yourself from here?"

"Shoot, I can get home by myself from anywhere. You know that."

"But you will go home, won't you?"

"Might as well, can't dance. How about you?" Pierson asked, his grin off his face.

Howie had thought of little else since his flight off the Mississippi trestle. He had debated his decision and knew he was right in seeing that his brother got home, but now that that task had been accomplished, he had no choice. He had to go back. He had to face Old Clyde and finish his commitment to the Corps, one way or another.

He couldn't explain it to Pierson, not that his brother would understand, but he knew deep inside his inner being,

Cobbs had to finish what they began. He couldn't run away from it any longer. He had met his obligation to his Momma and gotten Pierson home in one piece. Now, he had to attend to the other voice in his head, his Poppa's directive to finish what he had dutifully begun. So he said, "I'm going back to Iron Mountain."

"That's down right crazy," Pierson said. "How come?"

"It's something I have to do. Tell Momma I love her and that I'll be home soon as I can."

"You're an awful long way from Iron Mountain, Howie. How you plan on getting back?"

"Thanks to you, I don't expect I'll have any trouble at all." He held out his hand and took Pierson's in his and shook it in an awkward, self-conscious way. "I appreciate all you've taught me," he said.

Pierson looked at their hands clasped together and shook his head. "Shoot, Howbo, that ain't gonna do it." He threw his one good arm around his brother's neck, hugged him for a fleeting moment, then pushed him away. "See you!" he yelled and scaled the fence like it was hardly there.

"What you want me to tell Momma?" Pierson yelled from beyond the fence.

"Tell her—I'll be home when I'm home."

"See ya, Howbo, you bum!"

"The name's Howell, brother. Howell Madison Cobb!"

Howie turned back to the clamoring yard and spied a freight moving out of town not a hundred yards away. He had no idea where it might be heading, but did it matter? Make the mad dash and go along for the ride. Grab the bottom rung and swing on board. What would the good Captain Munk say when he found the Cracker parked on the commissary steps? Or better yet, answering roll call even if his name wasn't on the list?

He'd decide later. Right now he had to grab a rung, swing onto the cattle car, and crawl up the ladder for a top run out of Atlanta.